MW00467034

MURDER IS A DIRTY BUSINESS

A Grime Pays Mystery

TRICIA L. SANDERS

SOUL MATE PUBLISHING

New York

MURDER IS A DIRTY BUSINESS

Copyright©2017

TRICIA L. SANDERS

Cover Design by Rae Monet, Inc.

This book is a work of fiction. The names, characters, places, and incidents are the products of the author's imagination or are used fictitiously. Any resemblance to actual events, business establishments, locales, or persons, living or dead, is entirely coincidental.

All rights reserved. No part of this publication may be reproduced, stored in a retrieval system, or transmitted in any form or by any means (electronic, mechanical, photocopying, recording, or otherwise) without the prior written permission of both the copyright owner and the publisher. The only exception is brief quotations in printed reviews.

The scanning, uploading, and distribution of this book via the Internet or via any other means without the permission of the publisher is illegal and punishable by law. Please purchase only authorized electronic editions, and do not participate in or encourage electronic piracy of copyrighted materials.

Your support of the author's rights is appreciated.

Published in the United States of America by
Soul Mate Publishing
P.O. Box 24
Macedon, New York, 14502

ISBN: 978-1-68291-601-8

ebook ISBN: 978-1-68291-556-1

www.SoulMatePublishing.com

The publisher does not have any control over and does not assume any responsibility for author or third-party websites or their content.

Acknowledgements

Thank you for embarking on Cece's journey. I mean thank you, thank you, thank you from the tip of my pen to the tooth-marked cap. I hope you enjoy her story. I promise more, because you can't keep a woman like Cece (or me) quiet for long.

The kudos . . .

Without the love and support of my family, this novel would not have been possible. Ray and Amy, this one's for you. Thank you for respecting my writing time.

My sincere gratitude to Saturday Writers. The monthly meetings, fantastic speakers, and camaraderie of the group drew me in.

My Lit Ladies, Sarah Patsaros, Camille Faye, Margo Dill, Brandi Schmidt, and Grace Malinee, I would not have had the courage to follow this through without your gentle nudges. We are six women writing our truths into fiction.

To Thursday Writers, Scribe's Tribe, St. Louis Writers Guild, and Missouri Writers Guild, every writer needs a support system. Thanks for being mine.

To Deborah Gilbert and Soul Mate Publishing, thank you for "understanding" Cece and giving me the opportunity to send her out into the world.

Cheryl Yeko, I can't thank you enough. You are truly a Cover Art Coordinator extraordinaire. My apologies if I was a pain.

Rae Monet, Cover Artist, thank you for "getting" what I had envisioned for my cover art and transforming it into the real deal. Mwah!

To my writing buddies, past and present, Tricia Grissom, Alice Muschany, Candace Carrabus Rice, Dana Stiebel, Doyle Suit, and Jerry Swingle who read numerous drafts without whining, I am thankful for your talents, advice, and cheerleading.

To Barb Schmidt, you're always there for me. I love our Wednesdays and hope we have many, many more. (You also made it through my crappy first draft, but you need an acknowledgement of your own.)

To Dixie Dart, we have blazed trails together and you waded through my first draft, too. Here's to many more trails (and sluggish first drafts.)

My snark sister and co-procrastinator, Deborah Schott, our outings, lunches, and gossip warm my soul.

To Joy Wooderson and Amy Harke-Moore for proofing and editing the version I sent to my publisher. I appreciate you more than words can say.

To my first beta readers, Kim Beerman and Dee Doub, thanks for providing me the encouragement to keep going.

Margie Lawson, you helped me kill the clichés, power up my words, and urged me to change my main character's name. I am indebted. So is Cece. She is no longer a Sissy. Hugs!

Lee Dunn, my retreat buddy, you provided the serenity I needed to percolate my ideas, rest my brain, and finish the second novel. A big hey to Anna, Barb, Maggie, Bonnie, Judy, Vickie, and Julie, the amazing Dittmer ladies. Thanks for welcoming me into your group.

Finally, to Alecia Hoyt at Alecia Hoyt Photography and Kristina McGaughey at KM Makeup Design, thank you for the awesome headshots and makeup, respectively. You made me feel beautiful, and I so appreciate your talents.

If I have failed to acknowledge you for your participation in this endeavor, my sincerest apologies. I have schlepped this manuscript hither and yon across this great nation seeking input and feedback. It is not with malice that I have forgotten to mention you. Forgive me, my brain only holds so much data. Thank you.

Chapter 1

"My mother prides herself on her ability to marry well. All five times."
Cece Cavanaugh

My day started the way it had all week, cutting fresh lilacs from the bushes surrounding our patio. Dark clouds in the distance rumbled a spring warning.

"Cece." My husband, Phillip, stepped out onto the textured pavement, wearing khakis and a white linen shirt, not his usual workday attire.

I dropped two fragrant sprigs into the vase I held in the crook of my arm. "You're late for breakfast."

"Don't start," he said. "I'm not in the mood."

"Why aren't you dressed for work?" I reached for another cluster of lilacs and stopped. He never took a day off unless it involved a tee time, and he wasn't dressed for golf. "You're not ill, are you?" That was the last thing I needed. I had a hair appointment with my daughter's best friend Sarah, a library committee meeting, and a tennis lesson. My daily planner did not include nursing a sick, grumpy husband.

"I'm fine," he said, running a hand through his sandy, silver-at-the-temples hair. "We need to talk." He crossed the patio in five strides, carrying his morning coffee and an attitude.

When he began toying with the change in his pocket, a niggling thought crossed my mind. He had something on his mind, something that could spoil my day, and I aimed to cut him off.

"The travel agent from Kingman's delivered our tickets yesterday," I said. "She suggested a bike tour in Chianti."

Phillip set his cup on the table and pulled out a chair, motioning for me to sit. "Cece, I have something I need to tell you."

I stopped clipping and glared at him. "Don't you dare," I said, ignoring the chair. "We've been planning this for a year. We're going hiking, taking a cooking class, and don't forget the winery tours. You'll enjoy this trip."

"About the trip." The look on his face mimicked constipation.

"No excuses. We're going." I pointed the shears at him. "And when you finish breakfast, bring the luggage up from the basement."

A muscle in Phillip's jaw jumped. "My bags are packed," he said, the words coming out in a rush.

I stepped back, fear inching its way through my veins, carrying a burden straight to my heart. "You-You never pack yourself." I stumbled over my words. "E-Esther always packs you."

As if on cue, our housekeeper stepped through the door, carrying a breakfast tray. Phillip waved her off. "Not now, Esther."

She mumbled under her breath and walked back into the house leaving the door open a crack, her typical response when something went awry in the Cavanaugh household. Listen now, blab later.

Phillip pulled a letter from his pocket and dropped it on the table. "I'm leaving."

"What? Why? Our flight isn't until Sunday." My stomach started cartwheeling, end over end, over end. The bagel I'd eaten earlier joined the battle, threatening to make an appearance.

Phillip's gaze traveled to the table and then back to me.

I shifted the vase in my arm and smoothed open the letter.

"It's an itinerary? That's not Kingman Travel's logo."

"I'm not going to Tuscany. I'm going to Rio."

"Rio today? Then Tuscany on Sunday?" I asked.

Sadness clouded Phillip's face, followed by the clench of his jaw. I'd witnessed his guarded look before. "No," he said in a voice so quiet I strained to hear.

An impossible thought materialized in my brain. I dropped the vase. I dropped the shears. I dropped my dignity. The clatter crowded my ears. "If you're set against going, I'll cancel the trip." I felt myself struggling for traction on an icy slope. "Next year. The year after. We'll figure it out."

"I'm going to Rio with someone else."

"What the hell? You're joking?" Questions rushed from my mouth, and scenes of sultry women, husband-stealing women, dressed in sexy-near-nothingness clouded my vision. "Who?"

"Willow." Phillip glanced at his watch and headed for the door. "My flight leaves in four hours."

I choked off a laugh. The seriousness of his demeanor held me back. "Willow? That-That-That 'I stick my finger down my throat to stay so skinny' girl from your office? She's what? Twenty? We have a daughter older than her."

"Willow's none of your business."

"If you're leaving with her, then she is my business." I followed and grabbed him around the waist, resting my head against his back. "Why are you doing this to me? To us? To our family?"

"Don't make this harder." Unwrapping my arms from his mid-section, Phillip shrugged out of my embrace and went inside.

I kicked off my rubber gardening clogs and trailed him, step-for-step, across the kitchen, past a slack-jawed Esther, up the stairs to our bedroom. "What about the girls? Michelle will be devastated. Jessie will never forgive you."

He pulled a suitcase and an overnight bag from his closet, dropped them on our bed, and disappeared into the bathroom. "Don't be dramatic. Jessie's grown, and Michelle will understand. Eventually." The sadness in his voice betrayed the bravado of his words.

Hoping to find he'd packed for me, I opened the overnight bag, the Louis Vuitton he'd given me last year for my forty-seventh birthday. Instead, it contained chargers for his cell and tablet, a belt, and his golf shoes.

Ha! He can't even take his mistress out of town without thinking about golf.

I jerked out the shoes and shoved them under my pillow.

He returned, dropped his toiletries in my bag, and zipped it shut. "We'll talk when I get back."

"Don't do this." I reached for the bag, but he scooped it and the suitcase up and left me standing at the foot of our bed.

I plucked the shoes from under my pillow and charged after him. "That's my luggage. Come back here with my Louis Vuitton, you bastard." I stood on the top step of our winding staircase, clutching the golf shoes.

My husband hiked the strap of my overnight bag higher on his shoulder. "I'll pick up the rest of my belongings when I return."

"Like hell you will." I launched a shoe, and it ricocheted off his shoulder.

Midway down the stairs, he spun around. "Are you crazy?"

His words snapped the synapses of my brain, sending a bolt of white-hot anger straight to my heart. "Me? Am *I* crazy?" This time I aimed and sent the other shoe flying. It clipped his sturdy Cavanaugh chin and blood spurted onto his shirt. "What do you think?"

"Shit." Phillip grabbed his chin and dashed to the door. "I'd have you arrested for assault if I didn't think I'd miss my flight."

"Go ahead. I've got time." I ran down the stairs in my socked feet. When I hit the marble floor, my feet slid in opposite directions, and I crash-landed.

"You need to get a grip on yourself." He shook his head and hurried out the front door, dragging my luggage behind him.

I picked myself up and followed, stopping on the porch when I saw his new golf clubs leaning against the wall. The custom-made set his mother bought for his birthday.

Phillip dabbed at his chin with a golf towel and scurried down the sidewalk toward his Porsche.

"Hey, jackass, don't forget your clubs." I pulled the driver out and slung it at his car, followed by the pitching wedge.

"You crazy bitch, those clubs cost thirty grand. Stop it." Phillip scrambled after his precious clubs, a perfect imitation of a crab crossing scorching sand. I continued flinging.

I scored a direct hit on his ass with the nine iron. The sand wedge struck him on the ankle. I had let loose with the five iron when Angie Valenti, our neighbor who also happened to be a cop, rounded the side of the house. The club missed the side of her head and bounced off the garage door.

"Jeez." Angie jumped back. "You're supposed to use those to hit a ball, not your best friend."

"Phillip!" I screamed. "The cops are here. You wanna have Angie arrest me?"

By now, Phillip had gathered all the clubs, including the one I'd almost beaned Angie with, and shoved them into the car. He stopped at the driver's door. His cheeks were flushed, and sweat gathered at his hairline. Rage contorted his face.

"You're just like your"—he paused—"mother." He spat

the word off his tongue like he'd taken a mouthful of spoiled milk.

It was damn lucky for him I'd dropped the gardening shears on the patio. I darted after him, intent on bashing him in the mouth and making him sorry he'd uttered those horrifying words. Angie must have read my mind. Before I could reach him, she tackled me, pinning me to the ground.

Phillip ducked into his car, gunned the engine, and sped off down the street, tires squealing.

"Get off me," I yelled, my face planted in my bluegrass lawn. Just because she was a cop didn't mean she had to act like one. I arched my back and tried to buck her off, but she held steady. All those years of cop-training paying off.

"I'll let you up when you calm down." She didn't budge.

I unearthed my face. "He said I was like my mother."

"Better yours than that witch he calls Mother," Angie said, loosening her grip. "Hazel Cavanaugh makes your mom look like a saint."

"Ha!" I said. "That'll be the day." Hazel might have a high opinion of herself, but my mother held no opinion of herself. No self-worth at all. She had five husbands under her belt to prove it, not including the guy she was shacking with now. Angie relaxed, and I used the opportunity to squirm out from underneath her and scramble to my feet.

She stood and smoothed a strand of burgundy hair that had escaped the bun knotted at the nape of her neck. "What the hell happened?"

I struggled to draw a breath. "I-I-I can't do this. Not now."

Angie grabbed my arm, ushered me across the porch, past the empty golf bag, and into my living room. After she pushed me down on my sofa, she said, "Spill it, girlfriend."

I shut my eyes, wondering how my life had taken such a horrendous turn. They say as you grow older, you become more like your mother. I had already begun to see her crow's feet clawing at the corners of my eyes. Her voice often screeched out of my mouth when my youngest daughter, Michelle, stretched my nerves beyond their boundaries. Now, for the first time in my life, I had begged a man not to leave. Something I'd watched my mother do all too often. I felt a flush creep up my neck and bloom across my face.

Phillip was right.

The cushion next to me gave, and Angie's arm slipped around my shoulders. That was all it took for the dam to break. Tears rushed down my face. I lifted one shoulder, then the other. "Rio de Janeiro." My voice sounded far away. But not as far away as Phillip. "With Willow."

"The giant beanpole from his office? Why?"

I pulled away and frowned. "Do I have to draw a picture? He left me. For her. She's young and pretty and doesn't have hair sprouting from her chin."

Angie leaned back into the sofa. She was a striking woman, especially in her police uniform. No one would ever call her beautiful. Her nose was a tad too long and her eyes wide set, but she had dewy-pink skin, smooth and clear with a smattering of freckles across her nose and cheeks. Most women our age—me, for instance—envied her complexion. Particularly considering my face was blotchy and swollen from crying.

I pulled up the hem of my shirt and wiped my face.

"How tall is she, anyway?" Angie asked.

"I don't know. Tall. Stupid tall," I said. "She's like a freaking Amazon."

Angie disappeared into the bathroom and returned with a wad of tissue. "Bet she has feet the size of a barge."

"A cargo ship," I said, taking the tissue. "An ocean-going cargo ship."

"She's gotta be what, a foot taller than Phillip and at least twenty-five years younger?" Angie never missed an opportunity to get in a good insult. She only tolerated Phillip because of our friendship.

Bolstered by an idea, I drew myself up and wiped my face. "He'll be back. This is a midlife crisis. Men have them all the time. Don't they?" Even to myself I sounded pathetic.

"Gah! Don't do that."

"I thought we had a good marriage. What did I do wrong?" Other than a cheating husband, I had a good life. Emphasis on had. We owned a beautiful home in Harris Arbor, the classy side of our small community of Wickford, Missouri.

Sixteen years ago, when my younger daughter, Michelle, was born, I'd given up my nursing career and turned my attention to community projects, charitable organizations, and taking care of my family. As wife of the CEO of Cavanaugh Structure and Design, it was my job to make sure my husband had a home fit for entertaining.

Angie ran her hands around the back of her head and tugged her bun. "Listen to yourself. He's cheating on you. You didn't do anything to deserve this. Find yourself a damn good divorce lawyer and sue Phillip's ass."

She thought my husband was selfish and domineering, and she constantly urged me to stand up for myself. Angie was like tree bark, rough. I didn't know if it was because she dealt with criminals or because she hung out with cops, but she always said what she thought, straight to the heart of the issue with no possibility of misinterpretation.

Dave, Angie's husband, said her straightforwardness was what he loved most about her. He said he always knew where he stood, no questions. Dave, a plastic surgeon, had seen more boobs than Playtex and Maidenform combined. Half the women at our country club were his patients, and the other half would be, as soon as they spotted the first wrinkle or sag.

I sniffed and rubbed my eyes with the tail of my shirt again.

"Gross, use the tissue," Angie said. "Girl, you need to grow a set of balls. It's time Cece Cavanaugh stood up for herself." She clamped her lips together to emphasize her point.

I twisted a tissue in my hand and contemplated what she'd said. The more Angie talked, the more depressed I became.

"You've got two legs. Use them. He's controlled you long enough."

"What are you talking about?" I sniffled and blew my nose.

"When's the last time you made a decision?" Angie crossed her legs and began to swing a brogan-covered foot.

"I planned the trip to Tuscany."

Angie wagged her pointer finger. "You might have planned it, but who suggested it?"

"Hazel," I said, hanging my head. Damn my mother-in-law. Always sticking her nose where I didn't want it.

"So, about your last decision?"

When I didn't answer, Angie plowed ahead. "You can't remember because you don't make them, he does. He decides where Michelle goes to school, and who vetoed the sensible car and gave her a Mustang? He even chose the color of your Lexus. And the club? You wouldn't be hanging out with those vultures if it weren't for him."

Angie was right about the country club. I hated the fakey nice-nice. But it was the norm. Phillip expected it and so did Hazel. Lord knew we couldn't go against Hazel.

"I do make decisions," I said.

"Name one."

"Don't be condescending. You make it sound like I'm a twit."

"I see it all the time in the battered women I deal with."

I pushed off the sofa and swung around to face her. "You're comparing me with women who get beat up by their husbands? Phillip's never laid a hand on me."

Angie pulled me back to the sofa. "Calm down. I know he doesn't do you physical harm. But he's abusive all the same. It's called mental abuse. When you do make a decision, he overrules it. For God's sake, he even tells you what perfume to wear and how to dress. I've kept my mouth shut all these years to keep peace, but now you have the opportunity. Take it. If Willow wants him, let her pick up his wet towels and dirty socks."

I interrupted her rant. "I don't clean up after him."

"Huh?"

"I have a housekeeper."

"Oh, yeah. Whatever. He litters your brain with his mental refuse, and you let him. Tell the creep you're through."

"It's not that easy," I said. "He waited until Michelle left for school. I have to tell her and Jessie he's gone."

"What'd you expect?"

The phone interrupted my reply. "Now what?"

"Let it go to voicemail."

"I can't. It might be one of the girls. Or Phillip. Maybe he realizes he made a colossal mistake." At the thought, I tore through the house and snatched the handset off his desk. *Please let it be him. Please let it be him. Please let it be him.*

"Is Phillip there?" a male voice asked.

"No. This is his . . ." The word caught on my tongue. "Wife. I'm his wife."

The man cleared his throat. "Cece, this is Keith Jenkins."

My pulse tapped a staccato beat against my temples. Phillip's attorney. "He's . . . He's . . . He's already filing for divorce?"

"Divorce?" His voice hiked an octave. "Good grief, no."

"Oh."

Keith sighed. "Phillip's avoided my calls all week. I need his approval on a payment plan for the mortgage company."

"Payment plan?" The grandmother of all hot flashes crept up my back, breathed fire on my neck, and roared full force up and over my scalp. Beads of perspiration sprouted across my forehead.

Papers rustled on Keith's end. "Your mortgage is in default."

"There must be a mistake," I said, but after this morning, who knew what was going on? I leaned against the desk to brace myself.

"Cece, there hasn't been a payment in six months. You've got ninety days to get the mortgage current or your house goes to foreclosure."

Chapter 2

"He promised he'd take care of me. Liar! He promised we'd grow old together. Liar! Liar! He promised he'd never cheat. Liar! Liar! Liar!"
Cece Cavanaugh

After dropping Michelle off at school and going home to change into dress clothes, I sat in my car in the parking lot of Bonafide CSC, Inc., giving myself a pep talk in preparation for a job interview. Blech! My stomach roiled and lurched at the thought. Little waves churned into huge rolling whitecaps. If only someone would throw me a life preserver.

Two weeks had passed since my cheating liar husband walked out the door dragging my Louis Vuitton luggage behind him. He hadn't made a mortgage payment in six months, and he'd cleaned out our joint bank accounts.

I'd made hundreds of calls to Phillip's cell phone, the bank, a lawyer, and all I got for my effort was a sore finger. The bank wanted money, the lawyer wanted money. Hell, even Michelle wanted money. Spring meant prom, and prom meant big bucks I didn't have. I couldn't afford a pedicure for myself much less a designer dress for a sixteen-year-old. To make my Friday even more memorable, Esther quit when her paycheck bounced.

Earlier in the week, I'd cashed in savings bonds my grandfather had given me when my girls were born. If I made a budget and stuck to it, I could stretch the money a couple of weeks, but it didn't come close to what I needed for the mortgage. I teetered between selling an organ and hocking my grandmother's silver. *Kidney, anyone?*

I had scarfed down enough Chunky Monkey to freeze a rainforest and counted the days until foreclosure long enough. After rejecting Angie and Dave's offer of a loan, I decided it was up to me to alter my future. Angie suggested I look for a job and even offered up daily suggestions in the form of classified ads circled and stuck under my windshield wipers.

Career prospects for a forty-seven-year-old who hadn't worked in sixteen years looked bleak. The thought of getting a job scared me to the point I almost broke down and called my mother-in-law, but I came to my senses before I'd had to grovel. My life would have to get a whole lot worse before I invoked Hazel's evil spirit.

Bonafide sat in the end spot of a strip mall in the Three Pines Center. Havil Law Center occupied the storefront next door. That was where I saw Kim Anderson. She had exited the lawyer's office. I raised my hand to wave, but her manner stopped me. Normally dressed to perfection, she wore faded exercise clothes, and her long, black hair was pulled up in a messy ponytail. Her red, blotchy face did nothing to hide her distress. She scanned the parking lot once and then looked again.

Kim and my oldest daughter, Jessie, had been friends since grade school. Not wanting to embarrass her, I sank down in my seat, hoping she wouldn't see me.

She climbed into her car and sat for a couple of minutes. From where I sat, I could see her crying. She collapsed against the steering wheel, sobbing. Kim had no family, other than an absentee, alcoholic father. Maternal compassion surged through me. Maybe something had happened to her father. I couldn't stand to watch her suffer. With a few minutes to spare before my interview, I did what I do best. My kids likened it to interfering, but I thought it more like intervening, helping, mothering. Sharing the wisdom of my years.

Whatever.

I traipsed over to Kim's car and let myself in the passenger side. She jumped when I pulled the door shut. When she saw it was me, fresh tears streamed down her cheeks. She tried wiping them away, but they continued to flow.

I pulled her into a hug, as best I could with a console between us, and sat there letting her sob on my shoulder, my 'smartly dressed for an interview' shoulder. When she sniffled, I thought about the condition of my jacket and released her at once. I dug around in my purse and found a tissue. For her, not me. Though, these days it wouldn't take much to set me to blubbering.

"Now," I said, using my mother voice, the one that made Michelle's eyes roll to the back of her teenage head. "What's going on?"

"I don't know where to begin."

"Try the lawyer's office," I said, nodding in the direction of the building.

Straightening, she wiped her eyes with more force. "I filed for divorce."

She could have pulled a baseball bat from under her seat and smacked me in the head, and I wouldn't have been more surprised. I knew Kim and Brian had a rocky relationship. But divorce? Though, I'd been a bit naïve in the marriage department. Who was I to second-guess someone else's situation? Brian had always been a prankster and a flirt, and not too long ago the school administration had placed him on probation for an incident involving another teacher. The whole incident was hush-hush. Even Jessie didn't know the entire story.

"I thought you were seeing a counselor." Jessie told me weeks ago things were strained, but I'd hoped with counseling they'd be able to pull through the tough times.

"After I made the appointment, Brian refused to go. He said we couldn't afford it."

The clock in the Lutheran Church bell tower across the street started chiming, and I knew it was eleven. I didn't feel right leaving her, but I needed this job.

"Honey, I've got an appointment I'm going to be late for. How about you come by the house later? I'll make iced tea, and we can sit outside and talk." I glanced at Bonafide and saw the blinds move apart.

"Thanks, you're sweet, but I'm okay." She jammed her keys in the ignition. "My mind is made up. I want Brian out of my life. Jessie and Sarah are taking me for a girls' weekend. I think they're trying to cheer me up. Tomorrow is my three-year anniversary. Brian and I had a celebration planned at this new bed and breakfast, Harmony Inn. Needless to say, we won't be going. It's already paid for. Jessie and Sarah are picking me up at four. We're going to party all weekend, and I'll officially bury my marriage."

I sighed, recognizing the wall she'd built to hide her pain. The juxtaposition of staying at a place called Harmony Inn for a weekend to bury a marriage did not escape me. If it worked for her, I might have to book a room or a whole floor. "If you need anything, anything at all, you call me." She'd be in good hands this weekend. Sarah, now my hairdresser, had moved to Wickfield the beginning of their sophomore year of high school, and she'd fit right in. They'd all been best of friends since.

Kim nodded.

Not wanting to leave, I hesitated.

"Go," she said. "I'm fine. Really."

I had no sooner let myself out and watched Kim drive away when I saw Brian parked four rows down next to a Dumpster. He inched his SUV from his hiding spot and followed in the same direction Kim had gone.

I didn't think it was a coincidence seeing Brian in the same parking lot on the same day his wife went to see a lawyer. I grabbed my cell phone and tapped in Kim's number.

My call went straight to voicemail. I was torn between getting in my car and going after her or going on the interview. Since I had to have this job, I called my daughter.

"Jess, it's Mom," I whispered.

"I know, Mom. Your number comes up on my phone." She sounded harried. Working in an emergency room did that to a nurse.

I went back and got in my car for privacy. "I saw Kim coming out of an attorney's office."

"I can't talk now. I'm heading out to lunch," Jessie said, turning on her bored-daughter mode.

"Listen to me. Brian was following her," I said.

"He what?" Jessie asked, anxiety creeping into her tone.

"You heard me." I went on to tell her what I'd seen. "I tried to call her, but she doesn't have her phone on. He wouldn't hurt her, would he?"

"He's been acting odd, but no, he wouldn't," Jessie said. "I'll call her neighbors and have them watch for her. She should be heading home."

"Okay," I said. "Why didn't you tell me about Kim and Brian?"

"With everything you've been going through with Dad, I figured you had enough to deal with."

I blew out a breath and leaned back in my seat. "Are you kidding?"

"Look, I gotta go, but I'll tell you all about it later," Jessie said. "Sarah and I are spending the weekend with her."

I heard exasperation in her tone, and then I heard nothing. She hung up on me.

Brat!

~ ~ ~

Before going in for my interview, I checked my make-up in the rearview mirror and fluffed my hair. I gasped when I noticed more than a little gray sprinkled among my own blonde hairs. I had missed my appointment the morning Phillip walked out on me. Now, with my situation, there was no chance of getting a touch up unless I could talk Sarah into giving me a freebie.

Inside, away from the glaring sun, I stopped to give my vision time to adjust. I blinked once or twice, and I focused on a woman sitting behind a desk. The plastic nameplate read NANCY—SECRETARY.

She wasn't what I'd pictured as a secretary. I expected a plain-Jane sort. Nondescript in an unobtrusive way. Boring, yet efficient. Nancy—Secretary had plump, pouty lips, high cheekbones, and the nose of a veteran hockey player, lumpy and bumpy in all the wrong places. The absence of wrinkles around her eyes and mouth made me jealous. Not even one laugh line.

Frizzed-out hair, the color and texture of a withered sea sponge, framed her face. I guessed her age to be about thirty-five, maybe older if she'd been pumped and plumped. The *pièce de résistance,* her fuchsia tank top with plunging neckline left *nothing* to the imagination.

"Are you the Cavanaugh lady?" Her grating voice slung the words at me like a mop splashing dirty water across the floor.

I shrank into myself and nodded, hoping I was interviewing for her job, and she would be long gone before I started work, if I got hired.

"You're late." Nancy opened a folder and pushed a pile of papers at me. "Fill out this, this, and this."

I reached for a pen, an apology almost making its way out of my mouth, when I heard a loud crack, like a rifle. I jumped, but Nancy didn't flinch. The noise came from her. Her jaws worked overtime on a massive wad of gum.

A bubble escaped her lips and grew to the size of an orange. I watched in horror while the pink goo expanded. Another explosion appeared imminent, but she sucked it in and started over.

God have mercy. If we had to be stuck in an office together, I'd find a place to stick her gum.

While I worked on the forms, a round, little man appeared through the doorway behind Nancy's desk. When he stepped into the room, I swiveled my head and did a double-take. The theme song from *The Alfred Hitchcock Hour* popped into my head. I pushed down a laugh and almost choked.

"Scary, ain't it?" Nancy paused and burst another bubble. "Mr. Fletcher always creeps people out. But it's cool. He don't have to buy a Halloween costume." She erupted into giggles, followed by a fit of snorting.

Hitchcock's double cleared his throat. "Enough, Nancy. Don't you have filing?"

Nancy sank back in her chair and stuck out her lip in a pout.

"I assume you're Cecelia Cavanaugh," Fletcher said to me.

"Yes." I offered my hand, but he didn't accept. His eyes focused on Nancy's rear. She had left her desk and headed in the direction of a row of filing cabinets. A stuffed black raven perched atop the one closest to the window. Beady eyes glared across the room and made me rethink my employment choice. *Yeesh.* I retracted my hand and used it to smooth my skirt. "Everyone calls me Cece."

He shifted his scrutiny to me. "Cece it is. I'm Bruce Fletcher."

Starting with my sensible navy pumps, his gaze traveled up the skirt of my suit and landed on my chest. He paused, remaining fixed on my less-than-endowed boobs. I stayed in shape playing tennis and working out at the gym, but never in my life had a man ogled me that way.

He reminded me of one of those bug-eyed cartoon characters, and I wasn't flattered. The contents of my stomach swayed side to side from nerves, and his creepiness added to my anxiety. I made a mental note to buy pepper spray—a case of pepper spray—on my way home. Perhaps the lecher was harmless, but I wasn't going to take a chance.

Cece Cavanaugh, what have you gotten yourself into?

I coughed to get his attention.

He sputtered and met my stare.

After handing him my résumé and the papers I'd filled out for Nancy, I followed him to his office. He motioned for me to sit in one of the two walnut captain's chairs.

His desk and credenza looked expensive—teak or mahogany—with brass drawer pulls. A leather blotter covered most of the surface. Expensive was good. It meant he could afford to pay me, unless he spent all his money on office décor. He settled in his chair, a high-back leather job, trimmed in brass tacks, and scanned my work history. Very lawyer-like. I couldn't help but grin. *Perry Mason meets Alfred Hitchcock.*

In less than a minute, he slapped the desk. "You're hired."

"I am? But . . ." I paused, elated at the prospect of getting a job with the first ad I answered. Then my bullshit meter zoomed from green to red with nary a thought to yellow. I never dreamed he'd hire me on the spot. Was this a bad thing or a good thing?

"But you didn't interview me. I don't even know what I'll be doing." *Or how much you'll pay me.*

He hadn't told me the hours or anything about Bonafide CSC. Maybe I didn't want the damn job, not with a creepy boss like him. Who was I kidding? Short of prostitution or selling drugs, I would do almost anything to pay my bills. Well, not anything, especially not anything with him.

"If it makes you feel better, I can ask a few questions." He ran a chubby hand over his balding head, stopping to scratch a mole underneath his scant comb-over. "You dependable?"

"Yes." I leaned back in my chair, daring to relax.

"Got a good work ethic?"

"Yes."

"Good," he said. "I'm looking for a dependable person with a good work ethic to clean."

I stared down at my Boysenberry Bliss nails.

"Cleaning? Like dusting and vacuuming?" My manicure already showed signs of old age, chipped polish and little voids near my cuticles where the nails had grown out. I could have used a fill, but I needed a steady paycheck. A large paycheck. The stack of bills on my desk wasn't shrinking.

"Yes, ma'am. That's what we do," he said. "No job too gruesome."

Gruesome? Great. Last week I had a housekeeper, now I'm contemplating being one. Damn you, Phillip.

"Mr. Fletcher." I scooted forward, ready to vault from his office. "This may not be for me. I expected filing or answering phones."

I stood and grabbed my purse.

"For most of the jobs, you can name your price."

A quiver of excitement rumbled up my once spineless-spine. Maybe I could save my house. Before Michelle was born, I worked as a nurse and dealt with all kinds of messes. If it meant paying my mortgage, I could do it. I had checked into resuming my nursing career, but the training to get me up-to-date would take too long. I needed work now. Since my prospects didn't look promising, what choice did I have?

Desperation always outmaneuvered good sense.

"You can refuse any job you don't want," Fletcher added.

This sounded more and more like work I could handle, especially if I called the money shots. And the upside, if there was an upside, I wouldn't be stuck in an office with Nancy. That alone made me happier than a kid at recess.

"But, if you turn down too many, you're outta here."

"Well . . ." I looked down at my feet, hoping to see them moving toward the door. They didn't.

"Give it a try. The pay's good. If it doesn't work, walk away. No strings."

What did I have to lose? My dignity had left with my husband.

"No hard feelings?" I asked.

"None," he said. "We work on a contract basis around here. You're your own boss. I provide the jobs and bill the clients. I need someone willing to work." He came around to my side of the desk. "You want to work, don't you?"

"Yes." What I wanted to say was, *"Hell, no. I don't want to work. I want my life back. I want my husband back. I want all the cheating and lying to have been a bad dream."*

He grinned. "You up for a workout this afternoon?"

I sucked in my breath and prayed he meant a job. Before I could answer, he reached inside his jacket and extracted a paper.

I exhaled.

"The Bargain Hut. They've got a real shitstorm." He snorted and handed me the assignment. "Here's the address. The owner wants you there ASAP. Wear something you don't mind getting dirty. I don't reimburse for ruined clothing."

I scanned the information. It didn't tell me anything except the address and contact name, Clyde Johnson.

"Bargain Hut?" I searched my memory and came up blank.

"Yeah, over on South Main, across the railroad tracks, behind the auto parts store."

Oh, that Bargain Hut. Not exactly a side of town I frequented. "What do I need?" I asked.

"Standard stuff. Mop, rags, paper towels, disinfectant, and trash bags. Lots of trash bags. Clyde will provide the rest. If you buy anything, save your receipts. Main thing is you'll get dirty." He eyed me like a bulldog in a meat market. If he licked his lips, I'd be out of here, money or not.

Chicken flesh popped up on my arms. Apropos, considering I felt like a big chicken-shit. On my way home, I'd stop for pepper spray and maybe a restraining order. Was it too late to call my mother-in-law for a handout? No, I'd rather die a wicked, painful death.

"Before you leave, have Nancy show you how we do things. When you complete an assignment, turn in your invoice with your hours and expenses noted. She'll cut your check." He leaned his plump body against the doorframe, pulled in his ample gut, and hiked his pants. "Saves me postage, plus there's no squabbling over when you get paid." He ran his tongue over his front teeth like he was searching for a stray tidbit.

That did it. He could eyeball Nancy all he wanted, but this old gal was through. I sprinted across the office to the front door.

"This job may run in the neighborhood of six hundred dollars," Fletcher said to my back.

My feet stopped moving. My shoulders slumped. My hand stilled on the door handle. My brain screamed, "Jackpot!"

Chapter 3

"Cecelia doesn't deserve my son. When Phillip met her, she and her trashy mother lived in a car. A Ford Pinto of all things. What was my son thinking?"
Hazel Cavanaugh

Sleep eluded me as I tossed and turned in my king-size bed. Twice I reached across the distance and felt the cool sheet instead of the warmth of my husband. When I pulled his pillow to me, his scent lingered, bringing forth a new deluge of tears.

Around four-thirty, my hot flashes commenced with a vengeance. I slid to Phillip's side of the bed and languished in the coolness until the sheets were soaked with perspiration. In a fit of frustration, I gave up and trudged to the bathroom. Every muscle in my body ached. Even though I exercised on a regular basis, I'd found dormant muscles. My skin still tingled from the shower I'd taken last night, trying to remove the stench from my Bargain Hut ordeal. When Fletcher said the place was a shitstorm, he wasn't being facetious. In fact, a vandal had literally crapped on almost every surface in the Bargain Hut's unisex bathroom.

I had argued with myself all the way home whether to tell Michelle about the job, especially since one of the clerks recognized me as Michelle's mom. I prayed the girl would keep her mouth shut and decided to keep my secret. Telling Michelle that her dad had left was hard enough. She didn't need me whining about finances or upsetting her with our sudden decline in social status. And the longer she didn't know, the longer I could keep it from Hazel.

When I emerged from the bathroom, my cell phone chirped to life. I pulled my robe around me and answered.

"Hello?"

"You didn't clear your assignment."

"Excuse me?" I said.

"You're supposed to clear your assignments before you get more."

Ah, Nancy. I'd recognize her nasally whine anywhere. "I can stop by—"

"You got forty-five minutes. I told Fletcher I don't work on Saturday, but since you didn't do the paperwork yesterday, I gotta be here today. And you gotta pick up a key for the new job. You got two days to get it done."

"What's the assignment?" Even Nancy's sour attitude didn't dim the elation I felt about scoring another job.

"Forty-three minutes." Nancy exhaled into the phone. "Then I'm outta here whether or not you show."

"What. Kind. Of. Job," I said.

"Cleaning. A. Vandalized. House," Nancy said, mimicking my tone. "You want the key, you got forty-two minutes."

"Nancy—"

With the burst of a bubble and the slam of the phone crashing into its cradle, she was gone.

"—wait."

A horrendous headache hammered my brain. It took a great deal of effort and several aspirin, but I managed to dress in yoga pants and a light pullover, tug my hair into a ponytail, and stumble downstairs.

I was writing a note to Michelle when she shuffled into the kitchen.

"Where're you going this early?" she asked, trying to stifle a yawn.

"Errands," I replied. "Grocery store, cleaners, gas station, post office."

She narrowed her gray eyes. Eyes that reminded me so much of Phillip. My heart tightened in my chest.

"You look like you're going to the dump." Her blonde hair, still tangled from sleep, fell across her shoulders and spilled down the front of her tank top. At no more than five-foot, she had Phillip's build. Short and stocky. My girls were absolute opposites. Jessie had my green eyes and blonde hair. She had a lean runner's body and was taller than me. With Jessie, fitness came as second nature. Unlike her sister, Michelle counted every calorie and worked out like a fiend to keep the pounds from creeping up.

I switched the subject to Michelle. A tried and true tactic when dealing with teenage girls. "What's on your agenda today?"

Her face brightened. "Shopping with Gran. She's taking me into the city to look for prom dresses, and we're having lunch at the new bistro on Lehigh Street." She continued to outline her day with her precious grandmother.

Blah. Blah. Blah.

Of course, Hazel and American Express to the rescue. I sighed. Perhaps, I was a tad jealous of Hazel's affection. She had never shown me the slightest bit of warmth, and I had learned to return the sentiment. I appreciated Hazel for being a good grandmother to my girls, but it didn't negate the fact that Michelle was on restriction.

"Did you forget you're grounded?" Angie had brought Michelle home in a squad car three days after Phillip left when she'd caught Michelle ditching classes.

"Seriously?" Michelle stomped across the kitchen and flung open the pantry.

Rather than argue, I waited until she began foraging for breakfast. "Gotta go," I said. "See you later." I escaped to the garage.

In my rush, I tripped over a rug. My purse landed upside down, scattering the contents across the floor.

"Way to go, *grace*." I scooped up grocery receipts, cosmetics, and loose change, along with my wallet, and stuffed everything into my Versace tote.

~ ~ ~

In less than ten minutes, I made it to Bonafide. Nancy had the phone to her ear when I arrived. "You're such a bad boy," she purred into the receiver, ignoring me.

A few seconds passed, and she made no attempt to end her call. Her personal call. I cleared my throat. "Excuse me."

Irritated at the interruption, she mouthed, "Just a sec. Can't you see I'm busy?"

"I only need—"

"I said, wait." Her tone and the subsequent glare shut me up.

So much for Nancy worrying about the minutes ticking by. The key and a check lay on her desk in plain sight. She must have sensed my impatience, because she picked up the key and dangled it from her scarlet acrylics. New day, new color.

"But . . ." I pointed toward the key.

"Keep your panties on, hon." She giggled. "Not you, sweetie," she said into the phone. "You better not be wearing panties, big guy."

Covering the mouthpiece, she wiggled her finger toward a row of lime-green fiberglass chairs. "Sit."

"Are you kidding me?" I slung the strap of my purse onto my shoulder with such force it sent papers fluttering off her desk.

"Where were we?" She wrinkled her face into a scowl and lowered her voice to an ineffective whisper. "Oh, yes, I'm wearing a—"

I scooted a chair across the tile, making a noise much like a horny cat in search of relief. Nancy cupped her hand around the receiver and swiveled a full one-eighty. A scarred table beside me held an assortment of fine reading materials. I selected a copy of *People* and pondered the latest celebrity breakups, and Phillip and me, and what went wrong with our marriage.

I rifled through the magazine making as much noise as possible. When the pages began to tear, Nancy looked up and shot me the finger. My head felt like red-hot electrodes pulsing fire into my brain.

"What?" I shouted. "Give me the damn—"

Fletcher's door opened, and Nancy slammed the phone down. Too bad phone slamming wasn't an Olympic sport.

"Here ya go, hon." With a flick of her wrist, she launched the key across the room.

I stumbled to my feet and caught it in mid-air.

Fletcher glanced at the papers littering the floor by Nancy's desk and shook his head. "Morning, Cece. Glad you're taking the Cline house. Talk about a mess. Her daughter wants it cleaned pronto. Take a stab at figuring your invoice and bring it to me when you're done."

Hoping to avoid a lengthy conversation with Mr. Creepy, I slipped the key in my purse and assured him I'd take care of it.

He watched Nancy for another moment then retreated to his office.

"I hate it when he does that. Always sneaking around like he owns the place."

"He does own the place," I said.

Nancy tilted her head and yawned. "So?"

She pulled a paper from a file folder and pushed it across the desk. "You need to fill this out to close yesterday's assignment."

I completed the form and handed it back. She tore the address for today's job off a memo pad and scooted it to the edge of her desk along with my check. I snatched them up and plowed out the door, but not before honoring her with a one-finger salute. No one said I had to play nice.

Bi-atch!

~ ~ ~

With luck and the navigation system in my car, I located the client's home, a modest brick ranch in an older but well-maintained section of town. I didn't need the key after all. Someone had jimmied the lock.

The door opened with a gentle push.

"Hello?" I called. "Anybody here?" I waited, one foot on the threshold, the other ready to carry me back to my car.

"Mrs. Cline? Hello?" Stupid me. The house had been vandalized. But in case someone still lingered, I pushed into the living room, wielding my broom like a sword.

When no one jumped out, I did a quick walk-through to assess the damage. Cushions spewed stuffing from jagged slits. Books, figurines, and photos lay in a jumble on the carpet. Splinters of glass from a sofa-sized mirror glistened in the sunlight. My spirit plummeted to match my energy level. I forced myself to continue to the kitchen.

Cabinet doors gaped open, contents scattered on the quarry tile. Piles of flour, sugar, and cereal floated atop globs of ketchup and mustard. I found a glass that hadn't been shattered, filled it with water, and downed four more aspirin. *I will get through this.* The thought of returning to my clean, tidy house at the end of the day spurred me on.

In the bathroom, every lotion, shampoo, and medicine bottle lay empty, the liquids congealing in a gooey mess on the floor. The shower curtain hung in shreds and towels filled the toilet. A cell phone behind the toilet caught my attention. I put it in my pocket, intending to leave it on the kitchen table where Mrs. Cline could find it, but not until I cleared the clutter. I pushed down my queasiness and rolled up my sleeves.

In only a few hours a small blister had developed near the base of my ring finger. I held my hand palm-side up to inspect it, and a lump formed in my throat. Phillip's wedding vows came back to me: "Take this ring as a sign of my commitment."

I turned the platinum bands and remembered what the minister had said about Phillip and me starting our lives together and how the ring symbolized a never-ending circle of love. *What a load!*

Before I allowed myself another dive into the pity pool, I twisted off my rings and buried them in my purse. No sense taking a chance on knocking out the diamonds while I cleaned. I might have to sell them to make a mortgage payment.

My naked finger looked odd. I traced the groove and wondered if Phillip sported the same indentation. *Enough!* I shook off the melancholy and inspected my work. When I stopped for the day, the house was more than half done. I'd made excellent progress for an amateur. Maybe, just maybe, I could make this job work. My knees wobbled with fatigue, and my back bore the beginning of a telltale kink.

~ ~ ~

Before heading home for a soak in my tub, I stopped to replenish my supplies. I pulled into the almost-empty parking lot of a discount store, not the Bargain Hut. In my 'before Phillip left days,' I never went anywhere without makeup and had every hair in place, but tonight I was too tired to care how I looked. It wouldn't take more than five minutes to make my purchases and be on my way.

After today, I wouldn't go to any job without rubber gloves. Sticking my bare hands in someone else's toilet wasn't on my 'favorite things to-do' list. I'd also thrown away my mop after the Bargain Hut job and used the last of my paper towels.

Selecting the mop didn't take a lot of brain power. I grabbed the cheapest, sturdiest one I could find. Paper towels were a different story. The display contained at least fifteen different brands. I had never given paper towels much thought other than if they matched my color scheme. Now I worried about cost, strength, and absorbency. If I bought cheap, I'd have to use more. If I chose good ones, I'd have to pay more.

Decisions. Decisions.

"Oh. My. God. Cece Cavanaugh? What happened to you?"

The voice belonged to Bitsy Harris-Dodd, my mother-in-law's best friend. Bitsy's sing-song whine echoed through the empty store. I froze in the middle of the aisle, too far from either end to escape.

Of all people, why Bitsy? She spewed gossip faster than any of the busybodies at the country club, *and* she employed Esther's sister. Severe outages in the cellular network would be the only way Bitsy wouldn't know about my bounced check to Esther or Phillip's trip with Willow.

Wait a minute! Why was Bitsy at a discount store? Her family invented money. At least she flashed it around like they did. The Harris and Dodd families were the founders of the wine industry here. In Wickford, you either owned a winery or worked for a winery. The Cavanaughs were the exception. Phillip's grandfather made his money designing wineries. The whole of it fell into Phillip's lap as the only heir.

Bitsy clicked her tongue and interrupted my thought. "Is it true the wife is always the last to know?"

I pulled back and skewered her with a glare. "What did you say?"

She brushed at a speck on her linen skirt. "I wondered if you truly didn't have a clue about Phillip. His affair has been the talk of the club for weeks."

Her words drilled into my brain, but I held my tongue. I wanted to leave, but more than that I wanted to know what the old bat knew, and the most effective way to find out was to let her yammer.

"You cannot be shocked, darlin'," she drawled in her fake Southern accent. Bitsy was born and raised in Wickford, having only left a year or two to attend finishing school in Savannah. And a Georgia peach she was not. "If you think she was the first, you are deceiving yourself. Lordy mercy, but your husband does have a track record."

Others? There were others? Maggot! How could he do this to me? Hot tears built up behind my eyes. I bit my lip and commanded them to stay put. Bitsy would not see me cry.

She looked me over and smirked, like I'd stepped in dog doo. I *did* have a suspicious stain on my left tennis shoe, faded yoga pants, a pullover suitable for a linebacker, and hair that hadn't seen a salon in weeks. Not country club attire by any standard. I wouldn't even pass for a groundskeeper. They wore tailored uniforms.

"Speaking of hair," she said.

We were? I didn't remember hair being a topic of conversation, but my mind was busy processing Bitsy's news flash. I smoothed a few disheveled strands into place.

"What has happened to yours? My God, Cece, do you own a mirror?"

Bitsy whipped out her cell phone and hit speed dial. I prayed a ceiling tile would come loose, knock her on the head, and strike her with short-term memory loss before the call went through.

When it was apparent the ceiling would stay intact, I decided to gamble. "Bitsy, you're a bit out of your neighborhood, aren't you? Bet the old hens at the club would love to hear about your shopping expedition. Hazel wouldn't be caught dead in here, much less buying cleaning supplies."

Bitsy's pencil-lined brows shot up and her powdered cheeks paled. She glanced at her cart full of toilet paper, napkins, and laundry detergent. Then into her phone she said, "Uh, Mavis, darlin' you aren't going to believe it, but I dialed your number by mistake." She paused. "Sure thing. See you tomorrow at the club."

I pulled two packages of paper towels from the shelf and fled down the aisle, leaving Bitsy with her ruby red lips hanging open.

~ ~ ~

Darkness fell as I sped home. I hoped Hazel had dropped Michelle off and left. If my threat had worked, Bitsy hadn't told Mavis or my mother-in-law. I'd have to face Hazel soon enough, but not today. My temples throbbed at the thought.

The sight of the silver Mercedes parked behind Jessie's car sent my mood swirling into a dark, dark place. Heat rushed to my face. Hot flashes *and* my mother-in-law. I didn't know which was worse, but together they were hell squared.

By the time I reached the porch, I had put my emotions on hold and prepared to face my mother-in-law for the first time since Phillip left. I squared my shoulders and jammed the key in the lock. The door flew open.

Hazel stood there in her signature pink Chanel suit complete with satin, buckled Manolo Blahniks. One hand gripped the door, the other rested on her hip. My mother-in-law's battle stance.

"We were beginning to wonder if you would ever show up." She launched into full witch mode without taking a breath. "I've been trying to find you all day."

"My phone never rang," I said, the rebel in me rising to the surface. An ache snuggled up to my brain and unleashed a full-scale assault. I dug in my purse searching for my cell and came up empty-handed. Then I pictured the contents of my purse scattered all over the garage floor this morning. I must have overlooked my phone in the chaos.

I asked, "What's going on? Why are you here?" I peered around her into the empty hallway.

"What do you care? Especially since you've been out doing who knows what." Hazel stopped her verbal attack and stared at me.

My faded clothing reeked of sweat and pine cleaner, and my hair had long since given up on the ponytail.

Hazel squinted her brown eyes, stepped toward me, and sniffed. "You look like a street person. Where have you been?"

Was she trying to smell my breath? I clutched my purse to my chest to put some distance between us.

"None of your business." I pushed past her.

"No wonder Phillip left," she mumbled loud enough for me to hear.

"Phillip left because he couldn't keep his pants zipped." The minute the words were out, I regretted saying them. Divorce or not, Hazel would be part of my life until hell ceased to exist and then some. We had never been friends, never would be, but as long as she was in Michelle's and Jessie's lives, she'd be in mine. From the moment Phillip introduced me to his mother, she had belittled me at every turn. The first time I met her, she accused me of being a "gold digger." Who does that? A self-centered, pretentious snob, that was who.

I wondered about the longevity of Hazel's side of the family. Then I remembered Phillip's grandmother, Hazel's mother, lived to the cantankerous old age of ninety-five, and I do mean cantankerous. She made Hazel seem almost loveable. Ninety-five minus Hazel's seventy-three. *Ack! Could I take twenty-two years of Hazel's sniping?*

She followed me to the kitchen, heels tap-tapping on the hand-scraped hardwood flooring.

"Don't turn your back." Her voice echoed behind me. "I'm not finished."

Guess again. I kept moving toward the gathering room.

"Cecelia," her voice softened. "You need to know something."

If I didn't know better, I'd have thought she was backing down.

She touched my arm. "Wait."

I spun, my tennis shoes making squeaking noises on the floor.

Tears glistened in her eyes. *Don't do it, witch. You might melt.* The thought of her wilting into a puddle put a smile on my face.

"The girls . . ." Her voice caught.

My smile faded and I felt faint. "Hazel, what is it? What's happened?"

Jessie walked up behind her grandmother, tears streaming down her cheeks. "He's dead."

Over Jessie's shoulder, I saw Michelle crying.

For a few seconds, I allowed myself to imagine my troubles were over. No nasty divorce. No working myself into a frenzy. Life could return to normal. Well, a normal where I was a grieving widow. Then I looked at my girls and saw the expressions on their faces. Not a normal I wanted to live with. *What was I thinking? Wretched as he was, I still loved the man.*

I slumped against the wall for support and wrapped my arms around my chest.

"Phillip's dead?" I asked.

Chapter 4

"It's Mom's fault Dad left. She's always nagging him. If she was more like Gran, my life would be much better."
Michelle Cavanaugh

"Not Phillip," Hazel said, practically spitting the words at me. "Brian Anderson."

Relief spread through my bones. Even though Phillip dumped me, he *was* the father of my children. I'd never wish him dead. Impotent maybe, or with a herd of fleas invading his man parts, but not dead.

"Brian Anderson? Kim's husband?" My relief gave way to guilt. Guilt over what Kim must be feeling. She had filed for divorce; now her husband was dead.

Jessie nodded.

"They found him at the new bed and breakfast," Hazel said. "Harmony Inn."

My mind focused on Kim. Yesterday I'd seen her coming out of her attorney's office. I needed to be there for her. Then one thought led to another.

"What do you mean 'found him'?" I struggled to draw a breath, feeling a giant weight on my chest crushing my heart, my lungs. Twisting and squeezing.

"Murdered," Hazel whispered. "Jessie and Sarah found him."

I pressed my hand to my throat in an effort to eliminate the gnawing sensation. "What?" My hands trembled, keeping time with my knees.

Hazel sighed and patted her salon-induced platinum hair. "The detective called me when he couldn't reach you. And your daughter sat in the police station along with all the other Wickford riffraff. Like a common criminal."

The accusatory tone had returned to her voice.

Really? Like Wickford was crawling with disreputable citizens.

"Thank you for being here," I said, trying to sidestep a confrontation. Regardless of how much my mother-in-law and I clashed over the years, she made my girls her priority.

"Someone had to be," Hazel said. She leaned in close. "If you took care of your husband, he would not be chasing skirts in God-knows-where. And you-you're up to something not befitting the Cavanaugh name. I don't know what, but you can rest assured I will find you out, Cece."

Holy cripes, give me a break.

Hazel placed an arm around Jessie and ushered her into the gathering room. Angie sat on the sofa across from the fireplace. After witnessing my interaction with Hazel, Angie was doing a good job of remaining noncommittal. In any other circumstance, she'd be in Hazel's face telling her to back off. Michelle huddled in Phillip's recliner, a quilted throw around her shoulders. A cozy fire in the fireplace and the rhythmic tick of the grandfather clock in the corner countered the level of stress in the room.

Jessie eased onto the sofa, and Hazel excused herself to make coffee.

I knelt next to Jessie on aching knees and suppressed a groan. "Are you okay?"

She nodded, trying to stem the flow of tears with her shirt sleeve.

I reached up and wiped her cheeks. "What happened?"

"We don't know much," Angie said. "Kim's still at the station."

Angie picked at a button on her uniform, not making eye contact. Her role as my friend, neighbor, Jessie's second mother, and her profession as an officer of the law were in direct conflict.

"Oh, my God. They don't think she killed him, do they?" I asked. I turned to Angie, hoping she'd deny it.

Her face reverted to her cop expression. Blank.

Damn!

"Angie, is Kim a suspect?" I prodded.

"Too early to tell," she said. "The investigators will sort the details."

"I don't care about the details. Kim did not kill Brian," I said.

Jessie shivered. "He was lying on the floor covered in blood."

Hazel opened and closed cabinet doors in the kitchen, either assessing my grocery-shopping skills or snooping. I didn't buy her coffee-making endeavor. The only thing Hazel ever made was trouble.

"It was terrible," Jessie said. She buried her face in her hands.

"Does Kim need an attorney?" I pulled myself to my feet and stretched a kink from my back. "They won't question her without an attorney, will they?"

My mother-in-law interrupted the conversation and said, "I've already hired John Grayson. He's the best criminal attorney in the state."

Jessie cringed when Hazel said criminal. "Gran, Kim didn't kill him."

"No one's accusing her," Angie said. "But since they're separated, it's a natural assumption."

"What was Brian doing at Harmony Inn?" I asked. My mind reeled with possibilities. It didn't take much to conjure up the desperate things a wife might do when faced with a failing marriage. No, I made the leap with no problem at all. But, murder?

"Only Kim knows the answer," Angie said.

Hazel must have gotten bored because she disappeared into the kitchen again. She didn't do well when the center of attention focused on anyone other than her. It took me years to figure her out, but I'd finally arrived at the conclusion the world only mattered when it revolved around my mother-in-law.

"I knocked on Sarah's door at eight this morning, and then we woke Kim. Sarah and I went down for breakfast while Kim showered. We found him in the study," Jessie said.

"Oh, Jess, I'm sorry." I pulled her into another hug and squeezed tight. "Why was he there?"

Jess pulled away and shifted her gaze to Angie. "I don't know. I don't know anything."

It occurred to me and apparently to Jessie, that on- or off-the-clock, friend or not, Angie *was* a cop. "Should you be hearing this?" I asked Angie.

She shrugged. "The case has been turned over to the detectives. I'm not privy to the investigation. Unless Jessie implicates Kim or herself, it doesn't matter."

Jessie shivered and drew her knees closer to her chest. "I told the detective everything. I'm not incriminating anyone. Now will you guys leave me alone?"

Michelle brought the quilted throw she'd had around her shoulders and draped it over her sister. The unselfish act made me proud of my younger daughter. Maybe Michelle was growing up.

Even though it was late spring, the evenings still carried a chill. Someone had built the fire earlier, but the embers were dying. I stirred the ashes and added another log and some kindling. Everyone sat in silence while I poked and prodded the fire to life.

Staring at the flames, I tried to absorb everything Angie had said. "How did he die?"

Angie joined me and sank down onto the hearth. "Stabbed. Repeatedly."

Jessie winced and seemed to shrink into herself. "I checked his pulse." She shook her head and squeezed her eyes tight. "He was already dead."

"Did Brian spend the night?" I wondered if Kim and Brian arranged to meet at the inn or if he stopped by unannounced. Kim had been adamant about the divorce yesterday, and I had a hard time envisioning reconciliation a few hours later. But, he had been following her when she left her attorney's office.

Jessie toyed with the edge of the throw, rolling it between her fingers. "I don't know."

The grandfather clock began its familiar Westminster chime. The room fell silent waiting for the subsequent ten bongs.

"I'd better call it a night. Dave has an early consultation. Another trophy wife needs trophy boobs." Angie stood and touched my shoulder. "We'll talk tomorrow."

"I should go, too," Hazel called from the kitchen.

"I'll take Jessie upstairs," Michelle said.

Angie and Hazel gathered jackets and purses, and we walked to the foyer.

The girls hugged their grandmother and went upstairs arm in arm.

After they were out of earshot, Hazel leaned into me. "I don't know what the hell you were doing today, but you better get your act together." Before I could respond, she let herself out and slammed the door in my face.

"Bitch!" I seized the knob and started after her.

Angie clutched my arm. "Leave her alone, Cece."

"She knows how to push my buttons and one of these days, I'm going to let her have it."

"Where were you today? And what's with the B.O.?" Angie laughed and wrinkled her nose.

"Now you sound like her," I said, sniffing my armpit. "I need to ask you something, and I want you to be honest even if you think it will hurt my feelings."

"I've always got your back, and you know I'll always tell you the truth. Regardless."

"Did you know Phillip was having an affair?"

"Are you serious? I would have ratted the turd out in a nanosecond." She didn't hesitate.

I relayed the details of my run-in with Bitsy and how everyone at the club knew of Phillip's indiscretion. *All* of his indiscretions.

"Not everyone knows. Don't get yourself worked up," she said. "You know the old windbag loves to hear herself talk. All those wrinkle treatments have paralyzed her brain."

I slumped against the door as tears slid down my cheeks. "Angie, if he's been cheating all along, I'll never be able to set foot in the club again."

"Who cares? Most of those women are shallower than the kiddie pool."

"Thanks a lot."

"I'm not talking about you. Don't worry. There'll be other scandals. You know how gossip runs its course in Wickford. Rumors are like the manure pile out behind my father's barn. About the time the pile settles, he hauls another load and dumps it on top. In a week, you'll be old news. Bottom of the pile. What's important is how you handle it," Angie said. "Come on over. Dave's at a meeting. I'll mix up a pitcher of margaritas. We can get sloshed."

"I need to stay here. Can I get a rain check?"

She wrapped her arms around me and patted my back. "Sure thing."

We walked out on the porch, and I watched while she

clomped across my lawn. She gave a wave before heading up her driveway.

My pocket vibrated. What the heck? I shoved my hand into my pocket and pulled out the phone I'd found at Mrs. Cline's. *Great!* I headed into the kitchen to put it next to my purse, but before I set it down, it vibrated again. Thinking Mrs. Cline might be calling to find her phone, I answered, "Hello?"

"Who the hell is this?" The young voice sounded raspy, thick, and male.

I slammed the phone onto the breakfast bar. *Holy crap!* Who would talk mean to an elderly woman like Mrs. Cline? Was it a prank? Or was it the vandal, calling to terrorize her? My neck prickled. Before the phone could vibrate again, I wedged it between my purse and the fruit bowl to keep it from skittering across the counter.

My imagination had me in a tailspin. I double-checked the locks on the doors and closed the blinds. Wickford was a small, close-knit community. Sure, we had incidents like the Bargain Hut and even the occasional vandalism like at the Cline house. More often than not it was teenagers acting out, but bad things did not happen in our town. I'd lived here all my life and couldn't remember a single murder.

Until now.

I climbed the stairs, glad both my girls were home. A sliver of light peeked from beneath Jessie's door. She'd been through a lot today, and I wanted to make sure she was okay. I knocked lightly.

"Come in," Jessie said.

She was rooting around in her old dresser. "I know I left pajamas here the last time I stayed." She dug through stacks of clothes until she found them.

"I'll sit with you a while." She dealt with death daily at the hospital, but this was her best friend's husband. And what a shock to have found him. It was like a made-for-television movie.

While she changed, I turned down the comforter.

"Mom, Kim didn't kill him."

"I know," I said.

After she climbed in bed, I tucked in the covers and sat next to her. Seeing Jessie in her old room with all the mementos she had once held near and dear tugged at my heart. Even though she was twenty-five, I still felt the need to comfort my girl.

I zeroed in on photos tacked to her bulletin board. Jessie always took center stage, since I had taken most of the shots, but Kim rounded out the trio in every single picture. Jessie, Sarah, and Kim.

"Since Kim filed for divorce yesterday, I bet he decided to confront her. You said you saw him following her." She scrunched the pillow and fanned out her hair. It reminded me of years ago when Phillip traveled for his job. Both the girls would pile into my bed, one on each side of me. We used to talk like that all the time. A "mom sandwich," they'd joked.

"Could be," I said. "How did it get to this?"

"This whole separation thing came out of nowhere. One minute they're trying to get pregnant and the next Brian's in trouble with the school administrators. Then he moves out with no explanation. Kim didn't go into a lot of detail, but she was baffled. On top of everything, she suspected he was cheating." Jessie's voice carried a touch of bitterness.

"Why?"

"Little things, I think. Coming home late. Canceling plans. She thought Brian and . . ." Jessie hesitated and bit her lip. "Never mind."

"What?" I asked.

"Nothing. I'm tired and I'm not thinking straight." She rolled over on her side and pulled the comforter around her.

"Don't do that. What were you going to say?" I prodded.

"It's no big deal, and I don't need to go starting rumors. Especially not now. Not with Brian dead and Kim maybe being a suspect," Jessie said, her voice muffled through the covers.

I knew enough about my daughter to know when she was shutting me out. If I continued to nudge her, she'd never tell me anything. Jessie was always the daughter who confided in me, but only when she was ready. I could wait. Changing gears, I asked, "Do you work tomorrow?"

"Not 'til Wednesday."

"Why don't you stay for a couple of days?" I hoped she'd say yes. It would ease my mind to have her home while the investigation was in progress.

She pulled the comforter down and rolled to her back. "Do you mind?"

"It's been lonely since your dad left. A little activity in the house would be nice." I swallowed and forced a smile. "Not the kind of activity we had today."

She frowned and suppressed another yawn.

"Get some sleep." I kissed her forehead and stood. "We'll talk tomorrow."

"Mom?" Jessie paused. "We have to help her."

"What?"

"We have to do something."

"Such as?"

"I don't know."

"We don't even know if she's a suspect."

"The spouse is always a suspect," Jessie said. "You watch enough cop shows to know that."

"We can't fret over it," I said, patting her arm.

"If it was me, you'd do something, wouldn't you?" Jessie sat up in bed.

"That's different."

"Just because you didn't give birth to her doesn't mean she's not family. She doesn't even know where her father is. Do you think Brian's family will support her? If we don't, who will? Mom, she has to be scared. We know she didn't do it."

Jessie was right. If it were her, I'd do anything to prove her innocence. "Let me think on it."

"Love you."

"I love you, too." I flicked off the light.

"Leave it on, please," she said. "I might read for a while."

"Don't stay up too late." I turned the light back on and shut Jessie's door, knowing sleep would not come easy.

Across the hall, Michelle lay on her bed reading. She glanced up, her young face taut with concern.

I propped my shoulder against the doorframe and let my glance fall around her room. Posters of boy bands clung to the walls. The cornflower-blue coverlet lay crumpled in the corner near her closet. I said, "Your sister might need some company."

In the few days since Esther had left, Michelle's room had gone from organized chaos to a disaster zone. Despite Michelle's sloppy habits, Esther had been able to keep some semblance of order. Now clothes lay scattered on the floor like a bizarre jigsaw puzzle.

She tossed her tablet aside and swung her feet to the floor. The light from the lamp on the nightstand highlighted the golden strands of hair shimmering around her face. Sixteen. What had I been doing at her age? Not watching my parents' marriage implode—from what I knew, my mother and father had never married—or discussing murder.

I wanted to cradle Michelle in my arms and protect her from all the wickedness in the world. But we were walking a relationship tightrope. Right this minute, here in the safety of our home, we'd found balance. The slightest misstep could send us tumbling.

She padded across the hallway toward Jessie's room. At the door, she turned. Tears pooled in her eyes. "Do you think Kim did it?"

"Certainly not." My voice cracked, but I managed to keep my emotions in check.

While changing into my pajamas, I struggled with what Jessie had been about to say when she clammed up. Kim suspected Brian was having an affair and Jessie knew who Kim suspected. From the time Jessie was little, I always knew when she wasn't telling me the whole truth because she wouldn't look me in the eye. Not lying, but not telling me the whole truth. Several times during the evening, Jessie had avoided eye contact. My thoughts held no comfort.

Jessie was withholding something that had to do with Brian's murder.

Chapter 5

"Cece thinks Phillip walking out is the worst thing that's ever happened. Actually, marrying the idiot was the worst."
Angie Valenti

By noon, I had finished up at Mrs. Cline's. I returned home, showered, and put a bagel in the toaster, thinking the girls were still asleep and my early morning trip had gone undetected. I had also concluded that I needed to confront Jessie. Part of me remained conflicted. I knew Jessie would eventually tell me, but could we afford to wait? This was a homicide. In our town. If Jessie knew something about Brian's murder, she needed to . . . What did she need to do? I gave myself a mental smack. Whatever she knew, she needed to get it out into the open, and then we'd deal with it. Keeping a secret bottled up could come to no good for anyone. Especially Jessie.

When the patio door opened and Jessie walked in wearing a pair of my running shorts and a tank top, I deduced I was wrong about both the girls still being asleep and braced myself for a game of Twenty Questions.

Jessie kicked her shoes off and skirted by me without making a comment about my absence. And still no eye contact.

"Hold on," I said, grabbing her shirttail and pulling her to a stop.

She stilled. "What? I'm sweaty and need a shower."

I stepped in front of her, forcing her to look at me. "We need to talk."

"Why?" She dipped her head and concentrated on her feet.

"You know why," I said, cupping her chin in my hand. "There's something you aren't telling me. You were worried about Angie hearing something last night. And you started to tell me about Brian then clammed up. I know your tells, Jessie. You haven't made eye contact with me since I came home last night and you're still avoiding it."

"Mom, don't," she said. "It's not important."

"Bull. Sit down and talk." I turned her by the shoulders and pushed her toward the breakfast bar.

The patio door slid open again and Angie stuck her head in. "Hey."

"Hey yourself," I said.

Jessie wrenched from my grasp and trotted off down the hallway.

"We'll talk later," I yelled. "Don't make any plans."

"What's that all about?" Angie dropped her purse on the counter and helped herself to my bagel.

I debated telling her I thought Jessie had information about Brian's murder. In the end, I shrugged and said, "Kids, who needs them." The minute I said it, I wanted to eat my words. When Angie and Dave were younger they had tried for years to have a baby and resorted to every medical procedure known and nothing worked. "Yikes, I'm sorry."

Angie looked up from my bagel. "Huh?"

"What I said, about not needing kids. I wasn't thinking."

She waved me off. "It's been twenty years, Cece. I'm over it. Don't worry about hurting my feelings."

"But still, it was an insensitive thing to say."

"If I got upset every time someone said something insensitive, I'd be in my bed with a case of Valium. Get over yourself." She stuffed the rest of the bagel in her mouth and pushed away from the counter. "I gotta get to work."

"So, you stopped by to eat my bagel?"

She grabbed an apple from the fruit bowl and shoved it in her purse. "Nope, I needed fruit, too."

"If you hear anything about Brian's case, let me know. Will you?" I asked.

"Will do. Have you talked to Kim?"

"Not yet. I was gone all morning." In all the chaos, I had yet to tell Angie about my job. "I took your advice."

"My advice?" Her blank expression morphed into a quizzical one.

"Yes." I shook my head. Her short-term memory faded quicker than a pair of black jeans washed in hot water. "The ads you circled and left under my windshield wiper." Every time I left my car in the driveway instead of the garage, I'd come out and find the classifieds.

"Oh, those jobs." She flashed a toothy grin. "Did you get an interview?"

"Even better. I got a job. And I've already cashed my first paycheck."

"Get out of here," Angie said. "Fantastic. See? You don't need Phillip."

"I earned six hundred big ones."

Her eyes narrowed, and the grin that had sprouted on her face disappeared. "You got six hundred dollars for clerical work?"

"Not even close. You aren't going to believe what I had to do."

"You're not dealing coke, are you? That would get those biddies at your club slinging dirt. Menopause mama goes maverick."

Leave it to my cop friend to think I'd get involved in illegal shenanigans. "Do I look stupid?"

"Your husband is supposed to be the smart one. Big architect owns a fancy-schmancy firm and look where it got him. He's hanging out in Rio with a bimbo, and his home is on the verge of foreclosure."

"Thanks for the reminder," I said.

"What's the catch?"

I squirmed onto a barstool and lowered my voice. Brushing my hand in front of my lips in an effort to mask the words, I whispered, "I'm cleaning."

She stared at me, mouth gaping open.

Silence filled the room. "Well?" I said.

"That explains your outfit yesterday." She plucked an overripe banana from the bunch on the counter and peeled it.

I frowned at the almost empty fruit bowl and decided I needed to go to the grocery store as soon as my finances permitted. "My first job was at the Bargain Hut."

"The discount store over on South Main?"

"Uh huh. It was gross, I almost quit before I started." I shuddered at the memory.

"I went there on an alarm-sounding one time. It's filthy, I felt like I needed a shower when I left. Tell me, who buys stuff from places like that?"

I shrugged and told her about cleaning crap at the Bargain Hut and Mrs. Cline's vandalism, sparing no details.

"I can't picture Cece Cavanaugh cleaning." Angie laughed. "When was the last time you scrubbed a toilet?"

I gave her the granddaddy of all eye-rolls. "Friday, smartass. And it earned me a big, fat paycheck and got me another job."

"Cece, there isn't enough money in the world to make me scour a public crapper." She burst into a spasm of giggles.

I wanted to slap her. It was a good thing we were best friends. When she saw I wasn't amused, she plastered a serious expression on her face. It didn't work, and she launched into another round of laughter.

"When you want to talk, let me know." I busied myself making tea.

While I waited for the water to heat, I pulled the pile of bills from the junk drawer and splayed them across the countertop.

"Sorry, I shouldn't have laughed." Angie parked herself at my side and glanced at the array of paperwork. "This has been hard on you."

"That one check will pay the electric and part of a credit card." I thumbed through the stack, wishing it would disappear. While I totaled my debt in my head, the cell phone from Mrs. Cline's vibrated. I had totally forgotten to return the phone. I ignored it and continued my addition.

Angie eyed the phone and then me. "Aren't you going to answer?"

"No."

Angie shook her head.

"It's not mine. I found it on the floor at Mrs. Cline's and forgot to leave it for her. Someone called it the other night and I answered. It was a kid." The vibrating ceased. "A foul-mouthed kid. I even wondered if he was the one who vandalized her house."

Angie scooped it up and scrolled through the contact list. "Could be. I recognize some of these names. Real troublemakers." She shoved it in her pocket. "I'd better keep it. It could be evidence."

"But I need to get it back to Mrs. Cline," I said.

"Don't worry. I know this scumbag, it doesn't belong to your Mrs. Cline." Angie patted her jacket. "I gotta run. Talk to you later."

After Angie left, I powered up my laptop. Besides dropping off my invoice at Bonafide, the only activity on my calendar this week was a tea social at the club. After my run-in with Bitsy, I didn't mind skipping the occasion. Those women had no qualms when it came to spreading rumors and making me the gossip *du jour*. I cringed—had it not been for the events of the last couple of weeks, I'd be looking forward to sitting there and listening to their venomous chatter. What else does a self-absorbed, middle-aged woman do in the afternoon? My new budget didn't include hobnobbing with the rich and famous-only-in-their-own-minds crowd.

~ ~ ~

Jessie stayed in her room after her shower. It was a thin line between forcing her to talk and waiting her out. I decided to give her some space, but not too much. After all, this was a homicide, and there was a killer on the loose. Jessie needed to come clean.

Michelle had wandered in periodically and eventually landed in her room with a movie. I didn't realize until my stomach began growling that I'd never gotten around to eating lunch. While I was making a snack to tide me over until dinner, Angie walked in, dragging a disheveled Kim by the arm.

"You got any coffee?" Angie asked. "We need to sober this one up."

I looked from Angie, to Kim, and back to Angie. "She's drunk?"

To Kim I said, "What the hell are you thinking?"

Kim jerked her arm away from Angie and slumped on a stool at the breakfast bar. "I'm not drunk," Kim said, slurring her words. "I got a little buzz. And I'm thinking my husband is dead and no matter what everyone will think . . ." Her words became incoherent, and she crumpled to the floor.

I sprang into nurse/mommy mode and began checking vitals and trying to rouse her.

Angie crossed her arms and shrugged an unsympathetic shrug. "Great. Now she's passed out. At least she's not boo-hooing. I hate a crying drunk."

"Have a bit of compassion, will you?" I said. "It's not like she's some vagrant off the street."

"Hey, I brought her here instead of taking her to the station. I think that counts for something." Angie filled a glass with water and dumped it in Kim's face. "I could've let her sleep it off in the drunk tank."

Kim's eyes rolled open and she sputtered. I wiped her face with my sleeve and helped her to her feet.

"What the hell is wrong with you?" I said to Angie.

Angie looked at me with cop eyes. Or what I imagined disengaged cop eyes would look like. A look I'd never seen on Angie before.

"I gotta get back to work," she said.

And she was gone, leaving me with the chore of getting a tipsy Kim upstairs and into bed. It wasn't like Angie to be uncaring. Maybe I'd never seen her cop side in action.

~ ~ ~

After putting Kim to bed in the guest room, I went to work creating a bill for Bonafide. Fletcher told me to work up an invoice, so I winged it. If he balked, we could negotiate. I wrenched a legal pad from my junk drawer and jotted down the hours I'd spent on the project.

Fletcher paid me six hundred dollars for the Bargain Hut, but the job disgusted me. The nastier the job, the more I'd be able to charge. This latest project hadn't been a stomach-turner, though it made me ill to think how the vandals had damaged Mrs. Cline's possessions. Also, I'd used my own supplies. Fletcher made some allowances for supplies, but he had no idea what I'd hauled over there. My nursing degree hadn't trained me for the business world, but necessity proved to be one hell of a taskmaster.

Jessie came in while I contemplated my strategy. She edged by me, grabbed a handful of grapes from the fridge, and started out to the patio.

"Jess," I said.

She froze and slid the door back into place. Her shoulders bore the slump of someone who had a monster weight dragging them down.

I scooted out a barstool. "Come tell me what's bothering you."

When she turned, she had fire in her eyes. "Leave me alone, will you?"

This was so unlike Jessie it took me a minute to organize my thoughts. Jessie was a rock, my dependable child, the one who usually came to me with her problems. I knew she'd talk when she was good and ready; I hoped she'd decide the time was right sooner than later. She needed time to mull over in her mind what to do. I reined myself in and changed tactics, hoping to allay her uncertainties.

"Sorry," I said. "I know something is bothering you, but apparently you need to work it out, and I can appreciate that. I'll stop badgering you, if you give me your word you'll tell me when you're ready."

She inhaled deeply, and the tension seemed to drain as her shoulders relaxed. A smile, albeit a tiny one, quirked the corner of her lips.

"Deal?" I asked.

"Deal." She spotted the legal pad with my scribbling. "What's this?"

Confession time. "Let's talk about something else," I said. For my new endeavor to work, I needed her support. "Grab a drink and come in the other room."

"Do I need something stronger than iced tea?"

"Maybe. It hasn't been a banner week," I said.

She filled a glass and followed me to the sofa. "One I won't forget. It's not every day you find your best friend's husband dead."

"That's a memory you won't shake," I said. Like the

memory I had of Phillip walking out on me. Etched on my brain in indelible ink.

She nodded and took a sip of tea. "What's up?"

I rubbed my hand over the smooth, leather sofa and ignored her question for a moment, while I tried to frame my words. Phillip wouldn't win a husband-of-the-year award, but he was a good father. He may have turned out to be a maggot in the husband department, but he loved Jessie and Michelle. I had to protect their relationship.

Jessie listened while I told her about creating a budget and working to get a handle on my bills. When her eyes glazed over, I figured I'd better tell her my news before she dozed off.

"Bonafide CSC hired me for a couple of cleaning projects." I proceeded to give her a high-level overview of the job.

"Mom, don't get mad. But I can't imagine you working, much less cleaning up after someone else." Jessie shifted and folded her legs under her. "You're the PTA mom type, the classroom field trip chaperone. The one waiting with sugar cookies and milk when we came home from school. You aren't the mom who worked forty hours a week."

"Not an option now." I glanced around the room with its cherry accent tables and Persian area rug, wondering if I would ever be able to afford nice things again. This room was my haven, and I had never needed it more than I did right then. At least one part of my life held some comfort.

We sat in silence and sipped our drinks. I had done my best not to bad-mouth Phillip. My tongue would have teeth marks for a week. I was sure Jessie's thoughts were on Kim. My own mind was jumbled with concern about Jessie's secret and my anger at Phillip's infidelities. And I worried about Kim who was still asleep in my guest room. Nothing like murder to knock your troubles into perspective. Lack of sleep didn't help, either.

As I told Jessie more about my job, I kept the part about the Bargain Hut to myself. If she couldn't see me as a working mom, she would flip if she pictured me ankle-deep scrubbing crap in a public restroom.

"Mom, you look almost happy about working," Jessie said.

"It felt good to help someone else for a change." I still saw questions behind her green eyes. "Okay, so?" I asked. "What are you thinking?"

"Daddy will be back soon. Then you can stop worrying about money and bills."

I bit my tongue for the second time and suppressed a scream. No matter their age, kids focused on what they wanted to see.

"Jess, who knows when your dad will come to his senses? Or even *if* he will. His affair might be a fling, but if it isn't, I still have a mortgage to pay. Not to mention the back payments I have to catch up. I could lose our home."

I omitted the part about Phillip's multiple affairs. Having my daughters know he cheated once was bad enough. Neither of my girls understood the toll this had taken on my self-esteem. They both expected Phillip to waltz in and rescue me. Maybe I should have had my eyes open the last twenty-eight years. How could I not have seen what was right in front of me?

My own mother had bounced me around from place to place when I was a child. She'd latched onto one loser boyfriend after another. When the relationships ended, and they always did, Mom salvaged whatever possessions she could, and we'd sneak away in the middle of the night. Often, we slept in the car or a cheap motel until we'd wind up at my Grandpa Earl's trailer. There was no way I would subject Michelle to the life my mother had made for me. Now, it was up to me to keep this family intact, regardless of how I had to do it.

Jessie's laugh brought me back to the present. "I can't believe I'm going to ask this, but what can I do to help?"

I threw my arms around her. "Just give me strength. I need all I can muster to get your sister through her teens."

"And don't forget helping Kim."

I frowned. "Who, by the way, is upstairs sleeping off a bender. Angie picked her up and brought her here while you were showering."

"That doesn't sound like Kim."

"She was blotto and could barely stand up," I said. "But, at least I'll get a chance to talk to her when she's awake."

"Mom," Jessie said. "That proves we have to do something."

"It would help if you—"

"No," Jessie said. "It won't. It won't help anything."

Chapter 6

"Jessie's dad paid for my wedding dress and walked me down the aisle. I hate thinking bad about him, but who knew he could be such a loser?"
Kim Anderson

Before Jessie left to run by her condo to check her mail, she agreed not to tell Michelle about my finances or the job. *Who was I kidding? I begged her not to say anything, and she finally gave in.* Like her grandmother, Michelle lived for drama, and I expected a performance worthy of Broadway.

Earlier I had uploaded the photos I'd taken at Mrs. Cline's and was getting ready to run to the drugstore to pick them up. I had my hand on the doorknob when Kim wandered in, blinking away sleep.

"Are you leaving?" she asked. The slump in her shoulders told me I needed to stay. She had spent yesterday being questioned by the police, most of today on a drinking binge, and the last few hours sleeping it off. Her red, blotchy nose and cheeks wrenched my heart. I wasn't sure how much sleep she got, but she looked freshly showered and sober.

I encircled her in a warm hug. "Wasn't going anywhere that can't wait."

When she pulled back, a flicker of relief brightened her face. Then, in a flash, fresh tears pooled at the corners of her eyes.

I was the closest thing to a mother she had. Her own had died in a car accident more than fifteen years ago. To ease his pain, her father had become more than acquainted with alcohol. That was what surprised me when Angie brought her home. Kim wasn't a drinker, never had been. I knew because she had practically grown up in my home, my family became her family. Considering the circumstances, she wouldn't be turning to Brian's mom and dad for support. But drinking? Kim knew from her own family experience drinking didn't solve a thing.

I settled her at the kitchen table. "Have you eaten today?"

She shook her head.

"Sweetheart, you need something." I started an omelet with ham and a generous helping of cheddar cheese.

"Unbelievable. One minute I'm rethinking the divorce, and a couple of hours later he's dead," she said. "Why would anyone kill him?" She smoothed a damp strand of hair with a shaky hand. "Everyone thinks I did it."

"Not me." I wrapped my arms around her again. Right now what she needed was strength and support, not judgment. There would be a time and place to discuss her drinking binge.

"Can we talk about Brian?" I asked. Curiosity had always been my weakness. Nosiness, Angie would say. Though, in this instance, it was concern. Concern for a young woman I had watched grow from a freckled child to a confident woman. "Until the other day, I didn't even know you two had separated."

She nodded. "Give me a sec."

"Take your time. Let's feed you. Then we'll talk."

While she pulled herself together, I worked on the omelet. Every so often, she'd sniffle or sigh; but by the time I scooted the plate in front of her, she seemed calmer.

I brought a box of tissues from the hall bathroom. She'd need it, but I also worried I wouldn't be able to maintain a dry eye.

"I'm sorry I was such a mess earlier," she said, ducking her head. "I'm glad Angie brought me here. I owe her.

She could have taken me to jail, which would have made everything worse."

"Angie's a good person. She knows you're hurting."

"Jessie told me Mr. C. left." She stared at the plate. "Why do men act the way they do?"

Not trusting my voice, I shook my head.

"Would you let him come back home?" She had veered off her marriage and ventured into forbidden territory.

"Let's concentrate on you."

She sighed and cut into the omelet. "Okay."

"Why did you and Brian separate?" I felt my way through the maze of difficult questions I had been waiting to ask, not certain I wanted to hear answers that might dredge up my own situation with Phillip.

"I wanted to have a baby, and he kept putting me off. Finally he said yes. Gave in is more like it, because he didn't think we had our finances in order." She pulled a tissue from the box and folded it into neat squares.

"Anyway, I quit taking birth control." A blush spread across her cheeks. "He started coming home late saying he'd had a parent meeting or something to do at school. The meetings got longer and more frequent."

"Did you suspect cheating?"

She gave the slightest nod. "He'd come home long after I'd gone to bed and leave before I got up in the morning. I could feel something wasn't right."

How could I have missed the signs Phillip was having an affair? Kim had picked up the signals, and she was only married a couple of years. Why hadn't I? In retrospect, they'd been there, the late-night meetings and weekend business trips. I'd been too naïve to see them, or too complacent.

"Then the crazy teacher filed the complaint." Kim forked a mound of eggs into her mouth and chewed slowly.

"That's why he was on probation?" I asked.

"Yes. She claimed sexual harassment, and he retreated into himself. Nothing I said or did made a difference. It was like he gave up. On his job, his students, and on us. Nothing mattered."

"When I saw you at the attorney's office, did you know he was following you?" I asked.

"Not then, I didn't. He came by the house, but I made him leave. I wasn't ready to talk. I was afraid I'd lose my nerve. He can be persuasive when he sets his mind to it."

"And he left?"

"Yes, but I knew he'd be back. And I was okay with that. I needed time to digest my discussion with the lawyer without Brian derailing my thoughts," Kim said.

She had a faraway look in her eyes. I still remember the day she told us Brian had proposed and how happy she'd been. There had been a flourish of wedding planning, ending with a small ceremony in my backyard. Who would have ever dreamed it would end like this? I excused myself and poured us each more tea.

She leaned back in the chair and sighed. "I told the police everything about the divorce and the harassment complaint, and they still think I killed him."

"They would have charged you if they had anything. We need to give them a reason to look somewhere else. Right now, everything points to you, but someone out there had a motive. Who else knew he was going to be at the inn?"

She inhaled a ragged breath that caught in a sob. "I didn't even know until he called and asked to come by. I can't imagine who else would know."

"What time did you talk to him?" I asked, trying to keep her focused.

"It was late." She tapped her cell and scrolled through the calls. "Right before midnight." She laid the phone on the table and shivered. "If I hadn't taken his call, he'd still be alive."

"If he wanted to talk, he would have come to the inn whether you answered the phone or not. You're not to blame." I knew from experience about blame. I'd been beating myself up for weeks. Maybe Phillip deserved a better wife. Perhaps if I had nagged less and been more attentive to him . . . *Whatever.* I didn't believe I was blameless, but our failed marriage wasn't all my fault.

"Maybe not, but if he hadn't come over . . . ." A tear rolled down her cheek and clung to the top of her lip.

I didn't want to be cruel, but if someone wanted to kill him, he would still be dead. Another place, another time. This wasn't a freak accident. Someone wanted Brian dead, enough to murder him.

"You can't change fate." I waited for a reaction, hoping it didn't bring on a fresh round of tears.

She grimaced, but maintained her composure. "I know, but I'll always wonder."

She wasn't alone there. I'd been wondering what I could have changed in my marriage. I needed to take my own advice. "What happened after he called?" I asked.

"He wanted to talk, a chance to work on our problems." She picked at a piece of toast, sprinkling the plate with golden-brown crumbs.

I wondered if Brian's confession had been more than Kim could handle. On the other hand, maybe he did have a girlfriend and when she knew he was reconciling with his wife, she had taken revenge. Woman scorned and all that stuff.

"Jess said she didn't know he was there," I said.

"Everyone had gone to their rooms before he arrived."

"Did you two patch things up?" I didn't want intimate details, but knowing what frame of mind they were both in might speak to motivations or lack thereof.

"He agreed to see a counselor, if I let him move back home."

I tried not to let my personal situation cloud my opinion. Not an easy task. The day I learned about Phillip and Willow, the worst day of my life, still played in my head like a bad video. My opinion, for whatever it was worth, was married people don't fool around. Period. No matter the circumstance. No cheating.

"He admitted he was scared about us having a baby with our finances in such a shamble. I was, too." She laughed. "I guess it was too much for him. He said he left because he needed space. But it didn't explain his coming home later and later." A thread dangling from her jacket sleeve caught her attention, and she tugged at it until it fell free. "But he swore he wasn't seeing anyone else. He said this harassment thing was a joke. Jo Stewart, the teacher, was pissed. She came on to him, and he turned her down. But it was his word against hers. The administration had no choice but to take action."

"Did you believe him?"

Kim glanced up from the thread. "Don't ask me why, but I did. Marriage is important to me. I thought he had broken our vows. Maybe he was cheating. Why else would someone kill him?"

I didn't say anything. Was it possible he'd been cheating with Stewart and ended the affair? If she wasn't ready to let him go, that could explain the charges.

"I was supposed to meet him Sunday to move his stuff home. He said if our finances were in better shape we could consider a baby. He even said he had a plan to get us back on track. But he didn't elaborate." A strangled cry escaped her lips. She buried her head in her arms. "What am I going to do without him?"

Her words were muffled, but I understood what she meant.

I reached across the table and stroked her hair. Phillip had been my husband for more than half my life, and I didn't know if I could survive without him. But my vows were sacred, too. And he had broken them. More than once. There was no going back. Divorce might be the answer for me. But divorce or not, I couldn't imagine the loss I would feel if Phillip were dead.

"Did he give you any other reason to believe he was cheating?"

She raised her head and used a napkin to swipe at the tears on her cheeks. "I saw his truck at the salon where Sarah works, and at her apartment. More than once."

"She's your best friend," I said, realizing what Jessie was keeping from me. "Sarah would never betray you. There has to be an explanation."

"That's what Jessie said. I wasn't thinking straight. When he left, I fell apart. He wasn't himself. We've always been open, but he had shut himself off and refused to talk."

She placed a hand over her eyes. "After he left, I did something stupid."

Did "something stupid" equate to murder? "What did you do?"

She peered over her hand. "I called a number I found in his wallet."

Relief swept through me. "Is that all?" My voice echoed around the room.

"You thought I—?"

I intercepted and said, "No, of course not."

"Before he left, I found it and started following him. It wasn't Sarah's. I figured he was seeing someone else. Maybe more than one. When I called, a woman answered. I asked her why her phone number was in Brian's wallet, and she hung up. I called back and told her to stay away from my husband."

"No harm there," I said. A little intimidation never hurt anyone, especially a home-wrecker.

Kim slunk down in her chair. "It was more than once. Maybe a dozen times."

"Was it Jo Stewart?"

"I don't know. When I told him, he went ballistic. He said trust was a two-way street. We had a huge fight."

This was too much information for my brain to process. It sounded like Kim might have a motive. A trail of phone calls leading back to her didn't help if Brian was having an affair. If the police found out Kim had made harassing phone calls, how would it look?

The relief I felt earlier wavered, and there was still the issue of Brian's visit. "Let's talk about the night you stayed at the inn. Did you meet any of the other guests?"

"We were the only ones there, besides Amanda."

"Amanda?" I looked at the clock. I still had to pick up the pictures, but I didn't want to rush Kim.

"Sarah hired the masseuse from her salon to do our massages."

"Oh. So, back to you and Brian," I said.

Kim smiled. "We talked all night, and he left about five. I felt better. He assured me he was working on our money issue and told me not to worry. I was going to walk him to his truck—" The color drained from her face. "If I had followed him downstairs, none of this would have happened."

"Don't do this to yourself." I patted her shoulder. "No second-guessing. Okay?"

Before I could ask more questions, Jessie returned with her mail.

"Kim, I'm glad you're here," Jessie said, rushing in and hugging her friend. "You had me worried."

Before the girls veered off the subject, I posed a couple more questions. "Kim, do you think the teacher had motive? Another teacher, a disgruntled parent, unhappy student?"

"Mrs. C., I've been wracking my brain. He got 'Teacher of the Year' right before the harassment charge. If he had enemies, it's news to me. Everyone loved him. Everyone except Jo Stewart."

"What's her story?" I asked. "Does she live in Wickford?"

"I think so. I've seen her at the gym on weekends."

I tucked that bit of information in my brain. It couldn't hurt to check her out.

"What does she look like?" I asked.

"Oh, you can't miss her," Kim said. "Long, red hair, almost a copper color. She hangs out with two other women, an anorexic blonde and a bigger gal with dark, curly hair."

That description did it. I knew exactly who Jo Stewart was. I'd seen the trio numerous times. They were the annoying group no one wanted to be anywhere near, because they talked loud and nonstop.

"What was his plan to improve your finances?" I asked.

"Not a clue," Kim said. "He said he was working on a side business, but didn't want to jinx it."

Drugs crossed my mind, but I shrugged off the thought. Brian was smarter than that. Dealing drugs was a first-class ticket to losing his position as a teacher and a coach, a gamble Brian would not have taken. So as not worry Kim, I didn't speculate on this.

I bent and kissed Kim's cheek. "I'm going to leave you girls to talk while I run an errand. If you think of anything that might help, let me know."

"I will," Kim said. "Thanks for listening and for feeding me."

Chapter 7

"Honestly, there's been a murder, and she expects me to go to school. Could my mother get any more ridiculous?"
Michelle Cavanaugh

I wasn't ready to face Monday morning, but I showered and forced myself to put on my happy face. Kim had gone back to her place after dinner last night. Both my girls sat at the kitchen table, Michelle pushing cereal around a bowl, Jessie reading her tablet.

"Good morning." I filled the teapot and set it on a burner.

"Morning," Jessie answered without looking up.

Michelle averted her eyes and focused on breakfast. We had ended yesterday on good terms, but today she'd invoked the silent treatment. After another night of tossing and turning, I wasn't in the mood to deal with her.

"Anything in the news?" I leaned against the counter while my water heated.

Jessie held up her tablet. The headline screamed, "Beloved High School Coach Murdered. Estranged Wife Questioned."

"Will you call Angie and see what she knows?" The quiver in Jessie's voice was noticeable.

"She'll call us when there's news." Angie had always been honest and open. I knew, if possible, she'd keep us informed.

Michelle dumped her bowl in the sink and shuffled toward the patio, still dressed in her pajamas.

"Where do you think you're going?" I steeled myself for a confrontation. She wanted me to engage. Why not show her who wore the mom pants in this family? "It's a school day."

She turned around and pinned me with a frosty look. "Are you serious? I can't possibly go to school today."

"Of course you can. There's nothing you can do." Michelle didn't need spare time on her hands. Trouble seemed to find her.

"I didn't sleep at all last night. Look how puffy my eyes are." Michelle patted her face. "Do we have any cucumbers? I need something for the swelling."

"Spare me. Cut the drama and go get dressed," I said.

"Mooooommmmmm," Michelle whined.

"Now! Your sister can drive you to school."

Michelle planted her hands on her hips. "Are you freaking kidding me? Why can't I drive myself?"

"You're grounded." I poured my tea and hip-checked her on my way to the table. "End of conversation."

Jessie wadded a napkin and threw it at Michelle. "Move it, sister. I don't have all day."

Michelle curled her lip into a snarl and stomped out of the room.

What I wouldn't give to poke her in the butt with a cattle prod. She might not be in a rush, but I needed to get her out of my space before I clobbered her.

After the girls left, I turned on the television. Every channel carried Brian's murder as the lead story. Homicide wasn't commonplace in our community, and I still had a hard time believing it happened to someone I knew. The newscaster said no arrests were forthcoming, but police were investigating several leads. I hoped my daughter's best friend wasn't on the list, but in my heart, I knew she was.

Chapter 8

"I know her type. That Cavanaugh woman has never had to work for anything. Who cares if I make her life miserable. It gives me something to look forward to."
Nancy-Secretary

An accident had snarled traffic, which hampered my driving, but I arrived at Bonafide a bit after nine. Fletcher maneuvered into the lot ahead of me and extracted his bulk from a gold Fleetwood Cadillac, seventies vintage.

"Morning, dollface," he called. His navy pinstripe suit, pressed shiny, looked almost the same age as his Caddy.

I cringed and forced myself to walk through the door he held open. "It's Cece," I said through clenched teeth. Had he never heard of gender equality, sexual harassment, or plain old respect? To continue working for him, I'd need to develop the ability to shrug off his comments or else I'd blast him and get fired.

The smell of freshly brewed coffee greeted us. Not bothering to acknowledge our arrival, Nancy slammed the phone down the minute we walked in. Jumping from her chair, she scurried around the room, gathering documents from file cabinets, her jaws working at a feverish pace on a wad of gum.

Fletcher deposited a sheaf of papers on her desk and proceeded to his office. "Come on in," he said. "Nancy, get us a couple cups of joe, and unless it rings, stay off the damn phone." He shut the door behind us and waddled to his desk.

A fog of cologne followed him like a shadow. I liked a woodsy aftershave, but he smelled like a decaying pine forest. I suppressed a sneeze and veered the other way.

He motioned for me to take a seat while he removed his jacket and draped it over the back of his chair.

"Do you ever tire of people comparing you to Hitchcock?" I asked.

Ignoring my comment, he tugged his chair up to the desk. Pink scalp shone under thin wisps of hair crisscrossing his head. "Did you finish at Alva's?"

"If you're talking about Mrs. Cline, yes, I did." I reached inside my purse and extracted the invoice. Before I pushed it across the desk, I hesitated. *You can do this, Cece. Be strong.* I knew my numbers were in line, and I'd attached a copy of the receipts. I even had photographs. Since I wasn't sure if Fletcher had seen Mrs. Cline's house, I wanted to cover my butt with proof.

"What's this?" He reached across the desk and snatched the paperwork.

My resolve faded, but I dug in, determined not to let him intimidate me.

"Ummmm . . ." His eyes scanned the pages, and then he bolted from his chair. Bolt might be a strong word, considering his girth. The pine odor followed him around the desk to my chair. A vein in his temple pulsed. At the same time, his face turned the color of a ripe plum. He threw the papers down and bent over in my face. His aftershave clogged my nasal passages, but it was nothing compared to his rancid, hot breath. "Pull these numbers out of your ass?"

I thought I was going to be sick, but then my temper surfaced. I counted to ten before I spoke. *Okay, I made it to seven before I opened my mouth.*

"Did you go to Mrs. Cline's and see the actual damage?" I asked, my voice rising.

The grimace on his face disappeared, and he shook his head. "No."

I grabbed the invoice and shoved the photos in his face. "See this mess? The kitchen looked like a grocery store exploded. The rest of the house was beyond description. That's why I have pictures. I cleaned for two days to make it presentable."

He pulled the pictures from my grasp and thumbed through them. He snorted and grunted a time or two. Normal color gradually returned to his face.

"I've also attached receipts for my materials." I took a deep breath and continued. "My price is more than reasonable." By now, I was on my feet standing toe-to-toe with him. My hands shook, and my stomach lurched. I hoped I hadn't pushed him too far. I needed this job.

He reached over and stroked my arm. "Well, well, you're a fiery—"

A knock on the door stopped him mid-sentence; it saved him from getting a knee to the groin and saved me from losing my job.

He withdrew his hand, lumbered around the desk, and sat down. "Come in."

Nancy tottered in on heels that made my toes ache. "I hope I'm not disturbing you," she said.

From the childish grin on Fletcher's face, he enjoyed the diversion. On the other hand, maybe it was the view. Nancy wore a clingy blouse, sheer enough I could see the lace on her bra. Her microscopic skirt looked more like a second skin. If she sneezed, everything she held near and dear would be displayed.

She leaned over his desk in an exaggerated bend from the waist, allowing him an extended view of her cleavage.

"I made it the way you like it, extra strong, with lots of sugar," she purred while arranging his cup on the desk.

She pushed a cup toward me. "Cream and sugar's on the file cabinet." She turned and sashayed her assets back to her desk.

"Now, where were we?" Fletcher eyed the paper still in his hand. "Oh yes, the invoice." He pulled a calculator from a drawer and went to work.

The silence in the room was punctuated by Fletcher tapping the keypad. Numerous times, he stopped, cleared his throat, slurped his coffee, and continued punching numbers.

Beads of perspiration collected at the nape of my neck. They broke loose and rolled down my back. A hot flash in the making. I ignored my coffee and fanned my face in an effort to keep cool. "Mr. Fletcher, I think you'll find my prices are fair."

He motioned for me to come around the desk. "Yes, on the surface it appears that way, but let me show you how to calculate a job. First off, you accepted a job sight unseen without knowing how much to charge." He tugged at his tie and loosened it before continuing. "Second, you let me intimidate you. Your time is valuable, and you need to make sure your client is willing to foot the bill. *Before* you do the work."

Fletcher continued to drone on about what I should and shouldn't have done, but in the end, he had Nancy write me a check for the full amount I had requested. I did learn a big lesson. Three, to be exact. First, never accept a job sight unseen. Second, he was screwing with me, and I didn't like it. Third? Well, I took care of that on the way home. Mace in the form of a keychain. Job or no job, the next time Fletcher touched me, he'd get an eyeful, and it wouldn't be of my cleavage.

~ ~ ~

When I arrived home, I found Jessie at my desk working on my laptop.

"I stopped and picked up an accounting software package," she said. "I'm making a spreadsheet for you to track your income."

"Why?"

"Mother, you have to pay taxes on the money you earn, which means you'll need to keep a record of your expenses and income. You want to wind up in jail for tax evasion?"

Crap! I hadn't thought about that. One more area Phillip had taken care of. Why had I been such a dope? I should have been learning fiscal responsibility instead of taking tennis lessons.

"Good thinking." I waved my latest bank deposit slip.

Jessie inspected it and whistled. "Whoa, good work, Mom."

I lugged a chair next to her and watched over her shoulder as her fingers danced across the keyboard. "This isn't going to be too complicated, is it?" I knew I needed to step up to the challenge, but spreadsheets and databases and electronic gadgets made my brain turn to jelly.

"No, it's easy. Even a kid could do it."

Which meant I would fail. If it wasn't for Michelle, my iPod would still be lying on my desk in the box it came in.

"Mom," Jess said in a tentative voice. "I think Sarah and Brian were messing around."

I swiveled my head so fast it made me dizzy. Then I slowed myself. This *was* what Jessie was keeping from me. It meant she was ready to talk and I needed to listen. "Why would you think that?"

Jessie closed the lid of my laptop and pushed it aside. "Kim suspected he was cheating on her. Right?"

"Among other things. They were having financial problems and Brian had the disciplinary action on his record. He could have lost his job," I said.

"Brian got drunk a couple of weeks ago at a party and made a pass at Sarah. In front of everyone. She was tipsy and didn't discourage him, but that's Sarah. She's flirty and flighty. She barely tolerates Brian, but Kim already suspected he was cheating. Her paranoia kicked into overdrive." Jessie paused.

I raised an eyebrow. "Why do I get the feeling that's not the end of the story?"

"The morning Brian was killed, I saw . . ." Jessie's voice trailed off. She focused on a shaft of sunlight cutting across the kitchen floor.

"You saw what?" The blood in my veins seemed to accelerate. I shook my head to clear the thoughts running rampant in my brain matter.

"I got up early to go for a run," Jessie said. "When I started down the stairs, I heard voices. A man and a woman. At first I figured it was other guests, but when I got closer I recognized Sarah's voice. Then Brian's. They were arguing." Jessie pinched the bridge of her nose and closed her eyes. When she opened them, she looked down at her lap. "And I didn't do a damn thing. I went back to my room and closed the door, so they wouldn't see me."

"You can't believe Sarah killed him," I said.

"I don't know what to think. I confronted her, but she denied arguing with him. Mom, I heard her. I heard them. She said I was mistaken. I called Kim and asked if she and Brian had argued at the inn and she told me they were getting back together. I don't know what to believe."

"Jess, you have to tell the police what you heard," I said.

"No, I don't. We have to figure out who killed him. I'm not throwing Sarah under the bus to save Kim. They're both my friends."

I reflected on the other-woman theory. Maybe Sarah, maybe not. I'd come to expect the unexpected.

"Why would Brian move out with no explanation?" Jessie said.

I shrugged, knowing I'd never have to worry about my best friend sleeping with my husband. Maybe shooting him, but not sleeping with him.

"Being an adult sucks," Jessie said.

I put my arm around her and decided not to push her about Sarah. "Yes, but you get to drink wine and boss your kids around. Now, back to my spreadsheet. I have to learn what I'm supposed to do. Let me worry about Sarah and Kim."

Jessie worked on the program for a while then left to pick up Michelle. While she was gone, Fletcher called. He gave me the name of a builder who wanted to hire me. I did a happy dance and made the call.

Grant Hunter provided details on the work at his new development, Hunter Springs. We discussed price and his offer seemed fair for the amount of work required. He had two empty display units, freshly drywalled and in need of general cleaning, pronto. After giving me directions to the site and instructions for using the lockbox, he told me the job consisted of scraping drywall compound off the sub-floor, dusting, and mopping. His regular cleaning service had quit without notice and left him in a bind. Hunter hinted if I worked out and was agreeable, he would hire me when the rest of the condos were ready. I told him I'd swing by in the morning to take a look and if it matched his description, I could do the job tomorrow.

By the time Jessie returned with Michelle, it was all I could do to hide my excitement. When Michelle retreated to her room to change, I pulled Jessie aside and told her my good news.

"Wow, you're raking it in. Who knew clients would drop right into your lap?" She grinned. "A couple more jobs and I might even be able to borrow money for a new washer."

"Can you believe it? Cece Cavanaugh, entrepreneur."

I felt my lips curl into a smile. Something I hadn't had a reason to do in a while.

The ground beef I thawed earlier was now a meatloaf baking in the oven. Potatoes bubbled on the stove, and I'd prepared a salad and placed it in the fridge to chill. Life seemed almost normal in the Cavanaugh household. Phillip had rarely been home for dinner. His presence wouldn't be missed, not by me, anyway.

"Are you staying for dinner?" I asked Jessie. "Angie will be here."

"Sure." Jessie sat down beside me and scanned through the legal pad I had been working on. "I talked to Sarah, and I'm going over there later."

"With Kim?"

"No."

I was curious why she was missing from the mix. Did she decline, or did Jessie exclude her from the get-together?

She cocked her head to one side. "Don't look at me like that."

"Like what?" I asked.

"Like I'm sneaking around or something. I asked her, but she's exhausted."

"Oh." Maybe Kim was tired, but it was still odd.

"Brian's funeral is Friday. Do you think you can make it?" Jessie asked.

"I'll try. Depends on my job at Hunter Ridge or if Fletcher calls again. If I can make it, I'll see you there, but don't worry if I don't show." I drained the potatoes and dumped them into a mixing bowl.

"Mom," Jessie whined.

"I know I need to be there, and I'll do everything I can to make it happen. But my first responsibility is to our family," I said.

Since Kim and Brian had separated, would she feel

awkward at the funeral? Did Brian's family know the two of them were on the verge of patching things up? Going to the funeral would give me an opportunity to see who else showed up. Jo Stewart? I had to try.

Before we could continue our conversation, Michelle sauntered in and snatched an apple from the fruit bowl. "Gran's coming to pick me up. We're going to dinner and then shopping," she said, then bit into the apple.

"Not tonight, you're not." I didn't often pull rank where Hazel was concerned, but I wanted my daughter home. "Angie's coming for dinner."

Michelle swallowed the bite in her mouth, then narrowed her eyes. "So? If I stayed home every time Angie ate dinner with us, I wouldn't have a social life."

"Don't be smart. Dinner will be ready in a minute. Go call your grandmother and ask for a rain check. Then set the table."

Michelle threw the apple toward the trashcan and missed. It hit the wall and ricocheted onto the floor.

I sighed. "Clean it up, and then call your grandmother."

Jessie stifled a laugh. I shot her my best stern-mother look. She promptly rolled her eyes. At her age, my tactics didn't work, but it never stopped me from trying.

I was mashing potatoes when the doorbell rang.

"I'll get it." Jessie jumped from the stool and made a hasty exit.

I didn't blame her for not wanting to be in the kitchen. It wouldn't take much of a reason to get me to leave either.

Jessie returned with Angie and a tall, handsome, and just my age hunk of man.

Dessert anyone?

Chapter 9

"I knew bringing Case Alder to Cece's house would take her mind off Phillip. He could take my mind off Dave any day. Not really, but I don't mind looking."
Angie Valenti

Down girl. I reminded myself I was married, at least on paper. But a man like that sure could put ideas in a woman's head, not to mention a few other parts of her anatomy. Angie introduced the attractive man standing in my kitchen as Detective Case Alder, the lead investigator on Brian Anderson's murder. From the winks Angie kept sneaking my way, there was more than detective business on her mind.

"Valenti," Detective Alder said. "You got something in your eye?"

Angie sputtered. "Uh, yeah, speck of dust maybe." She jabbed a finger to one eye and massaged the lid.

"You need a tissue?" I asked, shaking my head. Why I would want to rescue her after Alder had caught her is beyond me.

"No, I'm good," she said. "I think I got it."

Oh, heaven help me. What a liar!

Detective Alder appeared to be my age, give or take a few years. He had eyes the color of my grandmother's Delft Blue china and brownish-black hair with a smattering of silver mixed in. Distinguished. I estimated Alder at six-feet-two in height. He had enough chin whiskers to qualify as a five o'clock shadow and a thick, full mustache, which brushed along the top edge of his lip. A tweed jacket and blue jeans, with a razor-sharp crease down each leg, rounded out the visual.

"I hope you don't mind Detective Alder tagging along." Angie pulled off her sweater and tossed it across the chair. "He has a few more questions for Jessie and . . ." She let the rest of her words trail off and focused on the potatoes. "You didn't say you were making mashed potatoes."

She reached toward the bowl, and I swatted her with a spoon. "Hands off."

Angie lost all focus when she was around food. That worked in my favor. She'd be too busy stuffing her face to worry about my love life. I hoped.

After drying my hands, I offered one to Detective Alder. "Detective, I'm Cece Cavanaugh, and these are my daughters, Jessie and Michelle." *Duh!* He'd questioned Jessie at the station yesterday.

He grasped my hand in both of his. For a split second, I thought he might kiss it. For a split second, I wished he would. My legs wobbled. *Damn knee joints.*

"Jessie and I have met." There was a slight bit of Georgia or South Carolina drawl in his voice. Umm, facial hair and a sexy Southern voice smooth enough to melt butter. Did I mention I'm a sucker for a man with facial hair? My, my. I didn't know if it was a hot flash or some healthier hormonal activity, but the temperature in the room grew warmer.

His eyes locked on mine, and my stomach fluttered. I hadn't felt butterflies in a long, long time. To tell the truth, Phillip and I had waxed and waned over the last couple of years and finally settled into a waned state. That was more or less what led to his boinking Willow and who knew how many others.

Jessie eyed me as if I'd lost my mind. "Detective, let's go into my *father's* study."

Alder released my hand and grinned, a slight twinkle in his eye. "Nice to make your acquaintance, ma'am."

The warmth of his hands on mine lingered. I needed to divert my attention away from his dreamy eyes. If I stared any longer, I might swoon. "Have you learned anything more about Brian's murder?"

"Not much," he said. "The medical examiner estimates time of death around six a.m. We've narrowed down our suspect list a bit, and we're still collecting evidence. Could be as simple as the wife or not. It's too early to say."

I stifled a curse. "I can vouch for his wife." I fanned my arm across the room. "We all can."

Angie coughed and shook her head. "Not now, Cece," she mouthed.

"Dammit, this is Kim we're talking about. She's like family. There is no way she would hurt anyone, much less kill her own husband." My bravado sank as tears built up behind my eyes. I pinched the bridge of my nose. "What about the teacher who filed the harassment charge? Or . . ." I grasped for other suspects, other ideas, other directions to steer the detective. "A student. Or another teacher. Maybe there's another woman. Or another woman's husband. He's a coach for goodness' sake. They make people mad all the time. Maybe one of his players didn't get a scholarship to a big-name school and the parent is out for revenge."

Alder patted my hand. "Trust me. I'll look at every possibility. It's in no one's interest to make a false arrest. I'm good at what I do."

I believed he would get to the bottom of Brian's murder. My main fear was at what cost.

He withdrew a notebook from inside his jacket. "Now, Miss Cavanaugh, could we find somewhere private to talk?"

"Right this way, detective," Jessie said, narrowing her eyes at me.

Alder followed her to the front of the house, looking over his shoulder as he walked down the hall.

I cuffed Angie on the shoulder.

"What?" she asked.

"Thanks loads for sticking up for Kim."

"Look, you know I can't make this personal. It's my job to stay as objective as possible and that includes not swaying Alder's investigation," Angie said by way of explanation.

"You saw how she was yesterday. She's under a microscope, and we're the only support system she has. And you. What was up with your tough cop act? You know damn well Kim didn't kill him, yet you were evil to her," I said.

"Cece, we can't baby her. This is a tough situation she's in, and she can't solve the problem with alcohol. Do. Not. Enable. Her."

"I know." My words came out on a sigh. "I feel bad for her, and all I can think about is finding out who did this and clearing Kim. There's got to be someone else who had a reason to kill Brian. It wasn't Kim." I cuffed her again. "And thanks for dragging Detective Alder over here without warning me."

"Sorry, I stopped by the station to drop off a report, and he cornered me. He knows I live next door, so he tagged along. I would have called but—well, he was right there. It seemed rude."

"Like you ever worry about being rude," I said.

"Plus, I knew you'd go ballistic and do something stupid like tell Jessie to leave, to keep him from talking to her," Angie said. "Don't even think about making his job more difficult."

"I'm not."

"Promise," she said.

I crossed my fingers behind my back. "I promise. Now can we change the subject?"

"Yes, let's get back to Alder. You could invite him to dinner. He's single," Angie said.

I glanced over to where Michelle was setting the table to

make sure she wasn't listening. She had headphones on and appeared oblivious to the conversation.

Angie winked several times in rapid succession. "And he's hot. Don't you think?"

"You got dust in your eye again?" Unbelievable. My oldest daughter was involved in a murder investigation. My youngest was perfecting the art of mood swings. Now my best friend was playing matchmaker for me and a detective. A hunky one. Phillip's side of the bed wasn't even cold yet. Did it get any better than this? My own personal soap opera hell.

Michelle finished setting the table and stomped off to her room to sulk. Lack of shopping affected her that way.

"You're killing me. What in God's name are you doing? He's here on an investigation."

"Suit yourself. It's your loss. You know what they say about falling off the bike and climbing right back on."

I rolled my eyes. "Like I need another bike. Rumor has it my old one had way too many riders."

Jessie returned while I was putting food on the table.

"Where's Detective Alder?" I asked, trying for nonchalance.

"He left." Jessie frowned. "He was here to question *me*."

~ ~ ~

Jessie came home from Sarah's around eleven. The cleaning supplies for the condo job were stacked in a neat pile near the door, and I was ready to load the car. I'd made sure Michelle was asleep first. I didn't want to have to explain myself.

"I'll help," Jessie said.

"A couple of trips should do it." I struggled, but I managed to kick the door open with my foot while juggling a mop, broom, and bucket.

"No, I meant tomorrow when you clean the condos."

She picked up the vacuum and headed to the garage.

"Really?"

"I don't have anything planned, and I need to get my mind off Kim." Jessie cleared her throat. "You should tell Michelle you're working. She deserves to know."

"I'll think on it." The teenage years were tough enough without having grownup problems dumped in your lap.

"Mom, you know I'm right. Now come on, let's haul this stuff to the car before I fall asleep."

After we'd finished, we climbed the stairs arm in arm.

"How was your visit with Sarah?" I asked.

"Good. I told her Kim stopped by, omitting the part about her being hauled over here by Angie," Jessie said.

"And?"

"And nothing. Let it go, Mom."

"She needs to come clean about her argument with Brian," I said.

"Sarah said it was nothing, and I believe her." Jessie stopped at the top of the stairs, crossed her arms, and gave me the glare.

I reached out and touched her shoulder. "Did you tell Detective Alder?"

"No, and I'm not going to. It's not my story to tell."

"Okay," I said nudging her toward her bedroom. "Get some sleep."

We parted ways. "I saw you making googly eyes at Detective Alder," she called over her shoulder.

I tried to think of a witty comeback, but she disappeared into her room and shut the door.

Googly eyes, my ass. What I had experienced was pure lust.

Chapter 10

"It makes me proud to see my mom exerting her independence. Now she needs to work on Michelle's attitude. The girl is too spoiled for her own good."
Jessie Cavanaugh

The condo job turned out to be a pleasant surprise. With both of us cleaning, Jessie and I finished by noon. We ate a late lunch and I dropped Jessie off at the house. She promised to pick Michelle up from school, if I wasn't back in time. Jessie was scheduled to work tomorrow. Tonight would be her last night at my house. I worried about her being alone while a killer was on the loose, but she'd pooh-poohed my concern.

Fletcher had called earlier and offered me another assignment. I headed over to check it out. He was turning out to be my ticket to financial freedom. Not only was he sending work my way, but he'd given my name to Grant Hunter. If Hunter gave me referrals, I could compound my income.

Traffic had picked up, and I prayed Fletcher would still be at his office. As usual, I hit every red light, and I had to pee. At the next intersection, my bladder won. I veered into the closest gas station and made my pit stop.

Fletcher's beat-up Caddy was nowhere in sight when I turned into Bonafide's parking lot. Just my stinking luck. He knew I was coming.

Nancy was still slaving away when I hurried in the door. Okay, she was filing her nails and yammering on the phone.

She raised her eyes and waved me in. *A wave instead of a glare. Progress.*

"I have to go," she said, then whispered into the phone, giggled, and finished with, "I'll talk to you later. Don't start without me, baby."

Listening to her was like tuning in to a porn show late at night, except I didn't have the option of changing the channel. Or maybe she was the porn channel as in 'dial-a-porn' or 'dial-a-bimbo.' I chuckled at my wit.

She smacked her gum a couple of times before asking, "What do you want?"

"Where's Fletcher?" My annoyance meter soared into the red zone.

"Left early." She pushed away from the desk and stood. Today's getup screamed Western. Annie Oakley does hooker in a hot-pink suede skirt and a sheer white blouse with dozens of tiny pearl snaps. The ones from her neck to her ample cleavage were undone. If Fletcher wanted to raise the image of his business, he could upgrade her wardrobe and enroll her in a twelve-step program for gum smackers.

He'd do good to trash the raven, too. It glared a beady eye, and shivers threaded their way up my spine. I knew it was stuffed, but who in their right mind kept a dead bird on their file cabinet?

"Ain't Norman a trip?" Nancy smacked her lips and stuck her finger in her mouth, snagging a strand of chartreuse goo, which she proceeded to stretch and twirl. When the gum reached its breaking point, she pushed it back in her mouth, chewed with a great deal of gusto and started the process over.

"Huh?"

"The bird, silly. Like Norman Bates in *Psycho*." Nancy clapped her hands and let out a cackle.

Like I knew Fletcher's bird had a name.

"Fletcher said he had an assignment for me." I ignored the gum gymnastics. "You know anything about it?"

She waved an envelope under my nose. "Bet that's what this is. Ya think?"

I snatched it from her hand and tore it open. Inside it was a slip of paper with the name Eve Taft and an address: 11252 Elm Street. I hadn't been in that neighborhood in years. A note scribbled in bold cursive letters read, *Client expects you at 8 am.*

"What kind of job is it?" As if I expected Nancy to know. Fletcher was the brains of the operation. She was the eye candy and a good filer—a good nail filer, that was.

She shrugged and strained to twist her lips into a pout. A difficult chore considering the wad of gum between her teeth. "Beats me. He never tells me anything important."

Go figure. Before Nancy batted another eyelash, I stuffed the envelope in my purse and headed home. Jessie had convinced me to level with Michelle about my financial difficulties, but now was not the time. I wanted to know for sure working for Fletcher would pan out. If I had to quit, then I'd be right back in the same spot.

Chapter 11

"It is my sincere fortune to have become acquainted with Cece. Though, how she became associated with the likes of Bruce Fletcher is a mystery."
Grant Hunter

Before heading home, I drove to Hunter Springs. If Grant Hunter was there, I'd deliver the invoice and ask about future jobs. His development called for more than five hundred units. I didn't know if I was capable of handling the whole project myself, but if Jessie wanted to help, I might have a shot. Michelle wouldn't want any part of it. I knew better than to make the offer. Plus, I still hadn't told her I was working.

When I arrived at Hunter's office, I frowned. Other than a lone, worn-out brown truck snuggled up next to the building, the parking lot was bare. I pulled open the front door and spotted a worker bent over a drafting table, engrossed in a set of blueprints, oblivious to my intrusion.

I cleared my throat and said, "Excuse me."

At five-seven, I was taller than the average woman, but when this guy unfolded himself to his full height, I gasped. He was at least six-five and perhaps weighed two hundred and thirty pounds. None of it was fat. His hair had weathered to a silver patina with threads of surfer boy highlights. Dingy, white painter pants and a chambray shirt with sleeves rolled up to his elbows completed the picture.

"Can I help you?" Coffee-colored eyes peered over a pair of reading glasses resting on the bridge of his nose.

"Any idea when Mr. Hunter will be in?" I asked. For the first time in my life, I felt petite.

"Mr. Hunter is in." A smile brightened his face.

At first I estimated him at sixty-five, give or take, but his cheery smile shaved off years, and I readjusted my guess to middle fifties. I glanced around the tiny office. My expression must have amused him, because he chuckled before extending a hand.

"I'm Grant Hunter. And who might you be?" he asked, grasping both my hands in his massive paws.

"I'm . . . I'm Cece Cavanaugh." I stuttered like a schoolgirl caught cheating on an exam. "I have an invoice. You know, um . . . for cleaning the condos."

"Sure. Have a seat, Ms. Cavanaugh." He swept a stack of magazines off a nearby chair. "Appreciate you taking the job on short notice."

"It was no trouble," I said. "Call me Cece, please." I handed him the bill and waited. While he inspected it, a burning sensation inched up my neck. I resisted the urge to fan myself.

"Looks good to me," he said. He reached into a drawer and extracted a checkbook. "How should I make it out?"

"Cece Cavanaugh. It's C-E-C-E and then C-A-V-A-N-A-U-G-H."

He wrote the check and ripped it out. "C-E-C-E Cavanaugh, it's been a pleasure. I looked over the units this morning on my way in. Excellent job."

"Thank you, Mr. Hunter. I take great pride in my work." *Holy hell, was I blushing?*

"Call me Grant." He removed the reading glasses and placed them on the table. "Any chance you'd be interested in a long-term relationship?"

My hearing must have been on the fritz. "Excuse me?" Had he propositioned me?

"I mean . . ." His face turned red. "I have . . ."

Great, I'd embarrassed him. What the hell was wrong with me? I was starting to act like my horn-dog husband.

"More," he said. "I have more units. A business relationship. That's what I meant."

I hesitated, trying not to appear anxious, hoping my face didn't appear as flushed as his.

"There's at least six months of steady work," he said. "Once these two are ready for display, we'll have contracts for the ones under construction. The last cleaning crew up and quit without notice. I was desperate until Fletcher gave me your name."

"How soon?" I couldn't charge a big fee for simple cleaning, but with Hunter having several communities under development, it could provide a steady income while I continued to look for work.

"Maybe two weeks. I can give you a rough timetable in a couple of days."

"Sounds workable." I resisted the urge to hug him. Not professional, considering I'd all but thrown myself at him.

"Terrific. I'll be in touch." He followed me outside and opened my car door. "Thanks again."

I slid behind the wheel and watched as he walked back to his office. When he reached the door, he turned and waved.

I smiled and tucked the check in my purse. Shifting the Lexus into drive, I headed home.

Chapter 12

"My mother might as well send me to a convent now. When my friends find out she's a cleaning lady, I'll never have a social life."
Michelle Cavanaugh

Jessie's reminder to tell Michelle about my job echoed in my head while I changed into my pajamas. My younger daughter and I needed a lesson on building trust, and I wasn't helping by withholding the news. But was this the right time? With kids her age, who knew? I decided to forge ahead. She already blamed me for Phillip leaving and accused me of being the bad guy. How much worse could it get?

Crossing the hall, I heard sobbing coming from Michelle's room. I tapped on the door. "May I come in?"

"Go away."

"Michelle, we need to talk."

She opened the door and glared at me through red-rimmed eyes. "Whatever. It's your house."

"It's been rough around here since your dad left," I said. "But we're still a family and families discuss their problems."

"Daddy didn't talk to us about leaving." She sobbed. "He didn't even say goodbye."

The morning Phillip left, he had waited for Michelle to leave for school before he packed his bags. By the time she came home, he was on a plane to Rio. I delivered the bad news.

"I can't speak for your father or his motivation, but give him some time. He's not thinking clearly, but he loves you." The reason was a severe mix-up in the location of his brain, but I didn't tell her. Several of our friends had suffered through one midlife crisis or another, but it never entered my mind Phillip would wig out on me. Maybe buy a motorcycle or a Piper Cub, but desert his family? Not in my wildest dreams.

He would come to his senses. He loved both girls too much not to be involved in their lives. Me, I didn't know where I stood in the whole equation, but I'd explore my options later.

"I tried calling his cell." She reached for a tissue and blew her nose. "It's turned off."

"He might not be able to get a signal," I said. "I need to talk to you about something else."

"I know I'm grounded."

"I'm not going to lecture you, and yes, you're still grounded." I stalled. "Although, you haven't been acting like it."

Michelle's eyebrows shot up. "What else can you do to me? I can't remember the last time you let me drive my car. God, Mom. You need to ease up. It's not like I robbed a bank."

"You need to curtail your excursions with your grandmother. It doesn't seem like punishment to buy new clothes and go to lunch and the movies."

"Are you kidding? Gran is going to freak."

"She'll have to deal with it." I might have been inviting a curse from the wicked witch, but it was a chance I'd take. Michelle would never learn her boundaries if Hazel kept rewarding my daughter's bad behavior.

"Whatever." Michelle flung herself across the bed. "Go away."

"I'm not finished. We need to discuss our money situation—or the lack of it."

This wasn't an easy subject for me. I hadn't dealt with finances since before I got married, when my mom's idea of steady income was bartending in a sleazy club. Michelle's only financial issues dealt with how fast and how often Phillip had been able to open his wallet.

"What about it?" Her eyes flickered with anger.

I leaned against her desk and motioned for her to sit up.

"We need to figure out a way to manage our bills with your dad gone."

"You're kidding." Michelle leaned forward. "Right?"

"I wish I was."

She sat up straighter and squared her shoulders. "We are not poor. We're Cavanaughs."

She was her father's daughter through and through, always believing in the invincible Cavanaugh name.

"Your father cleaned out our bank account, and we're in danger of losing the house, if I don't get a handle on the bills."

"Blame Daddy. Everything is always his fault. Like you never screw up."

Had I ever screwed up? Let me count the times. Heat lapped at the nape of my neck. "I'm not the one who left. Or emptied the bank account."

"Gran will help us. She has lots of money." Her face lit with the anticipation of Hazel riding to our rescue. "She already bought my prom dress."

"I know she'd love to help." She'd hold it over my head until she was dead and gone. "This is a whole lot more than a designer dress and fancy shoes. I need to work through this on my own. With your help."

When my words registered, she said, "That's what happened to Esther. You fired her."

"Esther quit," I said. No need to tell her I'd bounced the housekeeper's paycheck. "I couldn't continue to pay her.

We'll manage, if we both pitch in with the chores. We've been getting along without her."

"That's why we've been eating at home instead of going out."

"It's also why I've been working a couple of days a week."

Her mouth flew open at my revelation and then settled in a grim line. "Not funny, Mom."

"I'm serious. I had an assignment over the weekend and another one yesterday."

"You were working when Gran sprang Jessie from the cop shop, weren't you?"

"Yes."

"What kind of job?" She leaned in closer.

It wasn't going to get any easier. "I've been working for Bonafide CSC and a developer named Grant Hunter."

The corners of her mouth drooped. "You'll be there all the time, just like Daddy."

Her words stung. "No, that's the beauty of this job. It's flexible, and for the most part, I choose my own hours."

"What do you do?"

"I'm kind of a contractor." I hedged. She wasn't making it easy.

"Mother!"

"Today I prepared two condos at Hunter Springs for the interior design team."

"You helped decorate them?"

"No, I cleaned up after the workmen finished."

"You're the cleaning lady?" Her face turned a magnificent shade of scarlet. "Oh, my God! Gran will die." Indignation furrowed her brow. "Does she know? Mom, some of my friends live there. They will laugh me out of school. You have to quit. Did anyone see you?"

"Just your sister," I said.

"Jess knows about this whacked-out idea?"

"Yes, and she's supportive. She even built a spreadsheet to track my expenses."

Michelle jumped up. "How can you do this to me?"

"Do what?" I asked. "Keep food on the table and a roof over our heads? Something your father should be doing?" I hadn't meant to bring Phillip into our discussion, but it was his fault we were even having this conversation. He was supposed to be here taking care of us, not traipsing around Rio doing who knew what.

Damn him.

"Mom, you don't get it." Michelle's lower lip quivered. "It's embarrassing. I mean, we used to have a cleaning lady. Now you *are* the cleaning lady. Your friends at the club will love it. Forget being laughed out of school, we'll be laughed out of Wickford."

If words were straight pins, my balloon would have burst. What could I say? I preferred to think of myself as an entrepreneur, not a cleaning woman. But Michelle was right. I'd even scrubbed crap off a public restroom. Even Esther didn't have to do that, at least not in my house.

The way to win this battle was to drag out the heavy artillery.

"Come with me. I want to show you something," I said.

Michelle followed me to the kitchen. The deposit slips were still on the desk where I'd left them for Jessie to enter into the accounting program. I waved my checkbook under Michelle's nose.

"See the balance in my checkbook last Friday?" I pointed to the pitiful number and prayed she'd come to her senses.

"So?"

"Our bills add up to more than twice that. And there's no savings, no paycheck, no money to pay the rest of the bills this month, much less next month." My voice caught. "Michelle, what your dad did isn't fair to any of us. Now it's up to me to keep us afloat."

I slapped the deposit slips on the counter. "This is what I've earned in the last three days. And you know what? I feel pretty damn good about it."

It seemed like forever before she picked up the slips. She examined them for several seconds.

I breathed in a cleansing breath and waited. The inside of my stomach felt like a kaleidoscope of butterflies had crash-landed on takeoff.

She handed them back and said, "Someone paid you this much for three days' work?"

I exhaled, willing my insides to settle down. "Yes."

She didn't say a word. The set of her jaw reminded me of Phillip. She was like him, quick to anger and stubborn as a Missouri mule.

"When's your next job?" she asked.

"Tomorrow," I said. Deciding to go for broke, I brandished the legal pad with my plan.

"Do you want to see how I intend to pull this off?" I asked.

"Not really. But I guess you're going to show me," she said.

At this point, I was willing to accept any attention she paid me. It was better than her sulking in her room. I picked up the receipts and carried them to my desk along with the pad. Jessie still needed to show me how to enter the data, but I could pay bills. However, the stack wasn't getting smaller. If I paid two tonight, there'd be three in the mailbox tomorrow. It seemed like a vicious circle.

Michelle trudged to the desk with a handful of pita chips. "I have a ton of homework. Can you speed this up?"

The phone rang, and Michelle lunged to snatch it. So much for her homework. I didn't stand a chance.

Since she was still on restriction, I started to scold her, but when I glanced over, she wasn't saying a word. My heart pounded, thinking it might be the detective with more questions for Jessie. I knew Michelle wasn't talking to one of her friends. She wasn't chattering nonstop, and her mouth was set in a firm frown. Before I knew it, she stomped across the room and shoved the phone at me.

"It's Daddy."

My finger itched to press the off button. Stupid cordless phone. How are you supposed to get your point across if you can't slam the receiver? Could the person on the other end tell whether you press the button lightly or smash it down with the force of a sledgehammer?

I made Phillip wait long enough for Michelle to go to her room. What I wanted to say to him wasn't something she needed to hear. When I heard her door slam, I put the phone to my ear.

"Are you over your little midlife crisis? I need money, dammit. Now! Do you have any idea how many bills are due? How the hell do you expect me to pay them?" I stopped and waited for him to sally an excuse, but all I heard for my effort was a soft click. He must have been on a cordless, too.

It was just as well. No telling what might have spewed from my lips. Since he was at least making contact, I figured I'd better get my thoughts organized. I wanted to be reasonable and talk it out, not rant like a jilted shrew, but that was what I felt like. My Grandpa Earl used to talk about catching more flies with honey than with vinegar. I wasn't concerned with getting flies or being Phillip's honey, either. All I wanted was money and the promise he would continue to be a good dad. Once he decided to bed down with Willow, I drew myself out of the picture. Angie was right. I needed to see a lawyer to determine where I stood if it came to a divorce.

Chapter 13

"I knew there'd be sparks between Cece and Alder. Lord knows the spark with Phillip went out years ago. Though, Cece will never admit it."
Angie Valenti

The next morning, Angie stumbled through the door when I went to get the newspaper.

Eyelids barely open, she muttered, "Caffeine." She was attired in all the parts of her uniform and looked ready to serve and protect, except for the 'barely-opened-eyes' thing.

"I got tea." I grabbed the paper and followed her inside.

She groaned and rubbed her eyes. "Is it caffeinated?"

I nodded. "You're off to work early."

"Court."

"Don't write tickets. Then you can sleep in."

She followed me to the kitchen, moaning the whole way. "Like that would work."

After I nuked two cups of water, I spread the paper on the counter and waited for the tea to steep.

"Dave didn't make coffee?" I scanned the headlines for information on Brian's murder.

"No." She yawned. "Turns out the cell you found at the vandalized house belonged to a punk kid. We brought him in for questioning, and he confessed to trashing the place."

"That must be a comfort for Mrs. Cline. Did you arrest the 'perp'?"

"Perp?" She shook her head. "You watch too much TV.

To answer your question, we have him in the slammer." She winked. "That's not the best part."

"What's better than arresting a creep who trashed an old lady's house?"

Angie blew across the top of her cup, and then took a long swig. "Awwww, that's good. Not as good as coffee, but it'll have to do."

I drummed my fingers on the counter. "Well."

"Oh. Since the beginning of the year, we've taken more than eighteen reports of vandalism and another six burglaries. The victims were all senior citizens. You finding the cell phone was the break we've been waiting for."

"I remember seeing reports on the news about how the mayor was swamped with old people picketing his office. They thought he was more concerned with ticketing speeders than catching true criminals," I said.

"Spot on, and now he wants to give you some kind of commendation."

I groaned. "Tell me you're joking."

"Nope, he's holding a press conference tomorrow. The sooner the news gets out, the sooner he'll get all those old people off his back."

As if on cue, my phone rang. I answered and listened as the mayor invited me to his office.

"Yes, sir," I said. "I'm looking forward to it. See you in the morning."

I disconnected and said to Angie, "Terrific. Can't wait for Hazel and her minions to get ahold of this tidbit. One more thing for my mother-in-law to look down her pointy nose at."

"You worry too much," Angie said. "Focus on something else for a change."

That was all I needed. "Anything on Brian's case?"

She shrugged. "I'll check with Alder after court. Though, it's not looking good for Kim."

I cringed. "There's always the other woman theory, isn't there? Have they investigated the possibility Brian was having an affair? Or the teacher who filed the harassment complaint?"

Angie shot me her mind-your-own-business stare.

"I know . . ." My words caught in mid-sentence when Michelle trotted into the room, iPod in one hand, cell phone in the other.

"What in heaven's name did you do to your hair?" I asked, wondering if I was dreaming in some B-movie genre. My daughter's once wheat-colored locks now matched the ebony baby grand piano in the living room and stuck out in uneven spikes around her face. Black lipstick covered her mouth and mascara clung to her eyelashes. Huge silver crosses dangled from her earlobes. Barbie turned Goth.

Angie hiked her salon-plucked eyebrows. "Wow! Gotta run." She slithered out the door and left me stranded.

"I needed a change." Michelle grabbed a bottle of water from the fridge and headed for the backdoor.

I hurtled across the room and plastered myself against the door. "If you think you're leaving this house made up like Elvira, you've got another thing coming."

"Who's Elvira?" she asked.

I bypassed the explanation and pointed toward the hallway.

Michelle sighed, a long, deep sigh. A frown tugged at her lips. "Mother, I'm sixteen."

"So?"

"If I want to dye my hair, I'll dye my hair. Hell, if I want to shave my head, I'll shave it."

"Watch your tongue." I wagged a finger in her direction. "You won't have to worry about shaving it. If it's not back to its natural color in an hour, I'll do it for you." The girl thrived on pushing my buttons.

"If Daddy—"

"Your daddy is in Rio entertaining Willow 'what's-her-name.' The color of your hair and choice of attire isn't a priority with him right now." I pointed again and pursed my lips for dramatic effect. "Now get up to the bathroom and do whatever it takes to get that crap out of your hair. And while you're at it, take a bar of soap to your face and ditch the jewelry."

She stared me down.

My heart pounded against my ribcage. Phillip and I had stopped at two children because I believed kids should never outnumber the parents. Two parents, two kids. Now, I was in the minority. Thank goodness, Jessie was on her own.

Glaring, I carted out the big guns. "Michelle Suzanne Cavanaugh." Nothing like throwing out her full name and enunciating every syllable like a rabid English teacher to get her attention. It had always worked when my mom was in her lecture mode. If Michelle defied me, I'd be toast. I didn't know what to do next. She was already grounded and too old to turn over my knee.

"Get up those stairs. Now!" I stomped my foot for added insurance.

She rolled her eyes. "Oh, Mother. You're such a drama queen." She took a long draw of water, cranked the volume on her iPod, and turned toward the living room. "Getting rid of my tattoo won't be as easy as washing this rinse out of my hair," she said with a light, airy tone.

After I chased her up the stairs and verified she didn't have any tattoos, I sat down at my desk, determined to pay some of my debt. A quick bit of calculating left me gasping. Even with the new job, my unpaid bills added up to more than my balance, not including the back house payments or Michelle's tuition. The Cavanaughs needed more belt-tightening.

I created two piles for my bills—necessities and luxuries. Of course, electricity, water, and trash pickup were requirements. Cable, Internet, and the fitness center were frivolous. On second thought, I snatched the gym bill and put it on the necessity pile. Despite my dire circumstances, I worked hard for these thighs and didn't plan to sacrifice them. The lease agreement for Michelle's Mustang glared at me. It wasn't like she had a job. I didn't know if there was a penalty for breaking the lease, but I'd check. One car would work for the both of us, or I could extend her house restriction until her eighteenth birthday and not concern myself with her transportation.

It crossed my mind to suck it up and call Hazel, but I shook off the thought before it had a chance to fester. The evil banker would have to tie me to a railroad track in front of an oncoming train before I'd allow Hazel to ride in on her broomstick and rescue me.

Michelle was already late for school when she strolled into the kitchen dressed in her uniform. Her freshly scrubbed face had the pink sheen of a baby's bottom. Tiny pearls replaced the silver crosses. Her hair was still a bit darker than her natural color, and the bad haircut remained.

"Happy?" she asked.

"Not especially, but I guess the rest will fade out. Get your stuff. I'll drive you to school."

She slung her backpack over one shoulder and huffed all the way to the car.

My mother always said she hoped I had a daughter just like me. Who knew Mom would ever get anything right?

Mornings were becoming way too familiar, Michelle acting like a spoiled brat and me tiptoeing around her mood. We had made headway last night, until Phillip butted in. On the way to school, I plunged into the deep water, head first. Watch out mood, here I come.

"What did your dad want?"

"Nothing."

Her reply was short, but indignation oozed from her voice. If I left it alone, she'd talk when she was ready.

~ ~ ~

My next assignment was in a part of Wickford that consisted of older homes with a few businesses thrown in. I circled the block twice before I found the address. The lumbering Victorian had all the fancy gingerbread trim befitting a house of its era. I stopped on the opposite side of the street to take in the view. It sat square in the middle of a tiny yard, making it appear like a big-busted woman atop skinny bird legs.

The clapboard shingles were painted dove gray and trimmed in white. A spacious porch encircled the home, lending a simple Southern grace. It was the sort of home I envisioned sitting high on a hill overlooking a meandering stream, not perched on a busy street without even a view of the nearby river.

A driveway angled up the sloped yard to the house. I pulled in and stopped the car. From this vantage point, the house was imposing, at least three stories with a turret on one end, but the ornate fretwork softened the appearance and added depth to the gentle curves. I hoped this wasn't someone who wanted a housekeeper on a regular basis. At this point, with the Hunter Springs project on the horizon, I didn't want a job keeping house.

I decided to leave my supplies in the car until I scoped out the project. Fletcher told me I could refuse any job, but it was a bit early in my career to start turning down work. My bills would never get paid if I nitpicked every job.

The flagstone sidewalk bordered a row of boxwood shrubs and twisted where it approached the porch. At the steps, I dropped my keys and bent to pick them up. That was when I saw the sign. In fancy script lettering, a tiny rectangle read HARMONY INN.

I had never been here, yet the name sounded familiar. Too familiar.

Chapter 14

"That Cece is a hot number. If I was a few years younger, I'd turn on the Fletcher charm and go after a little action."
Bruce Fletcher

A slight breeze carried the fragrance of lilacs and honeysuckle. Instead of relishing the heady scent, my stomach clenched. My thoughts whirled while snatches of conversation from the past few days clicked into place.

"Girls' weekend."

"We're going to party all weekend, and I'll officially bury my marriage."

"Harmony Inn."

"He's dead."

I stood in front of the inn where Jess and her friends had stayed. The inn that had been in the news every night this week. The inn where Brian Anderson was murdered. I glanced at the porch and saw remnants of yellow and black crime scene tape fluttering from the columns.

Taking a step backward, I tripped over a flagstone and fell flat. Pain shot through my hip. It took a few minutes to gather my wits and find my keys. When I did, I limped to my car and called Bonafide.

"Nancy," I shouted into my cell. "Is Fletcher there? I need to talk to him. Now!"

I heard her smacking and chewing on her wad of gum.

"Just a sec. I think he's in the john." She covered the

receiver, but didn't bother to conceal her voice. "Fletcher," she screamed, "the Cavanaugh woman is on the phone."

I counted to ten and held my tongue. *What a pain! If she worked for me . . . never mind, she wouldn't ever work for me.* By and large a patient person, I had no tolerance for ignorance or stupidity, and she was twice as guilty.

Paper rustled in the background, followed by an earsplitting crash.

"Oops, sorry. Dropped you in the trashcan." She snorted then burst into the giggles. "Oh, here he comes."

Good grief, could the woman do anything right?

"Cece, what can I do for you?" Fletcher asked.

Nancy continued to crack her gum.

"Nan-cy?" I asked, enunciating each syllable. What I wanted to tell him didn't need an audience.

A loud bang echoed through the receiver, and I jerked the phone away from my ear. When I eased it back, the gum smacking had disappeared.

Fletcher cleared his throat.

"What am I supposed to do at Harmony Inn?" I had a hunch he wouldn't give me a straight answer. He knew what the job entailed. Why else wouldn't he write Harmony Inn on the slip of paper he left me?

"Umm . . . " he hedged. "Cleaning, dusting. Tidy the place. Talk to the own—"

"You know damn good and well what needs to be done, and it's not light housekeeping." My voice sounded shriller than I had intended. *Get a grip, girl.*

"Eve Taft. She's the owner."

I lowered my voice an octave. "There was a murder here."

After a pause, he said, "I believe so. That's why they called Bonafide CSC. The CSC does stand for 'crime scene cleaner.' Did I fail to mention that?"

In an effort to ward off a complete meltdown, I slowed my breathing and focused on a fly crawling on my windshield. "Uh, yes, Fletcher, you did. This is a freaking crime scene."

"Not anymore," he countered. "Cops released it this morning."

"Shouldn't the police clean it up?" The fly inched its way toward the open window, stopped as if to test the breeze, and then flew off. What I wouldn't give to sprout wings and flutter away.

"Not their job," he said.

"The coroner?"

"Nope."

"This doesn't fall under the jurisdiction of any law enforcement agency?" Call me skeptical. Not that I was in a position to know, but this job belonged to a professional.

"Once the evidence is collected, it's the owner's responsibility."

"No way." I considered the consequences of a family dealing with the aftermath. This whole scenario screamed wrong, wrong, wrong. Lose a loved one, and you're the one to mop it up.

"Sometimes neighbors or members of the church volunteer, but not always," Fletcher said.

"Can't her church help?" My voice sounded whiney, even to me.

"A few members offered, but they aren't available until the weekend," he said. "Taft hasn't been able to rent rooms since the murder. She can't open until it's cleaned."

"But . . ." My resolve crumbled. It infuriated me how after the authorities did their jobs, everyone packed up and left the mess.

"Cece, all I ask is for you to take a look before you say no. Please." There was a hint of wheedling in his voice. "If you don't want to do it, I'll find someone else."

"Blood's a biohazard, you know." Thoughts rambled around my brain, or maybe it was dollar signs lining up like cherries in a slot machine. In my case, I expected lemons.

"Didn't you say you were a nurse? You should know how to handle blood."

"I'm not making any promises." I hung up and sat in my car, trying to convince myself to go inside. It wasn't like blood made me squeamish. When I worked in the ER, I'd seen my share of gunshot victims, stab wounds, even casualties from horrific car crashes. But I'd never seen an actual crime scene, especially when I knew the victim. The thought of going in sent a chill of Richter proportions up my spine.

While I was talking myself out of taking the job, my cell rang. I hesitated, then answered.

"Hello?"

"Mom, you aren't going to believe what happened," Jessie whispered.

"You're the one who's going to be in for a surprise." She had no way of knowing Fletcher had hired me to clean the inn.

"Mother, listen to me. I can't talk long." Her voice sounded shaky. "The police searched Kim's house."

"Oh, Jess. Did they find something?"

"I don't know."

"Calm down. It's normal for them to check her residence. Right? Let's not freak out until we have something to worry about. Okay?"

"You're right. It's not like they arrested her. I saw it on the news while I was on break, and now it seems real." Jessie sniffled.

Talk about real. "Fletcher wants me to clean Harmony Inn. I'm there right now."

"No way. You're not going to do it, are you?" she asked.

I told her what Fletcher said about the authorities leaving the mess for the owner. "If I don't do it, who will? It's a lot of money to turn down."

"Mom, wait." She paused.

I could almost hear ideas churning in that head of hers.

"It's perfect. Maybe the police missed something," she continued.

"What's perfect?"

"Maybe they missed evidence," she said. "Evidence that could prove Kim is innocent. You'll be in a great position to search the house."

"I can't believe the police left behind evidence."

"But Kim's innocent! We can't let her go to prison. At least take a look around."

"I told Fletcher I'd check out the place, but I didn't commit to taking the job."

"You have to, Mom. For Kim. Hey, I'm being paged. Gotta go. Talk to you later."

I pulled on my big girl attitude, went to the front door, and rang the bell. A slender, young woman answered. A few strands of auburn hair had escaped the barrette at the nape of her neck, giving her a frazzled look.

"You must be the woman Bonafide was supposed to send over this morning," she snapped. "You're late."

"Sorry, I had to drop my daughter at school."

"I don't have all day. The police trashed this place, and I need it back to normal by the weekend." She headed down the hall, leaving me in the doorway. When she realized I wasn't following, she turned. "What are you waiting for? Come on."

"Whoa, slow down. I haven't accepted the job yet. Let me look, and then I'll make my decision."

My main concern was the possibility of blood-borne pathogens. There was a reason why medical professionals wear masks and latex gloves, and I needed to follow specific precautions to protect myself.

Even if I decided to take this job, I couldn't start right this second. Protocol had changed since I'd left the medical field. Jessie could help me with the details, but I needed to do some research. How does one remove large amounts of blood from carpet? Or drywall? I had experience in washing bloodstains from uniforms. A lot of bleach. I couldn't just swab down walls and floors with copious amounts of bleach, could I? How cozy would the inn be if it reeked of chlorine or made the guests' eyes water? Could I arrange the furniture to cover stubborn, unpleasant spots?

The Internet would come in handy for my research. Surfing in the privacy of my own home sure beat sitting in a stuffy library pouring over musty books and antiquated periodicals. I had considered dropping my Internet service to save money. Who knew it would be an asset for something other than shopping?

The woman hadn't bothered to introduce herself, so I asked, "Are you Eve Taft?"

"Yes. Sorry, I'm stressed beyond limits." Her shoulders slumped.

Yeah, not to mention the toll it had taken on Brian and his family. "I can't even imagine what it's been like," I said. I thought it best not to reveal my daughter had been here the night Brian died. Taft didn't need a reason to be suspicious of me.

"Let me show you the study. It's my main area of concern, and the cops left fingerprint dust everywhere." She led me down a hallway filled with antique mirrors and portraits of dour-faced men and women. Ancestors? I didn't see a family resemblance. Eve was pretty, with a strong square jaw, high cheekbones, and a flawless olive complexion. Nothing like the folks in the portraits. They were downright unattractive.

She stopped at a set of floor-to-ceiling pocket doors. "I haven't been in here since the mur . . ." Her voice trailed off.

A sense of dread settled over me as I braced myself for what I'd see. Brian's body wouldn't be there. His funeral was scheduled for Friday. But, it was a stabbing. A multitude of questions bombarded my thoughts. Was there a struggle? Did he fight back? Would there be a chalk outline where Brian had fallen?

Eve inhaled audibly, squared her shoulders, and pushed the doors apart. They squealed in protest, but opened to reveal a room shrouded in darkness. When my eyes adjusted, I noticed a few shafts of light slicing through the room from a gap in the drapes. Tiny motes of dust floated like lightning bugs, glistening when they intercepted a ray of light. A nauseating mixture of floral air fresheners did not mask the smell of dried blood.

A small gurgle caught in Eve's throat. She shivered and scanned the room. "God, it's hard to come in here." She paused, then reached in and flicked on the lights.

I stumbled backward. Two end tables rested on their sides. Shards of a broken vase lay scattered across the floor. The tulips it once contained had dried and adhered to the hardwood. No chalk outline of Brian's body. Maybe it only happened in the movies. Instead, I saw a bare area, surrounded by rust-colored blotches, on a lavish ivory and sage green rug.

"Is that where they found him?" I asked.

An affirmative nod from Eve answered my question.

Dried puddles crisscrossed the outer perimeter of glossed hardwood flooring and stopped at the door where we stood. She entered the room, and I followed, taking extra care where I stepped.

I noticed black powder along the edge of a library table. "Fingerprint dust?"

"Yes, and it's everywhere." She tilted her head back toward the hall. "I've been scrubbing in the kitchen since the police left, and it's going to take me forever."

I didn't want to break the news to her about the rug. With that much blood, there would be no way to salvage it. I hoped it wasn't an antique.

"Do the police have any suspects?" I asked.

"His crazy wife," said a younger woman who stood in the doorway.

"Wha—What makes you think it was his wife?" I stuttered, trying to keep my facial expression neutral so my emotions wouldn't show.

"She was here, wasn't she? And then he shows up. Unless it was one of those other women she brought." The woman moved with tiny, deliberate steps across the room, stopped in front of me, and squinted through tiny round eyeglasses. "Who are you?"

"This is the woman Bonafide sent over," Eve said. Nodding toward me, she said, "This is my sister, Carrie."

Carrie stiffened. "Why did you call them?"

"Can we discuss this later?" Eve asked.

"I told you, we can handle this. We don't need strangers butting in." Carrie glanced at me. "I don't mean to be rude. My sister rushes into things without thinking."

"This is more than we're capable of," Eve said.

"Of course, you're right." Carrie gave her a quick hug. "Whatever you decide will be fine." Carrie turned and left, muttering to herself.

I detected a bit of tension between the sisters, but I ignored it. They'd had their share of stress the last couple of days, and who was I to judge?

If I had met these women on the street, I would never peg them as sisters. As pretty as Eve was, Carrie was the opposite. Her lackluster brown hair was close-cropped, and her facial features matched the dour expressions of the women in the portraits. Eve had certainly gotten the attractive genes. I guessed Eve to be mid-twenties, maybe Jessie's age, and wondered if they knew each other. Carrie looked a few years younger, early twenties.

"I apologize for her attitude. This has been difficult for us. The sooner it's back to normal, the better." Eve rubbed the back of her neck. "I don't think we've slept since it happened. Today's the first day they've let us back in. Will you take the job? Please?"

"Let me make a few calls." Before agreeing, I wanted to see how much work it would involve and what precautions I needed to take. "I'll call you with my decision."

"Thank you. You don't know how much I appreciate it," she said.

Aside from the blood and tumbled furniture, the study had a comfortable, lived-in appearance. A large cocoa-colored leather sofa sat at one end of the room opposite two matching wing-backed chairs. The seat cushions on all three sported deep impressions from generations of backsides. However, considering what had occurred, I doubted I would be making a reservation any time soon.

"Your place is charming," I said.

Floor-to-ceiling bookcases covered two of the walls. Amidst the volumes of books, stood photos in ornate frames and high-quality knickknacks. Heavy damask drapes covered a third wall. Pewter lamps with stained-glass shades sat on the writing desk and library table, and a broken lamp lay shattered on the floor.

"Thanks. It's pretty much the way my grandmother left it. We've started renovations, but it's going slow. A few rooms at a time as our budget allows. It's been in my family since 1911. My great-great-grandfather built it." She led me down the hallway and stopped in front of a portrait of a pinched-faced young couple in vintage clothing. "Levi and Evelyn Porter," she said. "They would be appalled at the mess the police have made of their home."

What an odd statement. Wonder what they would have thought about a murder in their study, not to mention their great-great-granddaughters renting rooms to strangers?

"Can I see the rest of the house?" My curiosity had gotten the better of me. I wondered where Kim's room was in relation to the study and why no one had heard a struggle.

Eve led me to the second floor. "There are two bedrooms in use up here. This one," she motioned to a door near the stairs on the left side of the hall, "and one down at the end on the right."

The other two doors she ignored. Eve must have read the puzzled expression on my face. "We haven't started the renovation in those rooms."

She didn't offer to open any of the doors, and I didn't ask. If I accepted the job, I'd see them soon enough. One way or another. Stealth mode.

I glanced down the stairs. "Do you lock the entry door at night?"

"Of course, we lock the door. Why do you ask?" Eve's brow furrowed.

"Curious about who else had access," I said.

"What does our security have to do with you cleaning?" she asked.

"Nothing," I said. "Just don't want anyone sneaking in while I'm here."

Eve shook her head and headed up the next flight of stairs.

The stairway wound around to the third floor. I followed her to the landing where she pointed out the bedrooms in use were the two at the far end of the hall. Eve said the two in front were under renovation.

I checked my watch and saw my morning slipping

away. "I'd better be going. I've got a few errands and some research to do."

She followed me to the front door where we exchanged phone numbers. "I hope to hear from you soon," she said.

By the time I climbed in my car, the left side of my brain was in an intense argument with my right. Sensory overload. The last couple of days had been doozies. Now this. I needed the money, but at what cost? I didn't want to make Fletcher mad. He'd been generous in sending work my way, though he did manage to hide important details. That part bothered me. Was he always careless with relaying information? It didn't seem like a coincidence. If I continued to work for him, we'd have to come to an understanding concerning better communication.

The drive home didn't help make up my mind. I darted through the door and headed to the kitchen. While my laptop woke up, I poured a glass of tea and thumbed through the envelopes and circulars I had taken from the mailbox on my way in. More bills. I had finished paying everything except the outstanding mortgage payments. Now there was insurance for my Lexus, a water and sewer bill, and my Macy's charge. I was afraid to open the last. Michelle still had my charge card, and I'd forgotten to get it back. No telling the damage she had inflicted.

The answering machine on the breakfast bar blinked its wretched light. My guess would be bill collectors or worse, my mother-in-law. I scrolled through Caller ID and ignored the two calls from Hazel. She could wait and wait and wait. Whatever she wanted was pure trouble, and I was in no mood to argue with her. There was also a call from Fletcher, maybe he'd changed his mind and assigned the inn to someone else.

I sat down and started my quest. What should I Google first? 'Ten ways to make pesky blood stains disappear?' Or better yet, 'Mother's home remedies for removal of blood-borne pathogens?'

Chapter 15

"Cece needs a distraction. A man, a job, anything. She's not a creampuff, but it would be easy for her to fall back into the comfy life Phillip offers."
Angie Valenti

Great strides had been made in bioremediation since my tenure as a nurse. That was a fancy word for cleaning up and disposing of biohazards: blood, human tissue, and body fluids. In the old days, when you had your gall bladder removed, you could bring your gallstones home in a jar. Today, thanks to AIDS, HIV, and Hepatitis, no more gallstones on the mantel. In my book, that was a good thing. One less show and tell for Aunt Tilly to expound on during Thanksgiving dinner.

My Internet surfing netted a couple of facts. It required a great deal of work to make a crime scene habitable and hazard-free and the disposal of biohazards cost a small fortune. You couldn't toss blood-soaked materials in the trash, nor could you mop up the mess and call it clean. Thank goodness I was savvy in the blood-borne pathogens area with my training and all. I also discovered the few companies operating this sort of business raked in big bucks. Raking in big bucks appealed to me. I didn't doubt for a minute I had the stomach to handle it, but could I manage by myself?

The phone rang, and without thinking I picked up.

"Hello?" I mentally smacked myself for not checking the display. I still hadn't returned Hazel's call.

Nothing.

"Hello?" I repeated.

This time I heard faint breathing, then a soft click. I checked and the display read, "Unavailable."

A knock on the patio door diverted my attention.

"Anybody home?" Angie already had her head stuck inside the kitchen. When she saw me at the desk, she plowed in and slid the door shut with her foot. Her arms were loaded with bags and soft drinks. "I took a chance you'd be here and picked up a couple of subs." She dropped lunch in the center of the table and collapsed in a chair.

"Make yourself comfortable," I said.

"Already did." She removed the wrapper from her sandwich and rearranged the toppings.

"Thought you had court today," I said.

"Guy pleaded guilty. Makes my job much easier." After helping herself to a glass of iced tea, she said, "You look deep in thought."

"Research." I flicked off the computer and joined her. "Did you bring me something good?"

"Turkey with cheddar." She fished it out of the bag. "What are you studying?"

"Bioremediation."

"Bio-what?" she asked.

"Did you know when your investigators finish at a crime scene it's up to the family to clean up? Including the mess the cops and coroner leave behind?" I bit into my sub.

"Uh, huh. Why are you interested?"

"Harmony Inn hired Bonafide to do the cleanup. Fletcher gave me first dibs." I filled her in on the details of my conversation with Fletcher and Eve Taft.

"Wow! Are you sure? Knowing Brian might make it difficult."

"I thought about that," I said. "I need the money."

"It's a lot of work, and it's dealing with dangerous stuff." Her pickles slid out of the sandwich and landed on the table.

Without missing a beat, she snatched them up and pushed them between the layers of meat.

"Not much different than working at the hospital," I countered.

She tilted her head. "Yeah, right. It's not like he's still there."

"Maybe I shouldn't. It is kind of weird." I bit into my sandwich and wondered if I could distance myself. But it didn't matter. I had to have a job, and this one was available.

Angie said, "Give it a whirl. A lot of off-duty cops and firefighters clean crime scenes to earn extra money. I've never been interested, but there's always a first time."

With Dave's practice, extra money had never been an issue for Angie. I almost laughed at the visual of her cleaning a crime scene. She lived as extravagant a lifestyle as I had, except now mine was in serious need of a cash infusion.

She continued, "Just compartmentalize. It's what I do. You can't let it get personal."

The phone interrupted her sermon.

Glad for an excuse, I checked and saw Fletcher's number. "Hello."

"You gonna take the job?" he asked.

"Haven't decided." If I let him stew, it might up the price he was willing to pay. "You said I could refuse any job I didn't want. This one has some potential showstoppers, like blood. How do you figure I'm going to take care of that?"

"If you do it, I'll help you dig up whatever supplies you need."

He should have told me that before. But I was glad I did my homework.

"If I take it, I name my price. And I'd say we're in the neighborhood of . . ." I hesitated and looked at Angie.

She raised two fingers.

"At least two-fifty an hour," I said.

"Are you kidding?" Fletcher was tapping something on his desk, his forehead maybe.

"No. There's going to be a disposal fee, and I'll need to buy supplies." I might be taking a chance, but I assumed he didn't have anyone to give the dirty jobs to or he wouldn't keep calling me. Nancy had never mentioned anyone, and I'd never seen another person when I went to the office.

"Let me think about it. I'll be in touch."

"Don't think too long. Eve Taft isn't happy," I added before I hung up. She wasn't too upset, not yet, anyway, but he didn't need to know.

"You were tough on him, don't you think?" Angie asked.

"Naw, I'm not doing this half-assed. I could hurt myself or someone else." *Yikes, when had I made the decision?* "If I take this job, I'll do it right. Shooting him a lowball offer will hurt my ability for future negotiations. I'll have a hell of a time getting more. All my research makes it sound like a solid price." *Whew.* I didn't know when the businesswoman oozed out of me, but I liked her power. There was at least one part of my life I felt I controlled.

"You go, girl." Angie high-fived me.

"Oh, and I have the Hunter Springs project if I want it." She shot me a quizzical look.

I had forgotten to tell her about Hunter Springs. Careful to avoid mentioning a certain handsome developer, I explained. If Angie even thought there was a chance to fix me up with Grant Hunter, she'd be all over it. She was more about distracting my attention from Phillip than she was about getting me fixed up with Detective Alder. In her book, any man would do as long he drew the focus off my husband. As much as it aggravated me, I couldn't blame her. She and Dave had their happily ever after, and she wanted the same for me.

I didn't dwell on my latest job long, because I wanted to pick her brain about the investigation.

"Have you heard from the detective?"

She raised her eyebrows.

"About Kim," I said.

"I can't discuss it, other than to say she's a suspect," Angie said.

That didn't sound good.

"You do know something, don't you? Jess said the investigators searched Kim's house." I volleyed another question. "What's up with that?"

"Standard procedure."

"Did they find anything?"

Angie pressed her lips together and shrugged. "I do know they left with a laptop, a tablet, and Kim's cell."

"Her cell?" My heart kicked up a notch. Kim had made all those calls to the number she found in Brian's wallet. Now the police would know.

"Standard procedure."

"Have they investigated the possibility Brian was having an affair?" I asked.

"They'll explore everyone with a motive. They'll keep interviewing people to find out if anyone remembers information that can help pinpoint witnesses or motivations."

"Did they find anything at the crime scene?" *Crap!* I slapped my hand over my mouth. *Stupid, stupid, stupid.*

"You're not thinking about the money, are you? There's more to you taking this job, isn't there?" Angie's eyes bored into mine with accusation.

"Why would you say that?" I asked trying to maintain an innocent face. "You know my situation."

"Yeah, yeah. I also know your relationship with Kim. You're not going to let this go, are you?" Angie asked.

"I'm only thinking about Kim," I said. "You saw her the other day."

"Cece, Alder is good at what he does. If Kim is innocent,

he'll prove it. Do. Not. Get. In. His. Way." She emphasized each word by jabbing her finger on the table.

"But—"

"No buts. You go, clean the inn, and leave the investigation to Alder. He won't tolerate your interference."

I took another bite of my sandwich and tried to ignore her. I was already thinking about what I might find at the inn.

"Do you hear me?" she asked.

"Yes," I said.

"Alder won't think twice about arresting you for interfering. Swear to me you will leave this to him," Angie said.

"Sure," I said half-heartedly. I hated lying to my best friend.

"Promise?"

I crossed my fingers behind my back and told another whopper. "Promise."

What Angie didn't know wouldn't hurt her. And wouldn't put her job in jeopardy. She would spin into a tizzy, and I didn't need her upset with me. She and Dave were the only support system I had besides my daughters. Make that singular. Michelle still blamed me for Phillip leaving.

Angie picked up the remnants of her lunch and stuffed them in the bag. "I need to go back to work."

"She's innocent. I don't care what they found."

Phillip had always accused me of having to get the last word.

She no sooner pulled the patio door closed and the front doorbell rang. My luck it would be a salesperson or worse, a bill collector.

When I opened the door, I came face to face with Phillip.

Chapter 16

"Women! Just when you think you have them figured out, they go all middle-aged on you. If it's not hot flashes, it's the damn mood swings."
Phillip Cavanaugh

Phillip stood on the porch dressed in khakis and a polo shirt, collar flipped up. The gray at his temples was gone and the tips of his hair had highlights. Did he have gel in his hair? I leaned in for a closer inspection.

Crap, crap, double-crap. Salon job or not, I liked what I saw. I had rehearsed this moment in my mind a dozen times. In every instance, he'd looked like he hadn't slept in weeks and pleaded for my forgiveness. But here, in real life, he could have just wrapped up a photo shoot for *GQ*, and he didn't appear to be on the verge of begging.

I suppressed my hormones and dredged up the anger still boiling in my belly. "What do you want?" Tact wasn't one of my strong suits, and, truth be told, I didn't want him to think I'd been obsessing over him. I knew he wasn't here for a quickie, because there in his passenger seat sat Willow.

He slapped a large envelope in my hand. "A divorce."

I sucked in a breath and let it out to the count of ten, hoping my voice wouldn't betray me. I needed rational, not whiney. "Tell me one thing." I paused and searched his face, looking for even a glimpse of the man I'd married.

"What?"

"Is she the first?"

He flinched, and I knew what Bitsy said was true.

I threw down the envelope and flew at him, pummeling his chest with my fists, wanting to make him feel the pain tearing through me. "How could you?"

Phillip grabbed both my wrists with one hand and pushed me away. "What the hell is wrong with you?"

"Me? You're the one who cheated. Then you have the nerve to come back and flaunt her in my face."

"For heaven's sake, Cece. Don't make this difficult. We can't go back. You know it and I do, too. Even if it was possible, I don't want to." He picked up the envelope and shoved it at me. "Read it and give me a call. When you pull yourself together, we can have lunch."

Lunch? Was he kidding? "Oh yeah, let's have a burger and a beer on the patio of some trendy bistro. Makes it all better. I don't think so. Have you even considered Michelle?"

"I've made provisions for her. When you've had a chance to read it, call me. We'll talk to her together." He hurried back to the Porsche and Willow.

"Wait a minute, buster. I need money," I screamed across the front lawn. "If you can afford to fly off to Rio, you can help me pay these bills. What about the mortgage?"

He ignored me and revved the engine. I leaned against the doorframe and watched as he drove away, his movements animated as he talked to Willow, probably giving her a blow-by-blow of our conversation. *Pig!*

I slammed the door and cursed. Words spewed from my mouth that had never before crossed my lips. I knew things would never be the same, but Phillip filing for a divorce had never entered my mind. And he delivered the papers in person. What kind of sadistic jackass did that? A cheating, self-absorbed jackass. Why didn't I get to ask for the divorce? I was the injured party. I knew I didn't want him back in my life or my bed. The thought made me cringe, but . . . Had I expected to be friends? That didn't seem feasible, either. Maybe we could get together for lunch. *Ha! Fat chance.*

A tap on the door erased thoughts of begging my children to spend future holidays with me instead of with their dad and Willow. In an instant, the anger I had been searching for made its way to the surface. Was he coming back to gloat? Or perhaps Willow wanted to get her two cents in?

I jerked the door open. "What the hell do you want?"

A stunned Detective Alder stood on the porch, notebook in hand. "Caught you at a bad time, I assume." He scratched his head and shoved the notebook in his shirt pocket.

I tucked the envelope behind me and tried to laugh, but it sounded more like a strangled chicken gasping for its last breath. "Sorry. I thought you were someone else."

"The guy in the Porsche?" He glanced toward the street. "Glad I'm not him."

That makes two of us, I thought. But I said, "Jess isn't here."

"Officer Valenti said your daughter was staying a few days."

"Yes, but she went home."

He looked like he hadn't shaved in a day or two and tried to stifle a yawn. "I was hoping to save myself a trip."

"Doesn't look like you need to be driving anywhere." I wondered if he would think it forward if I offered him a cup of coffee. But, hey, he was a public servant. Throwing caution to the wind, I decided to invite him in. Maybe caffeine would do him good and keep him from falling asleep on the job. He needed to focus if he was going to find Brian's killer.

"If you're interested . . ." I stopped. Dumb thing to say. "I mean, I was getting ready to make a pot of coffee." I didn't know why, but I lied. I didn't even drink coffee. "Care to join me?"

His eyes twinkled. "I'm interested."

I dropped the packet of divorce papers on the hall table and led him to the kitchen. For a moment, I was all too aware of the view from his vantage point and wondered if there was too much jiggle in my wiggle. I hadn't been to the gym in weeks.

"Nice house. Always liked this neighborhood."

"Thanks. We . . . I like it." Jeez, I sounded moronic and made a mental note to work on my pronouns in the future. "We" was now "I." "Have a seat in the other room. It'll take me a minute."

I busied myself in the kitchen trying to find coffee. Right. I had never made a pot of coffee in my life. In the cabinet over the range, I found an unopened package of Phillip's favorite decaf. Alder needed the real deal, but maybe he wouldn't notice the difference. When I tore the flaps apart, the damn bag split open and coffee flew everywhere.

"Hope you're not in a hurry," I yelled while chasing coffee grounds around the counter.

"I can make time for a good cup of coffee," he replied from the other room.

Ha! Was he ever in for a surprise. I measured the grounds, filled the carafe with water, poured it into the coffeemaker, and crossed my fingers.

"So, what did you want to talk to Jessie about?" I asked. My hands shook while I pushed the buttons on the coffeemaker. It couldn't bode well for Jessie if he had more questions. He had already questioned her twice. A third time could not be good.

"Just have a few questions about the Andersons' relationship," Alder said.

I kept pushing buttons, nothing happened. No light glowing, no water flowing, no coffee brewing. What the hell? I checked behind the machine. It wasn't even plugged in.

"Jess is not one to pry into other peoples' business," I said. "Do you have any suspects yet?"

He didn't answer. "Detective, did you hear me? I asked if you had any suspects." His silence sent a current of adrenaline chasing through my system. My heart rate kicked up a notch. Oh, my God, did he think Jessie had anything to do with Brian's murder? I slammed the plug into the wall and forced myself to calm down before I went to face Alder.

I walked into the gathering room and the thudding in my chest slowed. Alder wasn't evading my question. He was sound asleep in the recliner, and he wasn't even snoring.

I sighed and went back to the kitchen, wondering if I could ever be in a relationship with another man. Wondering, would I even be able to trust another man?

Stop it. You're married.

The phone rang, clearing my head of nonproductive thoughts. Fletcher's number displayed on the screen.

"Let's talk price," he said without preamble.

"Okay." I still had misgivings about the whole thing, but I needed the money and wanted to stay in his good graces.

He started to quibble about my rate, but I held firm. This wasn't a backbreaking job like the vandalized house, but there were health dangers. Not that Brian Anderson had some sexually transmitted disease, but these days, who knew? Kim thought he was having an affair. Better for me to play it safe.

Fletcher sighed and agreed to my price. "You drive a hard bargain, Cavanaugh."

While we were on the phone, he gave me directions to the supply house where I could purchase everything I needed.

"Be sure to keep track of anything you trash. The owners will want to submit any losses to their insurance," he offered.

When he disconnected, I heard a shuffling noise and saw Detective Alder standing in the doorway.

"Sorry, I dozed off. It's been a rough week." He stretched and looked around the kitchen. "Where's that coffee?"

I motioned to a chair. "Sit down, if you think you can stay awake." I poured him a cup and inhaled the aroma. Even though I didn't drink the stuff I enjoyed the smell of a freshly brewed pot. I hoped he couldn't tell it was decaf. "Do you take cream and sugar?"

"No, straight up." His day-old beard must have been bothering him because he kept scratching his chin.

"Do you have any suspects in Brian's murder?" I asked.

"Still investigating. Trying to tie up loose ends about the wife," he said.

"That's why you want to talk to Jessie?"

"In my experience, when there's a rift in a marriage, best friends always seem to know more than the average person on the street." He downed a mouthful of the steaming coffee and winced. "Wouldn't you say?" He lifted the cup and took a smaller sip.

"I wouldn't know, but I'm sure Jessie told you everything she knew. Besides, Kim and Brian were getting back together. Rift settled." I felt my composure slipping, like so many times these past few weeks. Sliding down, leaving me feeling vulnerable.

"Maybe, maybe not. I have to explore all angles." His gaze caught mine and held me captive. Like he was examining my soul.

I started to shiver, then caught myself and changed the subject. Anything to lighten the mood. "Can I make you a sandwich? I have ham and turkey. It's not the deli stuff, but it's good." I rooted through the refrigerator, hoping Michelle hadn't raided it when I wasn't looking.

"Don't bother." He tilted the cup toward his mouth, but stopped and placed it on the counter. "I'll grab a bite on my way home."

Ignoring his comment, I reached for the bread. "It's no problem. It's my civic duty to keep our local law enforcement fed. That's what Angie tells me, anyway." I smeared mayo on two pieces of rye and piled up a sandwich big enough to make Dagwood jealous.

My cell phone chirped. I hesitated, then looked at the display and groaned.

"Where are you? Why aren't you here?" Michelle shouted. "You're supposed to pick me up, remember?"

Grounding Michelle punished me as much as it did her.

"Sorry, honey." I grabbed a plastic zipper bag from the drawer and shoved the sandwich inside. "I'm on my way. Give me a minute."

"Forget it. Delia's mom is here. I'll catch a ride with her." She hung up before I could answer.

Detective Alder rose from the chair. "Sorry," he said. "Better take a rain check. You're busy."

I pushed the sandwich at him. "Forgot to pick up my daughter. She's grounded."

"Responsible parenting. I like that. Makes my job easier." He picked up the sandwich and chugged down the rest of his coffee.

I kept Michelle's truancy incident to myself. "You want a cup for the road?" Why did I ask that? It wasn't like I was a restaurant and had paper cups sitting around.

"No, I'm fine." He smiled and pulled a card from his pocket and pressed it into my hand. "In case you talk to Jessie before I do, will you ask her to call me? Don't worry. It's routine."

I closed my fingers around his business card. The spark sizzling between us was palpable. "She's told you everything."

He withdrew his hand and backed onto the porch, his eyes never leaving mine. Finally, he turned and strolled down the driveway.

I leaned against the door. The view from my vantage point was exceptionally nice.

Alder turned and caught me staring.

I diverted my gaze to his face and waved.

"Thanks again for the coffee and the sandwich. And the nap," he said.

A pang of guilt hit me. I hoped the nap was enough to keep him awake, since my decaf wasn't going to do the trick.

The phone rang again. Figuring it was Michelle calling again or Fletcher with a last-ditch negotiation effort, I shut the door and headed to the kitchen.

I lunged across the counter and grabbed the phone on the second ring. "Hello?"

Nothing.

Aggravated, I checked the screen. *Number unavailable*.

"Who is this?" I asked, wondering if it was Willow calling to annoy me. Not wanting to give her the satisfaction, I disconnected.

Chapter 17

"OMG! My mother is such a liar. Yeah, she's cleaning, true enough, but she's cleaning shit, and now my whole school knows it. My life is over."
Michelle Cavanaugh

Michelle roared through the front door.

"Mother!" she screamed.

I heard her before I saw her, but by her tone of voice, we were headed for a showdown.

When she barged into the kitchen, I braced myself for the inevitable confrontation. She dropped her books on the table.

"Is it true?"

I wiped my hands on a dishtowel and placed it on the counter. "Is what true?"

She glared, anger coloring her cheeks. "Heather Ramsey couldn't wait to come to school today and announce to the world about you cleaning shit off the bathroom walls at the Bargain Hut."

"Michelle! I won't tolerate you cursing." My first instinct was to deny, but I'd always taught my girls to tell the truth. It was my theory that the consequences for honesty far outweighed the damaging effects of a lie. The fact that I'd told Detective Alder a white lie about making coffee weighed on my mind. Oh, and I'd lied to Angie about Harmony Inn. Nice example I was setting.

It had been almost a week since I'd cleaned the Bargain

Hut, and up until now, my debut in the working world had gone undetected.

"Well?"

"I told you I had taken a job."

"You didn't say you were a janitor." She jerked open the fridge and pulled out a bottle of water. "I had to hear it from a *scholarship* kid. Her stupid sister works there."

Oops!

Ah, one of the clerks had ratted on me. "I'm surprised it took this long."

Michelle stomped a foot, a technique she'd perfected over the years. "If she hadn't had strep throat it would have been all over school before first bell rang on Monday."

"Fortunate for me, I guess."

"Gran's going to have a coronary," Michelle said.

"Not with my luck," I said under my breath.

She swallowed a sip of water and continued her tirade. "What were you thinking? We will never be able to go to the club again."

"No time in my schedule for tennis," I teased.

"I'm not going back to school. They'll laugh me out of homeroom," she said, the whine in her voice cranking to a high soprano.

Okay, humor was not working.

"Everyone's cracking up because of you and your crummy job," she said.

Lakeview Academy awarded twenty scholarships a year to deserving children in the community who otherwise wouldn't be able to afford a private education. There had always been friction between the students on free tuition and those whose parents paid full fare. A scholarship kid had called out Michelle. It put her on the same level, and she wasn't happy. But like it or not, we *were* on the same level. I was a working mom. What I didn't tell her was that she might become one of those kids fighting for free tuition.

"Don't you think you're being a bit melodramatic?"

"You don't get it, do you?" She finished off the water and threw the bottle in the recycle bin. "We're Cavanaughs."

"You think you have an image to uphold?" My throat tightened. I ground my palms into my eyes and pretended to massage out a headache. Damned if I'd let Michelle see me cry. "Sorry if me trying to keep us afloat embarrasses you." My nerves began to unravel, but my mouth was just getting started. "Big newsflash, kiddo. Everything I'm doing, I'm doing for you. So you stay at Lakeview. So you have a roof over your head. So you can eat a hot meal when you come home from school."

I let her digest my words and started in again. "I can't sit around and wait on your father to do something."

Michelle's upper lip quivered. I wasn't sure if she was going to cry or if she was gearing up to launch into me again.

"I'd scrub sewers if it meant being able to take care of you. My first and foremost concern is making sure you have what you need. If you can't see beyond that, then I've failed as a mother." I didn't wait for her to respond. Pulling one of her tricks, I ran up to my room, slammed the door, and threw myself across the bed.

I don't know how long I lay there, but I cried until the tears wouldn't come. After allowing myself to wallow a while, realization hit me like a load of manure. No amount of crying could change what had happened or bring Phillip back. My tears didn't matter to him, and no amount of justification would make a spoiled teenager see I was trying to make ends meet for her benefit. And no amount of what-ifs would undo what Phillip's infidelity had done to my marriage.

With renewed resolve, I sprang from the bed. In the bathroom, I splashed cold water on my face. "You can do this, Cece Cavanaugh. Michelle may balk and squirm, but you're the mother. Now quit your whining and take control."

The woman in the mirror didn't look convinced, but I shook my finger at her. "You can do this."

Before I made it halfway downstairs, Jessie rushed in the front door.

"Did you find anything to help Kim?" she asked in her most dramatic voice.

"Jessie." I sighed. "I only agreed to take the job this afternoon." My hands would be full at the inn without snooping around for something to prove Kim didn't kill her husband. It wasn't like I even knew what to look for, much less where I'd find it. "And I can't risk losing this job. I need the money."

I followed her to the gathering room, noting Michelle was nowhere in sight.

"Mom, she didn't do it." Jessie dropped into the recliner where Detective Alder had dozed earlier. "Someone else killed Brian. We have to find out who!"

She was starting to sound a bit like the mynah bird my Grandpa Earl used to have. It repeated the same thing over and over and over. "You realize if the focus is taken off Kim, you or Sarah could become suspects," I said.

"So? I'm innocent."

"You're supposed to call Detective Alder. He stopped by to see you."

"Already talked to him." She quickly added, "Nothing important."

Nothing important? That was what you say when you have a stubborn hangnail or a festered splinter, not about a detective calling for more information regarding a murder investigation.

Still worried, I changed the subject to keep from causing her to panic. "What does Sarah think about everything?" In all the years the girls had been friends, they had always stuck together. If you saw one, you saw the other two. The line blurred between where one girl ended and the others began.

It didn't matter what happened; they were a united front. "And why hasn't she been here pleading a case for Kim?"

"She's at work," Jessie said, averting her eyes.

I smelled a conspiracy. No way was I convinced Sarah's absence was a coincidence.

"She hasn't even called. Not once," I said. If Kim was guilty, I was all for justice. But, if this was a witch-hunt to rescue Kim by throwing Sarah's friendship under the bus, I wasn't going to be a party to it.

"Mom, I said she had to work. Are you going to help or not?"

"I'm not sure what I can do. The police already searched the inn. All they left was a mess."

"But," Jessie said, "you'll have access to all the rooms. Maybe you'll find a clue that slipped through the cracks."

"Do you mean maybe I'll find something in Sarah's room to point the finger at her?" I couldn't help myself.

"That's not what I meant." Jessie cleared her throat. "If someone from the outside followed Brian, you might find evidence to identify the real killer. A matchbook or cigarette butt, maybe a strange jacket or something out of place. I don't know."

"Do I look like Matlock?" I asked.

She laughed, but I knew she was serious. She expected me to become Miss Marple and solve the case. If I was going to get dinner on the table tonight, I had to play along with her scheme.

"Okay, write down what you remember about the evening while I work on dinner." I started for the kitchen. "I assume you're staying?"

Jessie hopped up, hugged my neck, and grabbed a legal pad from the desk. "Thanks, Mom. You're the best."

"Don't thank me. I haven't done anything yet." I dug through the pantry until I found our usual fixings for nights when Esther was off. "Is pizza okay?"

My request fell on deaf ears. She was already engrossed in reconstructing the happenings at Harmony Inn.

Michelle sauntered into the kitchen while "Operation Save Kim" was in full swing. She had the packet of divorce papers from the hall table.

"What's this?" She pulled the contents from the envelope.

Before she had a chance to see the document, I snatched it away. "None of your business."

She stuck out her tongue and gave me the famous Cece eye-roll. The one I'd perfected. If I had a dime for every time my kids mimicked one of my bad habits, I wouldn't have to clean other people's crap, and my daughter and I wouldn't be at each other's throats. But I took it as a sign she didn't hate me.

"Put those peepers to work, and see if you can find mushrooms in the fridge." I gave her my mean mom face, which consisted of narrowing my eyes and scrunching my mouth into a tight "O."

Michelle watched as I slid the envelope inside my purse. "You're good at keeping secrets. Is this one going to jump up and bite me in the butt, too?"

Touché. I punched the dough I'd been kneading and ignored her. When I didn't answer, she went to work chopping veggies. Jessie must not have heard the exchange, or if she did, she chose to ignore it.

By the time I placed the pizza on the table, my sleuth had constructed an entire timeline starting the moment she entered the front door of Harmony Inn, complete with diagrams. I pushed it aside while we ate and talked about everything except murder, crime scenes, and divorce. Michelle even joined in the conversation without slinging barbs my way. It was refreshing. Another almost-normal family dinner.

After some arm-twisting, Michelle agreed to clean the

kitchen while I sat and listened to the theories and speculation Jessie had conjured up.

"We arrived around five," she said. "After checking in, we went straight to our rooms and put our bags away. I stayed on the third floor. Kim and Sarah had rooms on the second. When we finished, the owner had a wine and cheese reception waiting for us. We were in the study by six, munching on gouda and sipping pinot grigio."

"Brian was killed in the study," I said.

Jessie nodded. "It's hard to believe we were laughing and having a good time and a few hours later he would be dead in the same spot."

"Then what?" I asked.

"We stayed there talking for forty-five minutes or an hour, then the masseuse showed up." Jessie grabbed her purse and dug through it. "I still have her card." She waved it in the air. "Amanda Chandler. She's from Sarah's salon. Kim went first while Sarah and I stayed in the study."

"Kim told me there weren't any other guests at the inn."

"No, just us." Jessie continued, "I was next after Kim, and then Sarah."

"Did Kim come back to the study after her massage?" I asked.

"I don't think so. After mine I went to bed."

"Was Sarah the last one downstairs?" I turned the diagram to get a better look.

"Technically, I guess Amanda was. She told Eve she'd let herself out." Jessie studied the notes she'd made before dinner and tapped the pen against the table.

"What about Carrie?"

"Who?" Jessie pursed her lips.

"Eve's sister."

"Never saw her. I guess she could have been there. It's a big house."

I jotted a note on the paper to remind myself to ask about Carrie's whereabouts.

Michelle finished the dishes and joined us. "Maybe the masseuse killed him."

The girls looked from one another to me.

"What's her motivation?" I asked. "Did any of you even know her? I mean, besides Sarah."

Eyebrows shot up. There was enough suspicion going around, I shouldn't have added to it. I didn't like the direction we had veered off in, but I made a mental note to check out the masseuse.

"I met her once or twice at the salon, but I don't know anything about her," Jessie said.

"I'll be at the inn for a couple of days. Can I borrow your diagram?" I folded the paper and put it in my purse, right next to the divorce packet.

Before Jessie left, I asked her a few questions about current biohazard treatment. Satisfied I could handle the job, I called Eve and accepted. I told her to expect me tomorrow around noon. She sounded irritated I couldn't be there sooner, but I told her I had an appointment with the mayor and needed to stop at the supply house. My puny income was the only thing keeping my family afloat until I figured out how to squeeze money out of Phillip.

Chapter 18

"The mayor giving Cece a commendation is a joke. A joke that will get him voted out of office. Not a smart move on his part."
Hazel Cavanaugh

The mayor presented me with a certificate of appreciation, shook my hand for pictures, and ushered me out of his office in less than fifteen minutes. Short and sweet, the way I liked it. Local elections were a couple of days away, and he needed all the press he could get if he wanted to get re-elected. Though, solving a few burglaries and vandalisms wouldn't do much to conceal Wickford's first homicide.

When I arrived at Harmony Inn, my first visual was Eve Taft standing on the porch, arms crossed over her chest, engrossed in conversation with Detective Alder. I hadn't noticed the blue sedan parked at the curb when I drove up, or I would have kept going. He had a way of making me feel all giddy, and I didn't need the distraction. Not today.

Alder jotted notes in his book while Eve's left foot tapped a steady rhythm on the warped flooring. He didn't appear to notice my arrival, but she shot me a sour glance then jerked her head toward the front door. Either my tardiness perturbed her, or maybe she was annoyed because of Alder. Who knew? I had to keep from making an utter fool of myself in front of him.

I feigned interest in sorting through the supplies in my trunk while they talked. I hoped she had other work to keep her busy. Her hovering wouldn't hurry the process. Maybe

Alder would take her to the station for questioning. Then both would be out of my hair.

Fletcher had given me the name of a safety equipment supplier in St. Louis. For a tidy sum, I'd purchased biohazard collection bags, protective coveralls, shoe coverings, and gloves, along with the necessary disinfectants and sanitizers to neutralize the biohazards. The owner of the business even gave me a crash course on using the products. While he was at it, he contacted a local agency to help with the disposal.

As soon as Alder finished with Eve, I'd unload the car. In the meantime, I'd stay within earshot, in case he spilled any juicy details about the case.

"You're late!" Eve broke off the interview and pointed to her watch. "You said you'd be here by noon."

Busted! With no chance of hearing anything about Brian's murder, I hefted supplies from the trunk.

"Sorry." Gasping for breath, I dropped the box on the top step. "Drove to St. Louis to buy this stuff." I inhaled to slow my breathing.

Alder looked up from his notebook, a grin spreading across his face.

My knees went weak. *Damn, why did he get to me?* The blue eyes and moustache didn't help. I squared my shoulders, determined not to listen to the voice whispering in my ear. *What difference does it make? Phillip doesn't care. For once, do something for yourself.*

"What brings you here?" he asked, while Eve paced the length of the porch.

An annoying tug in my mid-section caught me off-guard. It was the unmistakable temptation of lust. My lips betrayed me and curved into my best "come hither" smile.

Stop it, you hussy. Pull yourself together and act respectable.

Thank goodness for the other voice.

"Bonafide CSC hired me to clean so Ms. Taft can reopen her business."

He folded his notepad and tucked it into his shirt pocket. The grin on his face disappeared into a scowl. "You're what?"

The sensation in my midsection evaporated. "I'm cleaning the crime scene. Someone has to do it. You'd think it would be the police or coroner, but no. The owner is left to deal with the dirty business." One of these days my mouth was going to get me in trouble. I climbed down off my soapbox before stupider words poured forth.

A muscle twitched under his right eye. "Don't you have a tennis lesson or whatever you ladies do to stay busy?"

"Ha. Ha. You're too funny." I bristled at his humor attempt and returned to the car for another load, with Detective Alder following close behind. This time my jiggle didn't worry me.

"This isn't cleaning for your monthly book club get-together. This is a crime scene."

"The crime scene has been released. If you'll excuse me, I have work to do." I pulled a box from the trunk of my Lexus.

"Give me that." He lifted the carton from my grasp.

How could one man be sexy and annoying all at the same time? I bent to retrieve more supplies.

"Don't worry about those. I'll get them. Point me in the right direction." He followed me to the porch and dropped the box where I indicated.

"Are you qualified to handle this?" He rooted through a box, pawing at the supplies. The expression on his face landed somewhere between amused and frustrated.

"I was an ER nurse for ten years. I think I know something about blood and guts," I said. "Unless you have a reason to make it an active crime scene, I'm going in whether you like it or not."

The left side of his moustache lifted. He opened his mouth, but then closed it. After an exaggerated exhale, he said, "Suit yourself."

Eve was still pacing. "You do remember I have a business I can't open until you're done?"

"Yes. I'll start in the study." I fished around in one of the boxes and removed a spray bottle. "This is supposed to be great for removing fingerprint powder." I glared at Alder. "I hope the cops didn't track it onto your carpet. It doesn't work great on porous stuff, but hard surfaces should clean right up."

"Not my problem." She tromped through the doorway and let the screen slam behind her. From inside, she said, "Detective, call me if you have more questions." She scurried off down the hallway and left me alone with Alder.

"I'm already late, and if you haven't noticed, she's got a huge case of the pissies," I said. I picked up a box and started for the door.

"It's none of my business, but—"

"You're right," I interrupted. Tears filled the corners of my eyes, but I fought to keep them in check. I'd be damned if I was going to cry today. "It's none of your business."

"Just be careful. It's nasty work." His voice had softened, but the set of his jaw spoke of his seriousness. He took the box from me and carried it inside. I stood for a minute, trying to figure out what had happened.

"Are you coming?" he asked. "I don't have all day."

It didn't take long for him to haul everything in. The study was the only contaminated room, and I had to make sure I didn't taint the supplies I was using. Every rag, paper towel, and rubber glove I used, even the protective gear I had to wear, needed to go in a bag when I finished.

"Thanks for helping," I said. "Sorry I snapped at you."

"No problem," he said. "I better go." At the screen door, he paused, then pushed it open and repeated, "Be careful."

I stood on the porch and waited until his car was out of sight. My divorce papers were still in my purse, right next to Jessie's reconstructed timeline. When Alder wrapped up this case, there would be no reason to have to see him. I needed another man in my life like I needed a boob job. Well, okay. Perky boobs might be nice. But another man, no way.

I heard banging coming from the rear of the house and I followed the sounds, hoping they would lead me to Eve.

"Shit, shit, shit." Eve stood at the refrigerator throwing containers into the trash, tears streaming down her cheeks. When she saw me, she wiped her face with the back of her hand. "What do you want?" she asked between sniffles.

"Sorry, didn't mean to interrupt, but we need to discuss the rug." I'd combed the Internet looking for ways to deal with it, but nothing I found indicated it was salvageable.

"Why?" she asked.

"Unfortunately, it needs to be disposed of. Even if the stains come out, which is doubtful, no amount of sanitizing can remove the hazard."

"What? It belonged to my great-grandmother." She slammed another container into the trash. "It's an heirloom." Then out of nowhere, she started screaming. An ear-piercing, nonstop shriek.

I yelped and jumped two steps back. In all my years I had never heard such a blood-curdling sound, except maybe in a horror movie. Either the woman was capital "C" Crazy or she had forgotten to take her meds.

I stood there for a moment at a loss. When she stopped, I said, "Sorry, I didn't mean to upset you. The rug is contaminated." I watched in amazement as she turned to the fridge and began to pull out more containers, as if nothing had happened.

"Well, clean it. Isn't that why you hauled all those boxes in here?" She had her hand on a container, and it slipped and fell to the floor. The lid popped off and pancake batter, complete with blueberries, skyrocketed into the air, spewing the gloppy substance everywhere. She stared at the mess for a second and laughed. Soft at first, and then rising to a hysterical level. "Great! Just frickin' great."

"I'm sorry I can't save the rug. It has to go." Batter dripped from the kitchen island and plopped onto the tile, spreading out into a lumpy mess. I resisted the urge to wipe it up.

She scooped the bowl from the floor and flung it at the trashcan. "You see all this food? It's ruined." She pointed to the refrigerator. "Someone hit a circuit breaker while the cops were here, and all of it is spoiled."

Before I could scurry away, she said, "We're paying you plenty. You'd think you could clean the damn rug."

Her insurance would foot the bill, but it didn't seem like the time to remind her. "It's a health issue," I said and turned toward the hall, leaving her to her bad day. I didn't want any part of her temper. The sooner this place was in order, the sooner it would be nothing but an awful memory.

After my departure yesterday, someone had closed the doors to the study. I couldn't blame them. Who wanted a constant reminder of such a dreadful event? I didn't know how Eve or her sister could come back after the police released the crime scene. It would have freaked me out.

Before beginning, I tore open a package of protective coveralls and tugged them on over my shorts and T-shirt. I opened a bio collection bag and gathered the tools to work on the rug. It was too big to roll up. The best way to dispose of it was to cut it into manageable pieces. To accomplish my task, I had purchased a carpet knife at the hardware store.

Pushing the doors open, I steeled myself for the sight inside. The same rancid smell permeated the air. The thick tapestry drapes cast a pall over the room. I threaded my way across the floor, avoiding the blood, pulled the drapes aside, and opened a window. The space needed an infusion of fresh air. I took a deep breath, then turned and stared at my surroundings. The contrast between the brutal crime scene and the hominess of the study still startled me.

When I looked up, Carrie stood in the doorway. "I apologize for Eve's meltdown. She went upstairs to rest and won't bother you again."

"Thanks. Sorry I upset her."

She started to come in, but I held my hand up like a school crossing guard. "Please don't. I have to make sure nothing more gets tracked out of here."

"This isn't necessary," she said. "We're quite capable of managing this ourselves."

"That's why you have insurance."

Her gaze swept around the room, until her eyes fastened on the beautiful rug with its enormous burgundy blotch. I didn't need to be a mind reader to know what she was thinking.

"Eve told you about the rug?" I asked.

Carrie nodded. "It's not an heirloom. I don't know why she said that."

"It's beautiful. I can understand why she's upset. You can file a claim with your insurance company to replace it." I didn't know what else to say, but I hoped to win her over. Having at least one of them on my side would make my job easier.

"I hope so." She stared at the room.

If it weren't for the spray of blood across the floor and furniture, it was the type of place where I'd like to curl up with a good book, a cup of tea, and a crackling fire. However, considering what had happened here, this was the last place I'd be able to relax.

"If you need anything, I'll be in the kitchen." She turned to leave.

"I do have a question." I wended my way through the mess, veering around the bloodstained rug, to the door. "If you have a sec."

She stopped and walked back. "Sure."

"Were you here?"

"What?" Her voice caught. "When?"

"Friday night."

"Why do you ask?" Her lips thinned into a grim line.

"Just wondering." I wanted to smack myself. It wouldn't do to make her suspicious before I had time to do some investigating. "Did you know him?"

"Me?" she asked. "Why would I know him?"

"Wickford's not that big." I laughed, trying to add some levity to my inquiry. "Not much happens without the whole town knowing before sundown."

"We moved back to Wickford a few months ago," Carrie said. "Our grandmother died last year and left the house to us."

"This must be horrible for you and your sister. Such a tragedy."

"Yes, it is. Most people see this strictly as a business, but it's also our home."

She excused herself again and left me alone.

After she was gone, I pulled Jessie's notes from my purse and flipped through them until I located the map she had drawn. Nothing stuck out. She noted the bedrooms where each of the girls had slept and crossed through several rooms to indicate she hadn't been in them. At least I knew who had slept where. Before snooping, I decided to finish my cleaning and pulled a notepad from my bag to itemize the damaged possessions. Carrie hadn't told me if she was here when Brian was murdered. I jotted myself a note to ask her again.

I flipped the page, listed the rug, and then fumbled in my bag for my camera to snap a couple of photos before destroying the rug. It took me almost an hour to cut smaller sections and stuff them in the bags.

After a thorough inspection of the room, I followed the blood. Most of the contaminated items were glass or ceramic and therefore salvageable. The runner on the library table had a fine mist of blood. It went in the bag, along with two tapestry pillows from the sofa.

The books worried me. Many of them appeared to be first editions or at least family mementos. One section of shelving contained keepsakes that must have belonged to Eve and Carrie: a few scrapbooks, photo albums, textbooks, and Wickford High School yearbooks. A trail of blood led to the bookcase. The lower shelves had two contaminated books. The center area revealed five more with splatter, and the top shelves produced none. Lucky for the Taft sisters, all the soiled books were recent releases. I added them to the insurance list.

Michelle had arranged a ride from school, so I continued through the afternoon. Working on the other stains took three more hours. I washed all the hard surfaces with heavy-duty cleaner and then used a sanitizer. Around six-thirty, I deemed the room decontaminated and sprayed it with a special pine-fresh deodorizer. Before I stepped into the hall, I bagged the rags, coveralls, booties, rubber gloves, and sealed the bags. I piled them on the porch for the disposal company to collect.

Carrie was nowhere to be found, and I didn't want to find Eve. Too tired to snoop, I let myself out and headed for home.

Michelle had dinner on the stove when I arrived.

"Yeesch, you stink." She wrinkled her face and pinched her fingers over her nose.

"I know. Do I have time for a shower before we eat?"

"Oh, yeah, cause I'm not sitting at the same table with you." She crossed her eyes and fanned the air.

"No need for all the drama." I kicked off my shoes, peeled off my shorts and T-shirt in the laundry room, and ran upstairs in my underwear. If I'd learned anything since Esther left, it was to save myself work, less to carry down on washday.

In the shower, I reflected on what Jessie had told me about the night Brian died. Something didn't add up, and damned if I knew what it was. But that was only part of the story. Maybe Sarah could provide some answers. I hadn't seen her since before Brian died.

My shoulders ached from all the cleaning, and my calves were tight and cramped. No doubt these were muscles I hadn't used at the gym, but then, I didn't remember the last time I'd worked out. I stood under the hot water and let it run down my back.

As a rule, sweats or a robe would have been in order, but I had questions, and I wanted them answered in person. I dressed in a pair of jeans and a light sweater. As soon as we finished dinner, I was going to have a talk with Sarah.

When we sat down at the table, I turned on the television to watch the news.

"Hey, isn't he the detective who questioned Jess?" Michelle asked.

Sure enough, Detective Case Alder was standing outside the police station answering a reporter's questions.

"Indeed, it is."

I watched him tell the reporter how he was working several leads and was narrowing down the suspect list. A blanket of dread settled over me. Was he closing in on Kim? Sarah? If he was narrowing down the suspects, did that mean Jessie was off the list?

After the interview, details of Brian's funeral filled the screen. The services started tomorrow at ten, and in lieu of flowers, the family requested donations to the high school athletic fund. Did "family" mean his wife or his parents?

Kim had no one, except for a missing-in-action alcoholic father. If she ever needed my support, it was now. I didn't know how Brian's folks were handling the situation, but my guess was Kim wasn't their favorite daughter-in-law.

The next segment zoomed right in on my face then widened to show the mayor shaking my hand.

"That's you," Michelle said.

I started to mute the TV, but she grabbed the remote. "No way. I want to hear this."

When a commercial came on, Michelle turned off the tube and glared at me. "How many ways can you ruin my life?" She shoved the rest of her dinner down the garbage disposal and slammed the plate into the dishwasher.

The phone rang while I was wiping down the table.

"I got it." Michelle snatched the handset and headed to the other room. "Hello?"

I added detergent and started the dishwasher.

"Guess it was a wrong number," she said, returning the phone to its cradle.

Wrong number, my ass. My money was on Willow. She had my husband, and now she wanted to make me miserable.

I needed to find out what Sarah remembered about the weekend Brian was killed. After dinner, I tried to call her for over an hour but never reached her. Was she ignoring me? She'd been cutting my hair since she graduated from cosmetology school a few years ago. Going to the salon would be the easiest way to talk to her. I called her salon. The soonest I could get an appointment was Saturday morning. That would have to do. Once I was in her chair, she'd have to talk to me.

Chapter 19

"I never dreamed I'd be attending a funeral for a murder victim right here in Wickford, but then I never dreamed I'd be considering a divorce either. If bad things come in threes, the third will be a doozie."
Cece Cavanaugh

Standing in my walk-in closet, I fixated on what to wear to the funeral. My paisley tea-length seemed too festive. Besides, it was Phillip's favorite. The beige sheath made my hips look big, and if I had a hot flash in the hunter-green sweater dress, I'd melt. Nothing in my closet appealed to me.

My best black dress still hung in the dry cleaner bag. It was an impulse purchase, and when I'd worn it to the theatre, Phillip commented he thought it looked okay but wasn't something he would have chosen. The memory of his disapproval was all I needed. I tore the bag away and slipped the dress over my head. Good, it still fit. Strappy black heels completed the outfit. Two turns in the mirror, and I pronounced myself appropriately attired.

Reaching for the bottle of Chanel Cristalle on my dressing table, I jerked my hand away. Phillip's favorite perfume. The one he'd bought and insisted I wear. Angie was right. I couldn't even pick my own fragrance. Damn Phillip, I couldn't make a simple decision about what to wear to a funeral. I swept the bottle into the waste can and went to Michelle's room to see what her selection offered.

After spritzing myself with a generous dose of Michelle's cologne, I headed to the church. Massive thunderheads rumbled in the distance, promising a spring storm. Appropriate weather for a funeral.

Turning onto Fifth Street, I noticed a black truck following way too close. I eased into the slow lane and waited for the other driver to take the hint and go around. Instead, the truck swung behind me and continued tailgating. Approaching the next intersection, I swerved into the other lane and turned onto Maple. I had too much on my mind to play chicken with a stupid driver. In my rearview mirror, I watched as the truck hung a U-turn and followed me. My stomach sank when I realized I was being followed. I stepped on the gas and hurried to the church where there would be plenty of people and I wouldn't feel vulnerable. As the church came into view, I lost sight of the truck.

St. Michael's Church, an imposing stone and brick structure, took up the entire block between Chestnut and Elm. At noon, each day for as far back as I could remember, the massive church bell rang twelve times, signaling the passage from morning to afternoon. My Grandpa Earl had told me, back in his day, it marked the time when work ceased for a small respite and folks went home for the noon meal. Nowadays people never gave it a second thought. With fast food restaurants popping up on every corner, and most families requiring two incomes, the pace barely slowed, much less came to a halt for a full-blown meal in the middle of the day.

I was halfway to the front door of the church when a thunderclap sent me scurrying back to the car for an umbrella. I stopped in my tracks when the black truck pulled through the lot and stopped in front of my car. Tinted windows made it impossible to get a look at the driver.

I marched right to my car, wondering if Phillip or his trashy girlfriend had hired someone to bully me into signing the divorce papers. I intended to send the message that they didn't intimidate me one bit. When I came up alongside the truck, the driver revved the engine twice and drove away. So much for bullying. I retrieved my umbrella and made a dash for the church. Before I made it halfway to the door the sky unleashed its burden. Huge, stinging drops pelted me.

Perhaps it was because I hadn't worn heels in a while and was concentrating on my footing, or because I had forty-eleven things on my mind, I wasn't paying attention. At the top of the steps, I ran headfirst into Detective Alder. My umbrella shuddered from the impact and sent a spray of water onto his overcoat.

He stepped back and pinned me with an icy stare. Even without the rain and dampness of the morning, I felt the chill. Quite a switch from the radiant smile he'd greeted me with yesterday.

"Good morning, Detective Alder," I said in a polite, yet reserved tone. Two could play his game. Besides, staying aloof would temper my hormones.

"I assumed you'd be here," he said.

"You know what they say about assuming."

"After I got back to the station yesterday, I asked myself why you'd be cleaning a crime scene. You live in a ritzy neighborhood and drive a Lexus." He grabbed his coat by the lapels and shook off the drops, all the while never taking his eyes off me. "It didn't take me long to figure it out. After your *tête-à-tête* with the mayor, my boss reamed me out because my guys overlooked the cell phone at the Cline house. The one you found."

I gulped. "I can explain."

He shook his head. "Save it. Are you really here for a funeral, or are you being nosy?"

"I don't need to justify myself to you. Kim is my daughter's best friend." I leaned forward and peered into his blue eyes. "Why are you here?"

"Are you interfering in my investigation?" He ignored my question.

"Officer, it's raining. Can we step inside and finish our conversation?"

"Detective," he said.

"What?"

"It's detective. You called me officer." He placed a hand on my elbow and led me into the foyer.

It was hard to be glib with a handsome, angry detective hauling me into church, but I tried.

"Potato, potatoh." As we entered the vestibule, my voice echoed above the soft murmurs of the mourners who were lining up to enter the sanctuary. Conversations stalled and all eyes focused on me and the detective holding my arm. More fodder for the gossip-mongers. Hazel would have an earful before the day was done.

I pasted on a half-smile, half-pout in a what's-a-girl-to-do pose and wiggled my fingers in greeting. No sense making a scene. I'd never be able to shake him in a room full of people.

"Where are you taking me?" I whispered.

"Where I can keep an eye on you." He nudged me through the door, down the aisle, into a pew, and then sat down, blocking my escape. "I don't know what you're up to, but I know you're up to something."

"Not that it's any of your business, but I came here to be with Kim."

"I'm making it my business." He slid a hymnal from the holder in front of us and flipped through the pages.

"I have to visit the ladies' room." I stood up and pushed his knee.

"Oh, no you don't." He reached for my hand.

Every nerve in my body stood at attention. I stole a glance at him as a smile crossed his lips. When he caught me looking, the smile disappeared, and he squared his shoulders.

"Let go," I said and sat down. "I'm not a five-year-old."

He released his grip. "You act like it." Then he crossed his legs.

The woman in front of us turned around and frowned. "Will you show some respect?"

I wanted to stick my tongue out at her and tell her to mind her own business, but we were in church, and it didn't seem like a polite thing to do.

"Fine," I whispered to Alder. But it wasn't fine. How was I going to find out anything with him watching my every move? "You can't hold me prisoner." My cell phone vibrated. I checked the display and found a text from Jessie. "Mom, are you here?"

"That's what you think. If you're impeding my investigation, I could take you down to the station and charge you."

"You wouldn't dare." I started my reply to Jessie and before I could hit the send key, Alder grabbed the cell from my hands.

"Try me."

The woman shook her head and turned around. "Will you please be quiet?"

People began to file in and fill up the rows. Extra chairs had been set up along the walls to accommodate the crowd. Jessie and Kim entered on the far side of the church.

"My daughter is here," I said, noticing Sarah wasn't with her. "She's saving a seat for me. Give me my phone. I want to tell her where I'm at." Poor Kim was about as welcome here as a skunk. Every head in the place turned in her direction, and the murmurs grew as she made her way to the front of the church. I had to give her credit; she held her head high and ignored the whispers. If she ever needed support, it was now. But Alder didn't budge.

"Not a chance," he muttered.

"Why are you holding me hostage?" I tried to keep my voice low, but dang he was stubborn.

"The service is starting." He put his finger to his lip and "shushed" me.

Jess kept turning around, watching for me. I tried to get her attention, but it wasn't as if I could stand up and wave. Alder had me corralled, and no amount of squirming would set me free.

Brian's parents and his younger sister were in the front row. Phillip and I had sat at their table during Kim and Brian's wedding reception, and I couldn't even imagine how they must be feeling. I didn't want to. The last thing a parent ever wanted to experience was the loss of a child. And I thought *my* life was in turmoil. The least I could do was take over a casserole or send a card, something to express my condolences.

With the huge turnout, it was difficult to tell if Jo Stewart was here. From my vantage point, all I could look for was long, red hair, and there were a couple of women who fit the description. Surely after all the trouble she'd caused Brian at school, Stewart wouldn't be dumb enough to show up.

I wasn't the only one looking over the crowd. Alder's eyes searched the room. When he found someone who interested him, he pulled his book from his pocket and jotted down notes. Too bad I couldn't figure out who had caught his interest. What I wouldn't give to get a peek at his observations. I'd love to know what he'd written about Kim, Jessie, and Sarah. And me. Did he consider me a suspect or a meddlesome housewife?

I paid attention to Alder's gaze roaming the room, but it was difficult to determine whom he was focusing on and writing about. His handwriting was too small and messy to decipher.

I knew he had a job to do. Angie had raved about him being a great detective. There wasn't a doubt in my mind that he would bring the bad guy to justice, but I didn't want him fixating on the people I loved.

The school must have cancelled classes because teenagers filled the pews. There was no doubt Brian was well-liked. My own tears were on the verge of letting loose as people filed to the podium to praise his accomplishments as a teacher, brother, friend. It was a moving service.

After the final prayer, I stood to leave.

"Wait," Alder said.

Dabbing at their eyes, people poured into the aisles. Kim and Jessie headed toward the door. Kim had her head low, and Jess had a protective arm around her as they talked in low tones. They shuffled by, caught up in the crowd, without looking my way.

"Excuse me, but I have to get to the inn." I'd had enough of his games, and I wanted to catch Kim.

People jammed the aisles, making for a slow exit. I looked over my shoulder and noticed the rest of our pew had exited in the opposite direction. That aisle appeared to be moving much quicker. Alder was playing nice with the older parishioners and allowing them to proceed before us. He had even engaged an older man in conversation, and the old coot was bending Alder's ear about the rain and arthritis. I fumed.

When Alder stooped to pick up a memorial card, I used the distraction to make my getaway. It didn't take long for me to scramble down the length of the pew and blend in with the swarm of people leaving the rear of the church.

Outside, the rain came down in sheets. I scanned the crowd for Jess and Kim, but with all the umbrellas and people rushing to their cars, it was impossible to pick them out.

"Thought you'd give me the slip, did you?"

By now, I'd recognize his voice anywhere, and it was getting old.

"Cripes, don't you have a murder to solve?" I asked.

The detective wrapped my arm around his. "Allow me to see you to your car."

I jerked my arm back. If I wasn't pissed, I might enjoy his protectiveness, but at this moment it seemed more like controlling. "I can manage, but thanks for your concern. Oh, and give me back my phone, you jerk."

He reached inside his suit and removed my phone. "There's no way I'm letting you out of my sight until you're in your vehicle and driving down the street."

"Whatever." I grabbed my phone and shoved it in my purse. "I'd have thought you had more important things to do than harass me." No wonder he wasn't married. His wife probably divorced him for being too bossy. I marched across the parking lot, dragging him behind me. We made it to my car in time to see Kim get in her car. Jessie followed her out of the parking lot.

"I hope you're satisfied."

He smiled.

Alder stayed with me until I had fastened my seat belt and started the car. He got in his sedan, pulled into the street and parked at the curb. When I put the Lexus in gear, a young woman stepped out of a red sports car parked next to me. Under other circumstances, she wouldn't have caught my attention, except for the big floppy hat and sunglasses. It was raining like crazy. She crossed the street to the church, bypassed the main entrance and entered through a side door. What was she up to? Being the nosy sort, I wanted to follow her but couldn't with Alder stalking me. I had to think of a way to ditch him. I glanced his way and noticed he was talking on his cell, not paying the least bit of attention to me or the woman.

The rain had let up, so I left my umbrella in the car and ran toward the back of the church.

Before I made it halfway across the street, I heard the screech of wet brakes behind me. I was not the least bit surprised to turn and see Detective Alder.

"I knew you weren't to be trusted," he said. "Where are you going?"

There had to be something I could do to get Alder off my back. After thinking for a minute, I plunged my hand into my purse in search of every woman's secret weapon when it came to men. With it, a woman could turn almost any man into a tongue-tied knot of nerves. I located the object of my search and pulled a tampon from my purse. "Some things are personal, Detective Alder." I pointed the tampon in his direction.

"Oh, sor . . . Sorry," he stuttered and diverted his eyes. His face flushed an unflattering shade of crimson.

"Now, if you'll excuse me." I stomped to the front door of the church and stood waiting for him to leave. My pumps were taking a beating today. It was a good thing I didn't have to dress up often. Satisfied he was gone, I slid into the church. A few stragglers still stood in the foyer talking. I peered around for the hat lady and not seeing her, I went into the sanctuary and stopped when I saw Brian's parents engaged in quiet conversation with her.

Now was as good a time as any to pay my respects to Mr. and Mrs. Anderson and find out how hat lady fit into the equation. When I was almost in spitting distance, Pastor Frank stepped out of a pew and cornered me.

"Cece, it's good to see you," he said. "We've missed you lately."

"Uh, yeah. About that," I mumbled.

"If there's anything you need to pray on, you know you're always welcome in God's house." He folded his hands in front of him as if already starting to pray for me.

Even my pastor knew my husband was cheating on me. "Thank you, pastor," I said. "I'll be in touch." I kept an eye on hat lady. She had stepped away from the Andersons. I caught a glimpse of her as she slipped out the same door she had entered.

"You know you don't need an appointment," he continued. "Stop by anytime."

"I will," I said. "I definitely will." Pastor Frank had married Phillip and me and had baptized both my girls. I didn't want to be disrespectful. I could catch up to the Andersons or try and corner hat lady in the parking lot. Before I could make my break, another couple had already corralled the Andersons. My option was eliminated. I excused myself from Pastor Frank with a promise to stop by for a prayer.

The sports car was gone by the time I made it back to my car. My brain kicked into information overload. I pulled a notepad from my purse and flipped to a clean page, which was a task in itself. Besides incomplete grocery lists and never-tried recipes, most of the pages contained a scribbled note or phone number. I found a clean sheet and started a new list titled "SUSPECTS."

Who were the suspects? Who wanted Brian dead? Who had motivation?

The first name I wrote on the list made me wince. I didn't want to think of Kim being a suspect, but I had no choice. She had motive, but others did, too.

KIM (wife):

Recently filed for divorce

Thought Brian was cheating

Wanted a baby, but did he?

Harassing Brian's girlfriend?

At the inn when murder occurred

Were there other things she hadn't told me?

SARAH (wife's best friend):

Brian came on to her

At the inn when murder occurred

Would she take revenge for her friend Kim?

What about the argument with Brian?

Why has she been scarce?

AMANDA (masseuse):

At the inn prior to the murder

Where was she when the murder occurred?

Knew Sarah, did she know Kim before that weekend?

Was she having an affair with Brian?

JESSIE (wife's best friend):

No way!

EVE (co-owner of Harmony Inn):

At the inn when murder occurred

No other known connection

CARRIE (co-owner of Harmony Inn):

Where was she?

No other known connection

JO STEWART (Brian's co-worker):

Filed a harassment charge against Brian

Had Brian had an affair with Stewart?

Was not at the inn when murder occurred. Where was she?

ANOTHER TEACHER/COLLEAGUE:

How did they get in and out of the inn without being seen?

No reason to believe it was another co-worker.

HAT LADY (snuck around at funeral):

Where did she fit into the equation?

Who is she?

Was she involved with Brian?

A fat lot of good my speculations were. I wasn't any closer to answering my questions. Someone, somewhere had the answers, but it wasn't me.

Chapter 20

"It's perfect that my mom is going to be at Harmony Inn. I'm not saying she's nosy, but if there's evidence, she'll find it."
Jessie Cavanaugh

The rain had stopped and sunny skies greeted me when I arrived at Harmony Inn. Even after stopping by the house to change out of my funeral clothes, I made it by one-thirty. I knocked several times, to no avail. The screen door was unlocked, and I let myself in, making noise, to keep from startling Eve or Carrie. They'd been through enough without me adding to their anxiety.

The study and office across the hall were both unoccupied. Carrie was at the top of the staircase with a carpet shampooer going full blast. From the expression on her face, she was involved with her task and unaware I was in the house. I tiptoed to the kitchen on the lookout for Eve, hoping to snoop before heading upstairs. No one to impede my progress on the first floor.

The layout on the three levels appeared to be identical. Two rooms in front and two in back with a central hallway down the middle. One room on this floor remained unexplored. I crept out of the kitchen and across the hall where I knocked with a gentle touch on the door. If I ran into Eve, I'd tell her I needed to ask what she wanted me to do next.

After waiting a reasonable time, I twisted the knob and pushed open the door to an ordinary bedroom with an old-fashioned four-poster bed, side table, and a dresser. In the corner, a straight-backed rocking chair served as a makeshift clothes hamper. Looked like the occupant could use a lesson in organization. I figured it belonged to Carrie or Eve. Which begged the question, where did the other sister sleep?

I pulled the door shut and made a note on the diagram Jessie had given me. All the rooms on the first floor had been identified: study, office, kitchen, and a bedroom.

When I climbed the stairs, Carrie was working on a stain near the base of the handrail. The more she scrubbed, the larger the spot grew. When she saw me, she switched off the machine and frowned. I thought about apologizing again for having to dispose of the rug in the study, but realized she wasn't angry with me.

"This damn spot won't budge," she said.

"Fingerprinting powder?"

She nodded.

"Umm, you shouldn't have wet it. It might never come up now." I fished around in my box of supplies and retrieved a spray bottle. "Try this. The salesman at the supply house said it's the best. Spray it on and let it soak in. Then get an old towel and try blotting. Pat it gently. Don't rub." I handed her the bottle. "I'll start in the front bedroom."

I reached for the doorknob but stopped. I remembered that I still didn't know where Carrie had been the night the girls checked into the inn. "Excuse me, but I was wondering . . ."

"Yes?"

"Never mind." No sense making her mad.

She turned on the rug cleaner, ending our conversation.

According to Jessie's diagram, Kim stayed in the room closest to the stairs and thus had easy access to the study. I pushed the door shut, so I could clean and snoop unsupervised. I had expected total chaos, considering how the police had left the study. They'd taken anything related to evidence and hadn't bothered to clean up. But this room was immaculate. The bed was bare, and all the towels were gone from the adjoining bathroom. Other than black residue on the surfaces, the room appeared to be waiting for fresh sheets and a new guest. I suspected Sarah's and Jessie's would be the same. Looked to me like one or both of the sisters had been busy.

After cleaning the furniture and woodwork, one spot of powder remained on the carpet. I managed, without much effort, to blot it up. Kim still had cosmetics and a curling iron on the bathroom counter. I tossed them in my bag. Jessie could return them later.

On the back of the bathroom door, I found a lace teddy. Had Kim been expecting Brian to show up? Or maybe he brought it for her as a peace offering. Some peace offering. If a man ever wanted to make up with me, he'd be better off bringing a pair of comfortable PJ bottoms and a worn-out T-shirt. His reward would be my undying love and a hot night in the sack.

I stuffed the lacy contraption in my bag and poked around more. Nothing pointed to premeditated murder, not that I knew the supply list of a would-be killer. I'd expected to find—what? A stray murder weapon or hidden blood stains, not a menacing curling iron and slinky undergarments.

Carrie was nowhere in sight when I stepped into the hall. I noticed she hadn't gotten the stain out, but it was lighter. The room opposite Kim's was directly over the study. It wasn't on my list to clean, but one peek wouldn't hurt. I expected a locked door, but the handle turned. The room was not vacant and not undergoing renovation. It contained an antique wrought-iron bed, an old-fashioned dressing table with a round mirror, and a floor-to-ceiling wardrobe. Someone lived here and that someone was not a guest. A nightstand next to the bed contained several prescription bottles. I opened the wardrobe and found it full of clothing.

Why did Eve tell me all of these were under renovation? This one wasn't. And why didn't she want me to clean it?

"Why are you in here?" A voice said from behind me.

I slammed the wardrobe door and spun around to face an irate Eve.

"Get out," she demanded.

"Sorry, I was checking to see if there was anything in here I needed to clean."

"The only room you need to be in is the one at the end of the hall." She jammed her hands on her hips. "Why are you standing there? Get out. Now!"

I'd pissed her off. Again.

I edged past her and headed down the hall.

She slammed the door, and I heard a key turn in the lock. If there was fingerprint powder, I guessed she'd be cleaning it.

Sarah's room was behind the one Eve booted me out of. Like Kim's, this one had no linens. Unlike Kim's, there were no personal belongings. If the police missed evidence here, it was so tiny I'd never find it. I imagined Detective Alder crawling around on the carpet with a magnifying glass. A quiver wormed its way through my midsection.

Stop it!

I dusted and tidied and then went to the third floor and did the same inspection where Jessie had stayed. The layout was identical to the bedrooms below. I collected Jessie's toothbrush and toothpaste and added them to my bag. Before I went downstairs, I checked the other doors. Both rooms were bare of furniture and in varying stages of renovation.

Carrie had resumed working on the spot in the hallway when I came down to the second floor.

"You want me to give it a try?" I asked.

"Sure, I'm not having much luck," she said. "I'd hate to rip up this carpet for one stupid stain."

I dropped my bag and accepted the cloth she offered.

She moved away and rested against the railing while I went to work. "Eve said she found you snooping in her room."

"I didn't realize it was hers." I continued to blot without meeting her gaze.

"We'll take care of our own rooms. You concentrate on the rest of the house. It's more important the public areas are ready for guests."

Now she had gone and piqued my curiosity. "Which one is yours?" I tried to act nonchalant and kept patting the carpet. The room on the first floor wasn't for guests. I'd lay odds it was hers.

It didn't work. She ignored me and focused on my bag. "What's in there?"

The lacy part of the teddy hung over the edge.

"Stuff your guests left behind," I said.

"What are *you* doing with it?"

She had no idea Jessie was my daughter. Telling her might set her off. I didn't need both women mad at me. "I found it when I was cleaning and put it in my bag," I said. "I know how busy you are. If you want me to deliver it, I'd be happy to." I didn't want to make a habit of doing grunt work for my clients, but considering the circumstances, I bet it was the only way she'd let me leave with the bag.

She studied me for a minute. "Okay." She reached for the banister and jerked her hand away. "Damn. This stuff is everywhere." She rubbed her hands on a rag and clomped down the steps.

I realized I'd been holding my breath and exhaled.

The spot she'd been working on started out over two inches in diameter. She managed to spread it to three times its original size. The salesman told me the solution would do the trick, if I didn't rub it all around. Carrie had already made a huge mess. I sprayed a generous portion on the spot and let it soak in. She had left a stack of old towels. I placed one on the stain and stood on it with both feet. I bounced up and down a couple of times without twisting. When I lifted it, some of the black had transferred. It took five more times before the stain faded. I fired up the rug cleaner and gave it a good scrubbing. When I finished, the spot was gone.

Score one for me.

Before leaving, I checked the study to see if my air freshener had worked. When I arrived earlier, the doors to the study were closed. I should have reminded Carrie to keep them open to help with circulation. But maybe it was still too disturbing to pass by and see where the murder occurred. I pushed open the doors and sniffed the room. The smell of pine still lingered. It wasn't overpowering like yesterday, and there was no rancid odor.

With the rug gone and bare wood exposed, the room echoed, but there was no visible evidence of blood. No one would suspect it had been a crime scene. When the sisters replaced the rug, the room would once again have a homey feel. News spread fast in our small town, and I was sure a murder wouldn't be good for publicity or revenue.

I surveyed the bookshelves and ran my hand along the wood. There was great literature on these shelves. It made my head spin. I withdrew a volume by Hemingway and let my fingers play along the spine. How many people had held this book? There were books by Proust, Maugham, and Fitzgerald. Even current authors like Stephen King and John Irving. It was a veritable storehouse of knowledge.

Scattered among the books were dozens of framed photos. I was too busy yesterday to pay them any attention. They were different from the formal portraits in the foyer. These were family pictures taken at picnics, birthday parties, and Christmases. Most of the photos were of a man and woman and two girls. I assumed they were family pictures. The adults were as stiff and dour as the portraits in the hallway. I picked up one of the photos to get a closer look.

It was a snapshot of two young girls sitting primly on the front porch of the inn, back when it wasn't an inn. The girls could have been bookends, except one was older by several years. Carrie was easy to spot; her appearance wasn't much different from today, just younger. The older girl didn't resemble Eve at all. The brown eyes were the same, but the girl in the picture had mousy brown hair and an elongated nose with a huge hump in the middle. Eve's was sleek and turned up at the end.

"I don't know if I'll ever feel comfortable in here." Eve crossed the room and stood staring at the center of the floor.

I dropped the photo, and it ricocheted off the shelf and clattered to the floor.

Eve jerked her head in my direction. "What are you doing?"

I retrieved the frame and returned it to the shelf, thankful it didn't break. "Sorry," I stumbled over my words. "Trying to clean up a bit of the mess the detectives left."

"Oh." She seemed placated by my response.

I continued to dust the shelf, taking time to look from her to the photo and trying to see a resemblance, any resemblance. I wanted to ask about the girls in the photos, but the glint in Eve's eyes stopped me. I wasn't sure if she was angry with me, her sister, or the situation.

"I hope that lunatic gets what's coming to her," Eve said.

"What lunatic?" I asked.

"His wife," she said.

"Kim?"

"You know her?" Her mouth twisted into a grotesque curve.

When was I going to learn to keep my mouth shut? With my track record, never.

It was too late to put the cat back in the bag. "Yes, I do. She's a friend of my daughter's."

A spark of recognition flashed in her eyes. "You're Jessie Cavanaugh's mother? She was here that night."

Her anger rose to the surface. Instead of lashing out, she crossed her arms and waited for my reply.

"I am."

"This strikes me as unethical. Your daughter is probably a suspect in a murder investigation, and you're cleaning the crime scene." Her eyes narrowed.

"The police finished here," I said. Why did she care? All she wanted was her business reopened.

"I think the detective might find it interesting you're related to one of the suspects." She drummed her fingers against her chiseled cheek.

"He knows, and he doesn't have a problem." Not much of one, anyway.

Carrie chose that minute to make an entrance. "Oh, I thought you went to your room," she said to Eve.

"She's related to Jessie Cavanaugh." Eve clicked her tongue.

Carrie glared at me, and then her eyes wandered to the teddy still hanging from my bag. "Leave it here. I'll take care of it."

"Doesn't matter to me," I said. These women were getting under my skin. Maybe I should have told them upfront, but what did it hurt if I returned the girls' belongings or cleaned the inn?

"If you're finished, I'll see you out." Carrie tugged the hem of her blouse.

"Before I leave, I need to complete the paperwork for your insurance," I said. "It won't take long."

Eve closed her eyes and massaged her temples.

"Eve, I'll take it from here," Carrie said. "You go on up and lie down."

I wondered why Eve needed to take to her bed in the middle of the day. After she left, I asked, "Is she ill?"

"She suffers from migraines."

I remembered all the pill bottles on the nightstand upstairs. That must have been Eve's room.

"You did a good job in here."

Talk about a mood change.

"Thanks," I said. "I was wondering . . ."

"Yes?"

"Were you here when Brian Anderson was murdered?"

"I saw you on TV. You didn't come here to clean, did you? I've got a news flash for you. Mind your own business and leave us alone." Carrie scooped the teddy from my bag. "My sister and I have been through enough without you sneaking around our home. Eve is not a well person, and your presence upsets her. I'm going to go check on her, and I'll be back. You do whatever it is you need to do. Then get the hell out of here."

"Fine, but your business will suffer until the murderer is found," I said. "No one is going to want to stay at an inn where a murder occurred, especially when the murderer is still at large."

She didn't respond, but left me staring after her. I sank down at a writing desk at the far end of the room. My hands shook. I could barely open the notebook where I'd been keeping my notes. Later I'd create an itemized listing, but I wanted to leave her with a preliminary inventory of everything I had disposed of. I also wanted to make sure she signed off on my hours. Fletcher had balked enough at my rate. I didn't need him questioning the amount of time I'd spent.

If Carrie or Eve contacted Fletcher, I could kiss my job goodbye. And Hunter seemed like a no-nonsense sort of guy. I had struck the deal with him and didn't need the word getting around that I was a busybody. I'd have to be more cautious.

It didn't take long to finalize the list: a couple of pillows, several books, a table cover, and the rug. Those were the items her insurance needed to replace. Then I totaled my hours and the supplies I'd brought. After adding everything together, I realized I'd still have a tidy sum left over once my supplies and the biohazard removal were paid for.

All the work I had done the last couple of days made me appreciate Esther even more. I still had to make good on the salary I owed her. I'd make writing her a check to cover the one I bounced a priority. My divorce papers also demanded attention, and I wanted to talk with Michelle and Jessie. To hell with Phillip. Let him deal with them however he saw fit. I needed to get control of my life and not wait around for someone else to tell me what to do.

Carrie returned as I finished my preliminary bill.

"Are you still here?" she asked, her voice carried an edge of hostility.

I pushed the invoice across the desk. "As soon as you sign this, I can leave."

She picked up the pen, scrawled her signature, and shoved the paper back at me.

I ripped off the original and left the duplicate on the desk. "I'm sorry if I caused Eve any distress. That was not my intention." The words grated across my tongue. But I knew I had to make nice with her.

"Get out!" she said. "Now."

I picked up my bag and stomped to my car.

~ ~ ~

As luck would have it, Fletcher's Caddy was in the lot when I arrived at Bonafide. And he was shuffling out the door.

"Hey, Mr. Fletcher," I yelled.

"Can't talk. I'm running late." He huffed toward his car

as fast as his stubby legs could carry him.

"I brought the invoice for Harmony Inn." I waved it over my head and veered off toward his car. He sure was quick for a stocky man.

"Give it to Nancy. I'll see it later." He jumped in the Caddy, slammed it in gear, and before I could blink, he was gone.

Blech! Now I'd have to deal with her and maybe not get my money until the middle of next week. I had hoped he would review it. I needed to be paid today. I shoved the paper in my bag and braced myself for another encounter with Nancy.

As usual, she was on the phone. I wondered if she'd had it permanently attached to her ear. She was already deep in either conversation or lust. I wasn't sure which. But the way she was cooing, I'd bet she wasn't talking to her mother.

"Sit down, hon." She covered the mouthpiece, to keep from spoiling the mood, I suppose. "I'll be right with you."

She called me hon. I must be growing on her. I sat in the hard, plastic chair again while she made kissing noises to the telephone. Fletcher might want to think about buying some of the sanitizer I'd used at the inn for her phone.

"Nancy, I'm in a hurry," I mouthed and waved the invoice. "Can I leave it?"

She put her finger to her lips and motioned for me to be quiet. What was with all the shushing? Twice in one day. I hadn't been shushed since I was in high school, a long time ago.

I crossed my arms and assumed a defiant pose. Maybe if I gave her the evil eye, it would creep her out and she'd hang up the phone.

Maybe not. She continued to coo and make kissy noises, oblivious to my menacing demeanor. When my patience gave out, I jumped from the chair, slung my purse over my shoulder, and stomped to her desk, making an extra effort to be noisy. She glared at me but didn't stop smooching into the phone. I grabbed the invoice and waved it in her face.

"I can't wait any longer," I said loud enough for the person on the other end to hear.

She excused herself from the phone and hung up. "I hope you're satisfied." Her lower lip curled into a pout. "Now he's upset."

Oh, for goodness sakes. What kind of man would get upset because his girlfriend had to hang up and go back to work? The world contained all kinds of oddballs, and this proved it. I raised my eyebrows.

"You don't even care, do you?" she asked. There was a picture frame on the corner of her desk, and she stroked it like a pet cat. I tried to peek at the picture, but she turned it facedown. So much for getting a glimpse of lover boy. I'd have to use my imagination. Not.

Two could play her game. "You're right. I don't. Your personal life is a little less important than conducting business for Mr. Fletcher." I shoved the invoice under her nose. Flicking it for good measure. "Make sure he gets this Monday morning."

"He won't be in Monday." She sniffed and plucked a tissue from her desk drawer and blew her nose. "Or Tuesday, either."

Double crap. The prospect of a prompt paycheck faded. Maybe Hunter would come through with more work. I'd promised the salesman at the supply house I'd pay him first thing next week. Fletcher had arranged for me to get credit, but the guy insisted on getting his money quickly. I hoped he didn't have a pal named Vito with a penchant for breaking kneecaps. If I was going to keep scrubbing to pay my bills, I'd need my knees.

"When will he be back?" I asked. If I had to, I'd find out

where he lived and deliver it in person. Fletcher was getting this bill today.

"Tonight." She didn't even blink when she said it.

"Didn't you say he wouldn't be back until Wednesday?" I felt like I was trapped in a warped Abbott and Costello movie. Third base.

"No, you told me to give it to him Monday, and I told you he wouldn't be here on Monday or Tuesday. You didn't ask about tonight."

You can't outwit a dimwit, no matter how hard you try. "Make sure you give it to him," I said. "Tonight." I put a little too much emphasis on the last word, and it came out like a command. To keep her from burying it under a stack of paper I said, "Please." It galled me, but I did it. Honest.

She grabbed the invoice, glanced over it and whistled. "You make this much for cleaning up blood? Maybe I ought to try it. If you can do it, it can't be too hard." She tottered to his office with the bill. When she returned, she said, "It'd beat filing all his stuff and letting him eyeball my girls every now and then." She adjusted her cleavage with the palms of her hands. "He'll see it when he comes in."

I wasn't sure if she meant he'd see her "girls" or the invoice, but I dropped the subject.

"Thanks," I said, squelching the urge to strangle her. Two crime scenes in one day seemed like overkill.

~ ~ ~

I had finished updating my spreadsheet when the patio door slid open. I jumped from my chair and screamed. A wave of relief settled over me when I realized it was Angie. Then she launched into me.

"What do you think you're doing?" she demanded.

"Catching up on paperwork," I said.

"You know what I mean. Case Alder cornered me today

about your escapade at the church."

"What escapade? I went to Brian's funeral." Angie knew I was working at the inn. It was no big secret. As far as the funeral, good grief, of course I'd be there.

"Alder thinks you're interfering." She threw her purse on the table and went to rifle through my fridge.

"Where'd he get an idea like that?" I asked. "And who does he think he is, running to you to tattle?"

"Cece, are you snooping?" she asked, her head still stuck in the fridge.

"Alder has a big mouth," I said.

Angie turned and narrowed her eyes into her don't-start-with-me stare.

"Hey, not my fault if I happen to stumble over evidence your guys missed. Like the cell phone at Mrs. Cline's." I curled my lip and tried to sneer.

"Don't even go there. Alder will fry your ass if he catches you meddling."

I slammed the lid of my laptop. "Maybe your investigators need a push to get on the right track. It's not like they found the killer yet."

"I'm not kidding. Mind your own business." She withdrew a plastic container and pried off the lid. "You gonna eat this mac and cheese?"

"No, go ahead."

Without heating it, she shoveled in a big, cold bite.

"But I don't know how old—"

She spit it in the sink and rinsed it down the garbage disposal. "Cripes, don't you ever clean out your fridge?"

"My maid quit, remember?" I stifled a laugh. "There's leftover Chinese."

"How old is it?"

"Not as old as the macaroni."

Like all leftovers eventually do, the takeout boxes had

migrated to the back of the fridge. When I unearthed them, I slid them across the counter. "Heat these up. I'll get you a plate."

When the microwave stopped, we sat down at the breakfast bar. Angie loved Chinese almost as much as my family. There were always containers in either her fridge or ours. We sat in silence while Angie polished off the General Tso's Chicken.

I changed the subject back to Alder. "What gave him the idea I was snooping?"

"The owner from the inn called him when she found out you were Jessie's mom."

"Oh, that snooping. Figures. She is a wee bit high-strung." I carried the dishes to the sink. "Somehow it slipped out I knew Kim. When Eve found out, she flipped. Then the sister came unglued. It was ugly."

"Have you got anything sweet?" Angie went to the pantry and rooted around the shelves, pulling out a bag of cookies.

"There's cheesecake."

She moaned and returned the cookies to the shelf.

"What's the deal with Alder?" I said. "He accosted me at Brian's funeral this morning."

"What do you mean?" A huge grin sprung from her lips.

"Angie Valenti, what did you tell him?" I threw a dishtowel at her.

"Just that you're available, if he's interested." She cut into the cheesecake and licked the knife.

"Stop it." I grabbed the knife and threw it in the sink. "You're sick and twisted."

"Takes one to know one." She winked. "Now tell me about Alder."

I didn't need my best friend trying to fix me up. "I'm still married, remember." I sighed. "Though, if Willow has her way, not for long."

"It would serve Phillip right if you divorced him. Have you talked to a lawyer yet?"

"Too late. He's divorcing me." I pulled the envelope from my purse and placed it on the table. "I haven't even looked at it yet."

She grabbed the packet and opened the flap. "Divorce papers? What are you waiting for? This is your chance to get away from the controlling S.O.B. once and for all. Get out now, while you have the chance, and don't look back."

I snatched the divorce papers. "You may be my best friend, but this is off-limits. And you can tell Alder I'm not interested. Not even one bit."

Angie grinned. "Sure."

"Oh, shut up."

Chapter 21

"I knew I'd have to face Mrs. C. one of these days. I'm ready for this whole thing to be behind me."
Sarah Crandall

The next morning found me sitting at the salon waiting for Sarah. She trudged in nursing a cup of coffee. Her hair was pulled back in its usual clip, but it poked out at odd angles like she'd gathered it in a rush and not bothered to use a comb or a mirror. Dark circles under her eyes hinted at a lack of sleep.

She sighed when she saw me sitting at her station. "Mrs. C., I wondered when you'd show up."

"You can't dodge my calls forever." I closed my magazine.

"I know," she said and led me to the shampoo area. This was my favorite part. My tensions drained down the sink with the water as she scrubbed my head. And I had plenty of tension to release.

While she washed my hair in silence, I wondered how to approach her about her recent distance. Where Sarah was concerned, I usually spoke my mind, but I didn't know what had happened to her in the last couple of days. There was uneasiness between us, and I felt the apprehension in her hands as she massaged my scalp.

She wrapped a towel around my head and motioned toward her station. Once I was in the chair, she gently combed through the tangles. Sarah had been doing my hair for almost four years, and I trusted her. Most of the time she filled me in on the latest gossip, or we talked about Jessie and Kim. Today she concentrated on my hair like she'd never seen it before. Every time I glanced in the mirror she averted her eyes.

"Honey, what's wrong?" I blurted out. Her obvious pain made all my mother hormones zing into action.

In the mirror, I saw her tense. "Nothing," she said and busied herself snipping the ends of my hair. "How short?"

"Get it off my neck," I said. "Between the hot flashes and the warmer weather, it's driving me crazy."

"You sure? You never liked it short."

"I'm sure." I tried to read her facial expressions, but her usual animation was gone. "Have you talked to Kim since . . .?" I stumbled over my words. "Since you stayed at the inn?"

"No."

"Can I ask you a question?"

She flinched, but didn't say no.

"What's going on between you girls?" I watched for a reaction. "Did you have a disagreement?"

"You might say that." She continued to snip my hair.

I eyed the scissors, hoping she wouldn't slip and nick my ear, or worse. Convinced that she was concentrating on my hair, I approached the next question. "What happened at the inn?"

She slumped against the chair and burst into tears. "It's my fault."

My eyes widened. "What's your fault?"

"I'm the reason Brian is dead," she cried.

Those were the last words I expected to come from her mouth. It took a minute for me to gather my senses. Other clients stared in our direction. Wickford wasn't a big town, and Brian's murder was still in the headlines. It would continue to be news until the killer was behind bars. Even after. Murder did not happen in our community. Ears perked up, and cell phones appeared from fancy designer handbags. The grapevine roared to life.

Sarah broke down, and the tears came in a torrent.

I motioned to the hairdresser in the next station. "Is there a quiet place we can go?"

"The spa." She pointed to a door at the rear of the shop. "It's closed today."

I gathered my purse and led my weeping hairdresser through the door. Sarah collapsed on a sofa, and I knelt in front of her. She was still crying, but at least she didn't appear to be out of control.

"Can you tell me what happened? Did you and Brian fight? Was he trying to hurt you?"

She sobbed louder.

I sat beside her and put my arm around her shoulders. "Sarah, if it was self-defense, you'd be justified."

She reared back and stared at me. "I didn't kill him." She buried her head in her hands. Then the hiccups came, big loud ones that jolted her body.

I got a cup of water from the water cooler. "Here," I said. "Drink this."

She gulped it down, almost choking as her hiccups grew stronger. She held the cup for more, and I obliged.

When the hiccups and tears were under control, she spoke.

"When Kim and Brian first separated, I was Brian's biggest advocate. I was all for them getting back together, and I thought Kim was crazy to even think he would cheat on her." She dabbed at her eyes with a tissue. "They've been a couple since our sophomore year of high school." She inhaled deeply.

"Go on."

"Kim convinced herself Brian and I were having an affair." She sipped her water and closed her eyes.

I needed to tread with caution. Too much pushing and she might stop talking.

"Were you?" I asked, praying she hadn't betrayed one of her closest friends.

"No. Kim and I are like sisters, you know that." She looked at me as if I had grown two heads. "Brian was a complete and total jerk."

She wasn't making sense. "Weren't you trying to help them patch things up?"

She sat up and stared straight ahead. "I was. At first. Then I found out what an idiot he was."

"How so?"

"He showed up at my building one night. I thought he had come by to ask me to talk to Kim, but he was there to see Amanda." Her eyes glowed with anger. "After I had defended him to Kim during the whole Jo Stewart mess, he starts sneaking around at Amanda's."

"I remember Jessie mentioning her. She's the masseuse who came to the inn?" I asked.

"Uh, huh. She lives in my apartment complex."

"Brian was seeing Amanda?"

Sarah shrugged. "She said they were friends."

The old "just friends" excuse. How many jilted spouses had heard that one? Every time I thought of Phillip and that tramp Willow, I felt like I'd been sucker punched. "You believed her?"

"I did until I saw him coming out of her apartment a couple of times and thought it was strange. He didn't know I saw him, but I cornered Amanda and she swore there was nothing going on." Sarah took another sip of water. "But he kept showing up. I caught him more than once sitting in the parking lot, and he'd make an excuse that he needed to talk to me about Kim. But I knew he was there to see Amanda."

"Kim told me she'd seen his truck in front of your apartment. That fits with what you're saying." Pieces of the puzzle were dropping into place. For the first time in a couple of days, I felt like there was a good chance Kim would be proven innocent. "Did you urge Kim to go through with the divorce because of how Brian was acting?"

"Yeah. Wouldn't you?" Her tears had dried. "When I told Kim to dump him, I think it set her off. I didn't want to involve Amanda."

"So, Kim thought you were trying to break them up and have Brian to yourself? Did you know they were going to reconcile?"

"Not until Jessie told me. Then after he was killed, I wondered if Kim hadn't planned it all. I mean, maybe they were getting back together, and maybe they weren't. Maybe she wanted a house full of suspects. I should never have agreed to go that weekend. If I hadn't, Brian might still be alive."

"You can't think Kim killed him?" I couldn't believe what I was hearing.

"What other explanation is there? Jessie didn't do it. I didn't do it. And Amanda didn't do it."

"I don't understand why you would ask Amanda to come to the inn. It's almost like you were trying to set Kim up," I said.

"It was Jessie's idea to hire her. I couldn't say no without giving a reason. I decided to ignore the whole thing with Brian. The less said the better."

"That's why you've been scarce, isn't it?" I asked. Things were clearer, but it still didn't prove Kim had killed him. I wasn't certain Sarah hadn't done it, but Amanda moved up a rung on my suspect ladder. Was it possible she had run into Brian at the inn and decided to put an end to the affair?

"It's too uncomfortable," Sarah said. "Kim was angry when we got to the inn. I figured the more space between us the better. I feel like I'm putting Jessie in an awkward position."

"Jessie said she overheard you arguing with Brian the morning he was killed," I said.

Fresh tears sprang to her eyes and she nodded. "It's not what you think. It's not about me and Brian. I told him he had to tell Kim about Amanda, or I would. Especially if he even dreamed of getting back together with Kim. He told me there was nothing to tell. That's what Amanda keeps saying. I insisted he tell Kim whatever was going on because there was *something*. Maybe not an affair. But he kept seeing Amanda for a reason. After he was killed, I figured he had told Kim, and you know the rest."

"So, you think he confessed to Kim and she killed him?" I asked.

Sarah shrugged. "No, but what else could have happened?"

"That's what I'm trying to find out." I knew I sounded exasperated, but this was like some ridiculous junior high love triangle—except someone got killed.

Sarah glanced at her watch. "I've got to get back to work."

"Is Amanda here?" I asked. "Maybe I could talk to her."

"She's off this week."

"How convenient," I said. Hmm, curious.

We walked back to her station with women staring gape-mouthed at us. I half expected Detective Alder to burst in and arrest Sarah.

"It's okay, ladies." I waved my hands in the air. "Nothing to get excited about. Little misunderstanding."

In the mirror, I saw Sarah's expression relax. I was glad she felt she could trust me.

"Amanda won't tell you anything?" Sarah brushed and blew my hair dry while she talked. "She's been avoiding me since this all happened."

"I have to try. She might have seen Brian at the inn or

saw him talking to someone. Anything to help us understand what happened," I said.

"I'm sure she's already talked to the police."

"Maybe she remembered something that might help Kim." I watched Sarah's expression, but she didn't react.

"Come by my apartment. We'll see if we can catch her at home," she said. "My shift ends at six."

"I'll be there around seven."

Sarah fluffed my hair and handed me a mirror. "What do you think?"

"I love it." And I did. She had taken off some of the length and layered it, which added fullness to my hair.

I fished out my wallet from my purse, and she laid her hand on mine.

"This one's on me," she said.

"Are you sure?"

"Yes. You don't know how badly I needed to talk to someone."

"I'm always available. You don't have to hold back with me. I've known you way too long for that. As for Kim and Jessie, you all need to sit down and clear the air."

"I know," Sarah said. "I'll try."

I hugged her and saw myself to the door, where I ran into Mavis Blevins and Bitsy Harris-Dodd.

These two malicious socialites were part of a trio usually rounded out by my mother-in-law. Hazel must have been up to evil deeds if she was skipping "salon day."

The older women at Highland Park Country Club traveled in groups. I think it was part of the creed. Or a protection strategy, in case the commoners caught them unaware and tried to steal their Prada bags. I also thought it was to keep them from talking about one another. It was hard to gossip about your haughty friend if she was sitting across the table, but let her miss the occasion and all bets were off. The upper crust women of Wickford cut their teeth on gossip and would give up their weekly pedicure for a juicy tidbit. With Hazel missing her standing appointment, there'd be a lot of Cavanaugh bashing passing through loose lips today.

"Hello, Cece. We haven't seen you at the club," cooed Bitsy. "Have you been busy?"

Mavis held a French-tipped finger to her seriously red lips and yawned.

I opened my mouth to answer, but Mavis cut me off.

"Bitsy, dear, we don't have time for chitchat. The planning meeting is at three. It will take that long to get you presentable."

Her barb pierced my already thin skin, exactly as intended. I was a long-time member of the club's planning committee. Someone had scheduled a meeting and hadn't included me.

I let her comment slide. Phillip was the sole reason I even belonged to the stupid club. He was an "old money" Cavanaugh. It was expected. He needed a place to wine and dine clients and to smoke expensive cigars. I was the trophy wife—*okay, I'm exaggerating*—expected to keep my mouth shut and make nice with the wives of all the wheeler-dealers. Since I wasn't from old money, if Phillip divorced me, the club would revoke my membership. No big loss, but it still stung.

Swallowing what I wanted to say, I responded, "Ladies, I'd love to stay and talk, but I've got to run." I veered around them and darted to the parking lot.

Bitsy called behind me, "Give Phillip our best."

The two cackled like a couple of old hens.

~ ~ ~

When I saw Hazel's Mercedes in my driveway, I knew my day had taken a severe turn for the worse. Bitsy and Mavis were rookies compared to my mother-in-law. Hazel's presence meant she was either interfering with my marriage or Michelle had called her. Regardless, I didn't like the prospect.

My eyes almost bugged out of my head when I entered my kitchen. A plump, white-haired woman was on her knees scrubbing my floor, and Hazel was sitting at the breakfast bar reading a magazine. Her platinum locks had that just-teased-sprayed-stiffer-than-a-dead-possum-on-a-winter-night look. Evidently, she had pulled one over on Bitsy and Mavis and gone to a different salon.

"Don't you ever stay home?" She acted as if it were normal for her to be lounging around my kitchen.

The other woman ignored me and focused her attention on the tile.

"What's going on?" I dropped my keys and purse on the counter and pointed to the stranger. "Who is she, and why is she cleaning my floor?"

"If you'd return my calls, you'd know. I don't want my granddaughter living in squalor. That's why I hired Beatrice." Hazel rolled the magazine and put it in her Gucci bag. "This place looks like a band of vagrants has taken up residence."

"Oh, no you don't. This is my home, and I make the decisions." The minute the words flew past my lips, I regretted them. My blood pressure jumped a notch or two in anticipation of her retort.

Hazel stiffened. I knew what was coming, and it felt like I had one foot on a banana peel and the other on an oil slick.

"Beatrice, you can finish in here later. See what needs to be done upstairs," Hazel said, her calm voice belying the storm brewing in her eyes.

The old woman struggled to her feet without making eye contact. "Yes, ma'am."

Hazel held her tongue until Beatrice was out of sight. "If you will recall, Cecelia, I paid the down payment for this place when Phillip was struggling to expand the business. As long as my granddaughter lives under this roof, I will have a say in what happens."

I started to spout off about how Phillip hadn't made a mortgage payment in six months, but I kept my mouth shut for fear she'd whip out her checkbook. In one flourish of her pen, the banker would be satisfied, and I'd be wedged even tighter under her thumb. Phillip hadn't told her, I was certain. If he had, she'd have put a serious dent in his head. No one besmirched the Cavanaugh name, not even the heir to her throne.

There was no need to tell her I couldn't afford to pay Beatrice. Hazel would foot the bill. Rather than start a war I didn't have a chance to win, I did what I'd done for all the years she'd been my mother-in-law—I shut my mouth and ignored her. She'd always had her way, and she would never change. Just because Phillip and I had separated didn't mean it would be different now, unless I eliminated my dependence on her and her Cavanaugh money. That was something I intended to do, even if it took me the rest of my life.

"Beatrice will be coming three days a week. Make a note on your calendar to expect her Monday, Wednesday, and Friday," Hazel said with an icy snip.

She was persistent. It didn't take a genius to realize the real reason for Beatrice's presence. Hazel didn't care if my house was a mess, and for the record, it wasn't. I wasn't saying she didn't care about Michelle, she did, but she knew I could keep house. I had done it for years before we hired Esther. No. Now that Phillip didn't live here, Hazel had no way of knowing what was going on. Of course, Michelle would be more than willing to clue her in, and Hazel wouldn't be above pumping her granddaughter for information. But by clamping down on Michelle, I had cut off my mother-in-law's pipeline, and it was killing her. The new housekeeper was here to keep the lines of communication going, in only one direction. Now I had to figure out a way around this housekeeper. I couldn't fire her because I wasn't paying her wages, but I could keep her out of my house. I just had to find a tactful solution.

Chapter 22

"Cece Cavanaugh. The woman drives me to distraction. I know she's interfering with my investigation. I'll have to keep an eye on her."
Detective Case Alder

After Hazel and Beatrice had gone, I decided the next time the housekeeper showed up, I'd send her packing. Of course, I'd have to answer to Hazel, but she couldn't put her social life on hold and play referee every Monday, Wednesday, and Friday. Sooner or later I'd wear her down, and she'd leave me alone.

I hoped.

Since Amanda lived in Sarah's building, I had no trouble finding it. Despite a misty drizzle, traffic was light, and I arrived on time. While I tried to find a parking spot, a truck whizzed past me, almost taking off my side mirror.

"Idiot," I mumbled, and then realized it looked like the black truck from the church parking lot. I found a spot and managed to wedge my Lexus between a Chevy Suburban and an ancient Volkswagen Bug. I cut the engine and heard metal crunching and felt my car jerk sideways.

"What the hell?" By the time I exited my car, I only saw a flash of black as the truck fishtailed out onto the street.

My rear bumper bore a black scrape from one side to the other. I ran a shaky hand along the damage and cursed myself for not being quick enough to get a license number.

If I called the police, I'd have to explain why I was here. If I filed a report, Angie would find out, and Alder was already suspicious. The chance of finding the truck was slim, since I couldn't identify the driver and didn't have a plate number. Other than knowing it was a big, black truck, I couldn't identify the make or model. At least the scrape was minor, but the black paint stuck out on the silver bumper. I resigned myself to living with the damage, but I wondered if the weird phone calls were connected to this truck. I wouldn't put it past Willow to call and hang up. And I was certain Phillip had hired someone to follow me, but hitting my car was another story. Was Phillip up to something more sinister? I didn't think so. He was the one who wanted a divorce. But then . . .

Sarah could wait a few minutes. I got back in my car and pulled the notebook from my purse. While the few details I had were fresh in my mind, I wrote down everything I could remember about the truck. It was large and black with tinted windows and a possible scrape down the passenger side. Some detective I made.

While writing, I saw a woman scurrying up the sidewalk. If I caught up with her, I wouldn't have to wait around in the drizzle while I buzzed Sarah to let me in. I considered taking my umbrella, but if I took time to dig around for it, I'd miss my chance.

I opened my door and had one foot on the pavement when a dark sedan pulled behind my car, blocking me in the parking space. The driver exited the car, slammed the door, and started toward me, head down against the rain.

"Hey," I yelled. "You're blocking my way."

"Damn right I am." Detective Alder raised his head and strode toward me. "We need to talk. Get back in." He headed around to the passenger side and climbed in.

"Why aren't you chasing criminals?" I pulled my now-damp leg in and jerked the door shut.

"Maybe I am." He twisted around in the seat to face me. "Why aren't you trying to locate the truck that hit me?"

"I don't do traffic." He paused. "Wait, you were in an accident? When?"

"Just now," I said. "A truck came out of nowhere and sideswiped my car."

His jaw tensed, and then he slung his door open and motioned for me to follow. "Did you file a report?"

I climbed out and met him by my damaged bumper. "No, it just happened. One more thing in my already crazy life. I didn't even get a license number or anything," I said.

"Can you describe the vehicle?" he asked.

"Big and black. That's about it," I said.

"Did you see the driver?"

"No. By the time I realized what had happened, the truck was gone. Don't make a big deal out of this."

He wrote what I had said in his notebook and slapped it shut. "I'm still going to call it in."

"Okay, I guess. But why were you following me?" I asked.

"Who said I was following you?"

"You mean it's a coincidence you showed up in this exact spot?" My neck began to ache. I wanted to talk to Amanda and get home. At this rate, I'd waste all of my time explaining myself to Alder.

He didn't bother to mask his annoyance. "I'm the detective. I solve crimes. If you're in a location where I'm working a case, I'd say it's not a coincidence."

"Oh." I couldn't think of anything else to say.

For a moment, he looked like he was going to crack a smile, but he pasted on his stern cop face. "What brings you to the neighborhood?" he asked.

If he was staking out Sarah's apartment, it meant he regarded her as a suspect. "Sarah's like family, and she's my hairdresser." I didn't dare mention I was here to talk to Amanda. If he thought I was trying to horn in on his case, he could bring me up on charges, impeding an investigation or something. Angie would kill me.

He didn't make a move to leave. Instead, he continued to stare.

"I like the new hairdo. It's shorter." He shook his head as if trying to dislodge a thought. "What am I going to do with you? Will it help if I beg you to stop whatever you call yourself doing? If your friend didn't kill her husband, my investigation will provide the proof. But if she did, I will do everything necessary to see her brought to justice. If I have to arrest you in the process, I will. Do you understand?"

I didn't like his tone. He acted as if I was a child who needed to be dealt with. This conversation wasn't going anywhere, and it was getting late.

"Excuse me, but if you're finished giving me the third degree, I need to go." I turned to leave. He reached out and placed his hand on my arm. His touch was light and sent a jolt through every nerve in my body. I shook off his hand and rubbed the spot he'd touched. A flutter lingered.

"Cece, this isn't a game. I can't prove you're here for any reason other than what you said, but I'm telling you to stay out of my investigation."

He's right, of course. I shouldn't mess in his business, but dammit until he turns his attention in another direction, what choice do I have?

Ignoring him, I ducked my head and ran for the building. A woman pushing a baby stroller jogged up the sidewalk and made it to the door before me. The door closed, and I heard the latch engage. Stroller woman had stopped to pick up her mail. I knocked on the glass, hoping to attract her attention, but she either didn't hear or chose to ignore me and disappeared down the hall.

I located Sarah's name and pushed her buzzer.

A few seconds later, her voice crackled through the speaker, "Hello?"

"It's Cece. I'm downstairs."

"Come on in." The buzzer sounded. Before I opened the door, I glanced over my shoulder. Alder stood in the parking lot, shaking his head. I didn't wait around to see what he would do.

Sarah met me in the hallway. "I'll show you where Amanda lives."

I followed her and waited while she knocked on the door.

"Do you want me to stay?" Sarah asked.

"Since I don't know her, it might be best."

It would panic Sarah if she knew Alder was staking out her apartment, so I didn't tell her. No need for her to be more upset than she already was. I didn't think she had anything to do with the murder, but if she did, then Alder needed to do his job. I wondered if he had someone watching Jessie's apartment. As soon as I was finished, I'd give her a call.

When Amanda let us in, I had the oddest sensation I'd seen her somewhere. It wasn't her spiky bleached hair that nagged at me, but something not readily identifiable set my teeth on edge. I shook the feeling off. As often as I'd been at the salon, we'd probably crossed paths there.

Clothes and accessories lay everywhere, piled on chairs, the couch and even strewn on the breakfast counter. There wasn't a square inch of floor visible. It was a carpet of jeans, T-shirts, bras, and towels. The rest of the apartment looked stark. No decorations on the walls, no photos.

"What do you want?" she asked Sarah while watching me suspiciously.

"This is Mrs. Cavanaugh, Jessie's mom," Sarah said. "She has a few questions about . . ." Sarah's words drifted off.

"About?" Amanda prompted.

"Can we sit down?" I asked.

"I guess." Amanda moved a pile of clothes, hats, and shoes, clearing a space for Sarah and me, then sat across from us. "What's this about?"

"I have some questions about the night you did the massages at Harmony Inn," I said.

"Why?" Her nostrils flared.

"Just trying to sort out the time frame," I said. "Did you see anyone when you were leaving?"

"Are you a cop? Because I told the detective everything I know." She stood up. "Unless you're with the police department, I don't have to talk to you."

"No. Of course you don't. I'm trying to help Sarah's friend. And Sarah. Other than Brian, there were five or six people at the inn that night, including you."

"I was hired to do a job. I didn't see anyone other than my clients and the lady who runs the place." She opened the door. "If that's all you want to know, I need to study. I have a test on Monday."

"About you and Brian," I said. "Were you having an affair with him?"

Amanda glared at Sarah. "I thought we were friends. I told you, there was nothing going on between me and Brian. Nothing. You have to trust me and leave me alone. Now get out. Both of you."

I opened my mouth, but Sarah gave a slight shake of her head and patted my arm. "I guess we should go."

I followed Sarah to the door. "Please think about it," I said to Amanda. "If you can think of anything that might help, please let Sarah know."

After Amanda shut the door behind us, Sarah said, "She's super stressed right now. I forgot she's in the middle of her exams. I'll see her Monday, if you want me to try to talk to her some more."

"Let me think it over. I may have a few more questions. But it bothers me she got defensive." I moved Amanda a few steps higher on my suspect list. She was hiding something, and I aimed to find out what. Something about her apartment bothered me, but I couldn't quite flush out exactly what it was.

"Call me," Sarah said. She hugged me and saw me to the door.

This was getting complicated. I hated to consider it, but Kim's name remained at the top of my list. I didn't even want to think about Jessie being on the list. If Brian had been making unwanted advances toward Amanda, then she could have a motive.

By the time I left the apartment, the drizzle had turned into a downpour. If Alder was still staking out the building, he'd found a good hiding place. I didn't see his car anywhere.

I was drenched before I reached my parking spot. The temperature had taken a nosedive, and I didn't have a jacket. I slid behind the steering wheel and turned on the heater. The air on my cold skin made my arms turn to gooseflesh. When I needed a good hot flash, nothing.

There was still time to run by Kim's to see what she knew about Amanda. The trip across town in this weather wasn't appealing, but I wanted to talk in person. I called and told her I was on my way.

Traffic was almost nonexistent when I merged onto the highway. The county had grown, but this area still had pockets without businesses or streetlights. In some places, the black pavement was almost impossible to see in the rain.

The roadway narrowed due to construction, and orange barrels blocked the third lane addition. I slowed down and concentrated on my driving. The dreariness of the day made it difficult to navigate the car through the obstacles. A few speed demons whizzed by in the passing lane.

I focused on my driving and mulled over my meeting with Amanda. It dawned on me why she looked familiar. Before my brain gelled around the memory, my car lurched forward. I glanced in the mirror and saw nothing but headlights and a gleaming grill.

What the hell?

I pressed the accelerator and sped up. The headlights backed off, then grew bigger. I braced for another impact. Even though I couldn't make out the vehicle, I knew it was the black truck.

Who the hell is in the truck? I tried to focus on my rearview mirror to see if I could see the driver. As I watched the truck gather speed, my heart thumped against my ribs. The driver slammed my bumper again, pushing my car forward.

I kept my foot on the gas, intent on maintaining my speed, but the truck eased off, increasing the distance between us. The sooner I got off the highway, the better. But it was miles before the next exit. I glanced in the mirror and saw the lights approaching at a rapid pace. This time the driver didn't back off but swerved around my car and cut in front of me.

I veered to keep from rear-ending it, and my car plowed through the construction barrels and off the roadway. The pavement gave way to gravel and then mud. I braked and tried to maneuver the car, but I couldn't remember if I was supposed to steer in the direction of the skid or away from it. Or was that for ice? The scene seemed to play out in slow motion. I planted both feet on the brake and gripped the steering wheel.

The car stopped with a bone-jarring jolt and a flurry of deploying air bags. My breath came in gasps and coughs. When I oriented myself, I was right side up, but the Lexus faced downhill at a precarious angle. The air bag pinned me against my seat. Frantic, I fought to mash it out of the way, and, at the same time, search the seat for my cell phone. In the rearview mirror, I saw lights pulling over on the shoulder. A wave of panic rose in my throat, followed by a surge of nausea.

Is the driver coming to finish me off?

Chapter 23

**"If Phillip or Willow is trying to scare me into signing
the divorce papers, they're doing a damn good job."**
Cece Cavanaugh

A red light pulsed in the darkness. It seemed like hours
before someone wrenched open my door.

"Cece, are you okay? What happened?"

Alder's voice sounded warm and welcoming. Giant
tears rolled down my cheeks when I saw his face.

"I think I am." I tried to wiggle from beneath the steering
wheel. "That truck ran me off the road!"

"The black one from earlier?" Alder asked.

"Yes, it's been following me." My chin quivered. "I
think someone is trying to hurt me."

"Don't move," Alder demanded. "I'll call an ambulance."

"No, I'm fine. Help me out of here."

Alder freed me from the Lexus and carried me to his car.

"This isn't necessary. Call Angie. She'll come get me."
I stared at my car and winced. The front end wasn't visible,
because of the way it had plowed into the embankment, but
it looked bad. Big bucks bad.

"You've got a nasty bump on your head," he said. "If
you won't let me call an ambulance, I'll take you by the
hospital to get you checked out."

Alder deposited me in his car, snapped my seat belt, and
tucked his jacket around me. He climbed in the driver's seat
and eased onto the highway.

I touched a sore spot on my forehead and felt a knot rising under the skin. "Ooowww."

"Sit back." He spoke in soft, reassuring tones. "We'll be there soon."

"Where'd you come from?" I twisted around in the seat to get a better look at him. "Were you following me again?"

"I was on my way home. You're lucky I came along when I did. There are all kinds of creeps willing to help a stranded female."

"Yeah, I think I'm in the car with one," I said.

"Funny. Do you remember what happened?" he asked.

I thought for a moment. "It was raining. I slowed down in the construction zone, but the truck came out of nowhere and cut me off. I swerved and lost control. It was the same truck that hit me at Sarah's, and I saw it at the funeral yesterday."

"You've seen it before today?" he asked.

"At the funeral," I said.

"Why didn't you tell me?" he asked.

"I don't know. I thought it was a coincidence," I said.

"Coincidences don't smash your bumper or run you off the road."

"If you were following me, you should have seen it." My head hurt like hell and arguing wasn't helping.

He grunted. "I told you I wasn't following you."

"Right." I laid my head against the seat and shut my eyes.

Alder shook my shoulder. "Hey, don't fall asleep. You could have a concussion."

"Just resting my eyes." I ignored him and turned toward the window.

I woke surrounded in warmth. I snuggled under a denim jacket and breathed in the woodsy aroma. It felt good against my cheek. I startled and remembered I was riding in a car, Alder's car. The tires bumped against uneven pavement. I pushed out of my cocoon and sat up.

"We're almost there," he said.

He turned off the highway and into the hospital lot. I wondered if Jessie was working. "I should call Michelle."

"Already done. I called Officer Valenti and asked her to let your daughter know."

"Thank you."

He parked in the area reserved for emergency vehicles and jumped out of the car. Before I knew what was happening, he opened the passenger door and scooped me in his arms. Again.

"This is not necessary," I said.

He wrapped the jacket around me and kicked the door closed with his foot. "Beats waiting for a wheelchair."

He smelled good. I resisted the urge to lay my head on his shoulder and throw my arms around him. He was a cop doing his job, and I was the hapless victim.

Jessie met us at the entrance. Her eyebrows shot up a notch when she saw me in Alder's arms. "Mom, are you okay? Angie called and said you'd been hurt."

Alder answered for me. "Nothing serious, she bumped her head. Nevertheless, she needs a doc to check it. Might have a concussion." He deposited me in a wheelchair and took back his jacket. "I'll go make arrangements to tow your vehicle and get a report in on that truck."

"Okay." He was such a contrast, gruff and demanding one minute and compassionate and caring the next.

"What truck?" Jessie asked.

"It's nothing," I said, giving Alder the stink eye. "It was raining and some idiot was driving too fast. Yada, yada, end of story."

Alder caught my message and left without blowing the incident out of proportion in front of my daughter.

Jess knelt down and examined the knot on my head.

"It's not serious. I bumped it." Jessie didn't need my drama.

"What are you doing with him?" She had accusation written all over her face.

"I think he's been tailing me. He cornered me at Sarah's tonight. I think he might be watching your place, too."

She sighed. "I guess you're lucky he came along when he did."

After I had been poked, prodded, and deemed fit to return to ambulatory status, Jessie wheeled me to the waiting room. Detective Alder jumped to his feet when he saw us.

"You're still here?" I asked. This was going to be the part where he grilled me with questions. I wasn't in the mood. I wanted to go home and crawl in bed and let the pain pills go to work on my throbbing headache.

"I went back and secured your car." He pointed to my purse in the chair next to where he'd been sitting. "What's the verdict? Concussion?"

"No, just a banged-up head. She needs to get some rest," Jessie said. "I'd take you home Mom, but I have three more hours on my shift."

"I can drop you at home," Alder piped in.

"It's out of your way," I said.

"Not a problem," he replied.

"How bad is my car?" As if I didn't have enough worries, my insurance rates would skyrocket, and I'd have to figure out what to drive while mine was in the shop.

He frowned. "I'm not a mechanic, but you'll be lucky if they don't total it."

I squeezed my eyelids and wondered how I'd gotten myself into this predicament.

Jessie dug her cell phone from her pocket. "I'll call Michelle. She can come get you."

Alder held up a hand. "Don't bother your sister. I don't mind. It'll take a half hour for her to get here." He grinned. "Besides I already called Officer Valenti about your accident. I told her I'd bring you home."

Crapsticks. He'd give me the third degree in the car, and it would be impossible to say no when he was being pleasant. I'd look like a witch with a capital B. At least it would match my mood.

Jess raised an eyebrow and hesitated before turning the wheelchair over to him. "I'll call you in the morning. Take a couple of Ibuprofen before you go to bed. You're going to be sore and bruised tomorrow." She bent down and kissed my forehead, opposite side of where I had a knot the size of a golf ball. In my ear, she whispered, "What do you think you're doing?"

"Nothing," I said, hoping she couldn't read my mind. "Call your sister and tell her I'm on my way."

Alder was quiet on the ride home. The rain had let up and driving wasn't as treacherous. Not to mention there was no construction on this stretch of highway. He turned the radio to a talk show and concentrated on the road.

I hated talk radio. If I couldn't listen to a good country song, I'd as soon not turn the damn thing on. The host on this talk show was boring. Rather than sit and be annoyed, I decided to engage Alder in conversation.

"For your information, I'm not trying to hamper your investigation." There. It was out on the table. I wanted to see if he'd bite and hoped he'd share information, in case Jess was a suspect.

"I'm not talking about this with you. Except to tell you to butt out. Now!" He gripped the steering wheel tighter and made no effort to turn off the radio.

Why did he have to develop an attitude? It wasn't as if I was running around like Sherlock Holmes. Okay, I was. But he seemed intent on pinning this murder on Kim, or maybe Sarah.

"But have you considered maybe—"

He jerked the car to the shoulder of the road and turned toward me. "I repeat. I am not discussing this case with you."

"I want—"

"Topic closed," he interrupted. "Do. You. Understand?" He enunciated each word to drive home his point.

"Yes, Detective, I do." I reached over and turned the radio off. "I hate talk radio."

"I don't." He turned the radio back on, gunned the engine, and pulled onto the highway, narrowly missing a speeding tractor-trailer. We drove the rest of the way in silence—except for the blabbering of the talk show host.

The motion of the car must have lulled me to sleep. The next thing I knew we'd come to a stop and the overhead dome light glared. I shook off the drowsiness and sat up. Alder had opened my car door. Before he scooped me into his arms, I noticed the Porsche in the driveway in front of Alder's car.

Phillip was home.

Chapter 24

"Divorce is not an option for my parents. My grandmother will not tolerate it. There has never been a divorce in the Cavanaugh family."
Michelle Cavanaugh

"Oh, my God. Put me down. Phillip's here." I struggled to get out of Alder's arms. "What is it with you?"

"Calm down. If I drop you, you'll give yourself a concussion for sure. Not to mention, all your squirming is killing my back." Alder started up the sidewalk, and I watched in horror as my front door opened. "So, the Porsche guy is your ex? That explains why you were pissed the other day."

I started to clear up the misunderstanding about the status of my marriage, but an evil thought crossed my mind. Phillip had someone else, maybe I'd play it up. Alder grunted and shifted me in his arms. I slid my hands around his neck and snuggled against his chest. *Hussy! Take that Phillip, you low-life scum-sucker.* Alder drew in a breath. If he knew what I was doing, he didn't let on. Jeez, he had no way of knowing I was trying to make Phillip jealous. I was heading deep into uncharted territory, and my GPS was clearly malfunctioning.

Before we reached the door, I released my grip on his neck and forced my head off his chest. As much as I wanted to hurt Phillip and rub his face in it, I didn't want Michelle to see me snuggling up to Alder.

"What the hell is going on?" Phillip, never one to mince words, stood, hands on hips, on my front porch. Okay, in reality it was still his front porch, but since he chose to leave and not pay the mortgage, I figured I had squatter's rights.

If Alder was shocked to see Phillip, he didn't let on. He eased me to my feet. "Just doing my duty, pal."

In the glow from the porch light, I saw a frown on Phillip's face. "I can take it from here, pal." The air crackled with tension, or maybe the gnashing of rival testosterone. Whatever it was, it gave me the willies.

Alder gave a half-salute and turned to leave, but then stopped. Without saying a word, he drew me into an embrace and planted a kiss right on my lips. For a moment I froze, and then a groan escaped my throat as I returned the kiss. He felt warm and safe and smelled like fabric softener and aftershave. I melted in his arms, until a spark of reality ignited in my brain. Or maybe it was Phillip's eyes boring a hole in the back of my head.

As quickly as Alder had embraced me, he let go. "Take care of your head, Cece." The spring in his step as he headed to his car told me everything I didn't want to know. The last thing I needed was another man in my messed-up life. What was he thinking kissing me in front of Phillip? Something had definitely changed between us. I felt it and was certain he did, too.

"What the hell was that all about?" Phillip's booming voice stirred me back to the real world of Cece Cavanaugh and not some fantasy.

"What do you want?" I bit my tongue and forced myself to remain civil.

His presence here was wrong. I had a packet of divorce papers to prove it.

"Who was that guy?"

Ignoring his question, I ducked my head and pushed past him. The warmth of Alder's kiss still lingered. I pressed my fingertips to my lips and thought, *Cece Cavanaugh, dangerous road ahead. Steer in the opposite direction.*

Phillip tailed me down the hall, but not before I noticed his gym bag and tennis racquet in the foyer.

"Get your mother some ice," he said to Michelle, who sat at the breakfast bar eating popcorn.

With an audience, I knew he'd drop the Alder inquisition. Too much Willow ammo for me to fire back.

"Michelle called and told me you'd been in an accident. I was headed to the hospital when Angie stopped by. She said you were already on your way home." Phillip gently clutched my arm and led me to the back of the house.

Angie knew Alder would be bringing me home, and I'd lay money she'd set Phillip up to witness our arrival. I didn't know whether to thank her or kill her.

My body screamed in pain as I slid into the recliner. I wanted everyone to leave me alone. Disappearing would have suited me fine.

Michelle handed me an ice pack. "You okay, Mom?"

I planted it against my goose egg and smiled. "I'm fine. Feels like my brain was scrambled."

Phillip cleared his throat. "You better head on to bed, pumpkin. Your mom and I need to talk."

A grin formed on Michelle's face, leading me to believe she thought Phillip and I were going to patch things up. A notion I intended to put right out of her head.

"Michelle, go to bed. Your dad and I have some business to settle," I said.

She stood on tiptoe and kissed her dad, then pecked me on the cheek. "Love you guys."

When Michelle was out of earshot, Phillip launched a verbal attack. "Now tell me what the hell is going on?"

"What?" I massaged the ice around my forehead, trying to numb the pain. "Who wants to know? My soon-to-be ex-husband or Willow's lover? Or the jackass who's trying to kill me?"

"We're still married," he said. "Wait, what did you say?"

"I said, the jackass who's trying to kill me," I shouted, then lowered my voice to keep Michelle from hearing.

"What are you talking about?"

"Your thug who keeps following me around town. The thug who ran me off the road tonight after he sideswiped my car in a parking lot. That's what I'm talking about." My head pounded with each word.

Phillip stared at me, then shrugged. "You clearly have brain damage."

"Asshole!" I shouted. "I know what you're trying to do. Between you and Willow, you're trying to intimidate me into signing those divorce papers."

He shook his head. "I don't have a clue what you're talking about."

"Don't deny it," I said. "Willow keeps calling and hanging up on me. And now you have a truck following me around trying to bully me. You can stop. I'll sign the damn divorce papers. I'm done."

Phillip knelt on one knee in front of the recliner. "Cece, I swear to you, whatever you think is going on, I'm not involved, and neither is Willow. You know I would never hurt you."

"Now there's an understatement." I pushed him out of the way and pulled myself out of the recliner. "Leave me alone."

"Are you making all this crap up thinking I'll forget about lover boy?" Phillip stood up and followed me.

"Seriously?" I asked. For the life of me, I didn't know why, but I didn't tell him Alder was a cop. The kiss wasn't a part of Alder's job, but it was an added bonus. "This conversation is over." I headed for our bedroom, and in a whisper, I mumbled, "Chew on that, pal, and leave me a check on your way out."

Phillip pulled me to him. "Talk to me, babe. We can make it work."

"Make what work?"

"Us. We belong together." Phillip winked and his dimple appeared.

Boy, he was smooth. In the past, when we argued, this was the place where I'd start to cave. He'd kiss me. I'd start crying. Then he'd stroke my shoulders and continue his sweet-talking. Before I could say no, *N-O,* we'd be in bed.

Phillip bent in, but I twisted away and dug deep for the strength to hold my ground. Tears already blurred my vision. If he sensed my weakness, it would all be over.

He turned on the charm. "Don't be like that, Cece. Come on. Willow was a mistake. It'll never happen again. Whoever that clown is, get rid of him. We'll start over. Like it used to be. Better."

"It won't work."

Phillip cut in front of me. "Come on. You can't give up on me."

"Don't do this." I threw the ice pack in the sink. My resolve weakened.

He must have seen my spine turn mushy, because he drew me against him and sprinkled kisses across my face.

"I'm sorry. It didn't mean a thing." Tears rolled down his cheeks. "Cece, you're the one I love."

I kissed back. His embrace was as familiar as my old robe, soft and warm. My determination crumbled, and tears started to flow. I almost believed him. My brain engaged before my hormones took over.

"Stop." I pushed away. "I'm not doing this. Not now. I need time to think."

Phillip leaned in and kissed me on the forehead. "It's your head injury. Let me help you up to bed."

"Oh, no you don't." I straightened. "I'm going to bed, but you're leaving."

He patted my fanny as he followed me down the hall.

At the bottom of the stairs, I turned and glared at him. "I mean it."

He gave me a dimpled grin and winked. "You're right. Sleep on it. I'll call you in the morning." By the time he ambled out the front door, he was whistling a cheerful tune.

Chapter 25

"If I wait around for Cece to decide what she wants, she'll be too old to enjoy herself. A little intervention never hurt anyone."
Angie Valenti

Angie must have been spying from her porch. The minute Phillip's vehicle was out of sight, she barged in my front door as if delivering a search warrant. If she'd had a SWAT team with her, I wouldn't have been surprised.

"What happened?" She was almost drooling. "Did you send him packing? Serves him right."

"You are not my friend." I feigned resentment. "You set me up."

"Not you, girlfriend. Phillip acted all concerned about your welfare. I omitted a few details. Big deal." She continued to blabber as she followed me to the kitchen. "I knew you'd be weak, and he'd be on his best game."

I spun around. "He kissed me, you idiot."

"Well duh! You knew that was coming. Was he all remorseful and sorry? Did he cry?"

"Not Phillip. Alder kissed me right in front of Phillip. And Phillip kissed me. But I kicked him out." I sunk onto the bar stool and sighed.

Angie's mouth hung open. "This is better than I hoped for. Did 'His Highness' have a meltdown? I would have paid to see that."

"What? Have you lost your mind?"

"I wanted Phillip to get a taste of his own medicine. Alder kissed you? Like a peck on the cheek or a full-blown, 'melt your panties' kiss? The kind where you swoon?" She wrapped her arms around her shoulders and made kissy noises. "He's a good catch. All the gals at the station are after him."

"Get off it, Ang. You should have seen the look on Alder's face when Phillip came out on the front porch." I cringed. "What did you tell him, anyway? Did you tell him I was divorced?"

She smiled. "Um, only that you were my best friend and that you were available."

"I am not available."

"I also told him you'd play hard to get. Have you talked to a lawyer or even looked at the divorce papers?" Her face tightened. "Cece, what are you waiting for? Your marriage is over. Do you *really* want Phillip back?"

I stared at a spot on the breakfast bar until my vision went fuzzy. "I don't know what I want." I thought I did. Too much kissing in one night could cause a girl's brain to go numb, or maybe it was my head injury. "Leave me alone. I can't deal with this right now."

Angie hugged me. "Get some rest. You'll figure out what you want. And if it's Phillip, your head may be more messed up than I thought."

She left me alone to ponder my marriage.

I had been wishy-washy when it came to my divorce before tonight, and now I was even more confused. First, there was Alder's kiss. It meant nothing, right? Then why was I still obsessing about it? And there was Phillip. Why did he have to come back, and why did I have to respond to his kiss?

The divorce papers remained in my purse unopened. I decided it was time to read them and talk to an attorney before I made a decision.

I checked the front door to make sure Angie had locked it on her way out and noticed Phillip had scooped up his gym bag and racquet. He must not have been too broken up, if he could think about playing tennis. And if he wasn't sleeping in my bed tonight, where was he sleeping?

Chapter 26

"My mother's attitude is different. I'm not sure what's going on, but she's acting all weird, and I don't think it has anything to do with her accident."
Jessie Cavanaugh

My eyes were scarcely open the next morning when Michelle bounced into the kitchen, grinning. When she saw me alone, her smile faded. "Where's Daddy?"

"Good question." The question had kept me awake most of the night.

"What?" Her firm jaw and inquiring eyes looked like her father's. My heart ached. I wanted to hug her, but her stance warned me to back off. "You made him leave, didn't you?" Her accusation hung in the air like smog.

"Honey, there's a lot you don't understand." When I was growing up, my mother had been the poster child for all the wrong ways to deal with men. And I had sworn I'd never be like her. Not that it stopped me from making the same mistakes. "I hope you never have to learn the hard way."

"Oh, poor you. It's always you, you, you. I'm not a kid, Mom." Her eyes bored into mine, then softened. "Daddy was worried last night. He loves you, Mom. And you treat him horribly."

Once Michelle made up her mind, there was no changing it. She would never understand the rift between Phillip and me, regardless of what I said or did. I'd have to live with her accusing attitude until she saw for herself it wasn't a one-sided conflict.

It was my own fault she couldn't see my side. I had kept silent when I found out about Phillip's other affairs. No wonder Michelle was angry with me. In her eyes, her dad was her hero and I had driven him away. Mom was the bad guy. Not Dad.

Michelle still wore her pouty face when Jess arrived with bagels. My head throbbed like I'd been beaten with a sack of rocks, but a bagel slathered in cream cheese would make me feel better.

"Pretty shade of blue," Jess said as she prodded the knot on my head.

I winced and drew back. "Be careful, it hurts."

Alder had arranged to have my car towed to a nearby body shop. I'd have to call the insurance company and arrange for a few estimates. In the meantime, I'd be driving Michelle's car. Nothing screamed middle-age crazy like a woman my age driving a bumblebee-yellow Mustang.

"So what's up with you and Detective Alder?" Jess asked.

"Nothing," I fired back, a little too quickly.

Michelle shot me a look. "Yeah. Why'd he bring you home?"

"My car went off in a ditch, and he came along. End of story." They didn't need to know he kissed me. Hell, I didn't want to know. Maybe it was the medication I'd been given at the hospital. It was probably a drug-induced hallucination. My head might be woozy, but my lips still felt the impression of his kiss.

"Oh right! Maybe he's why Daddy left." Michelle pushed away from the table.

"Michelle Cavanaugh," I said, through clenched teeth. "You know better."

"Do I?" she shot back. "I'll be in my room."

I started after her, but Jessie took hold of my arm. "Let

her go, Mom. It won't do any good. Go relax on the sofa, and I'll make you a cup of tea."

When the tea was ready, Jessie joined me. "What were you doing out there in the first place?"

"I was on my way to Kim's." I jumped up and grabbed the phone. "I better call her."

"Settle down. When you didn't show, she called your cell." Jess smeared a glob of cream cheese on a blueberry bagel and tore it in half. Between bites she said, "When you didn't answer, she called me. It still doesn't explain why you were on the highway."

"I went to Sarah's, and it was easier than coming through town." I sat down and sipped the tea. My stomach roiled from the pain medication, but the tea felt soothing. "Sarah went with me to talk to Amanda, the gal who did your massages. I thought she might have seen or heard something the night Brian was killed."

Her eyes widened. "Did she?"

"I don't think so. She got huffy when I asked a few questions." I set my cup down. "But I think she knows something. Amanda is the reason Brian and Sarah were arguing when you overheard them at the inn. Sarah said they both denied anything was going on. Kim thought Brian was trying to make her jealous, but I wonder."

"It's possible. He called me a couple of times and left messages. But I figured all he wanted was to cry on my shoulder, and I felt like it would be disloyal to Kim."

"You knew he still loved Kim, though. What if another woman was in love with Brian and thought he reciprocated the feelings? Or maybe he was harassing someone?" I asked. I'd been tossing around an idea about jealous women. "Like the teacher who filed the charges."

"She fabricated her story." Jessie smoothed her hair. "Who knows? We could speculate all day and still not know what happened."

"True enough." But it didn't keep me from turning it over in my mind. "Any chance you'd run a few errands for me?"

"Sure." She leapt from the chair. Her concern only went so far.

~ ~ ~

Jessie went to the store with my grocery list and left me resting. Her undivided attention was nice, but I knew it wouldn't last. She had a life, and I felt guilty for imposing on her. I also felt guilty about all the indulgences I had allowed myself in the past. It wouldn't be much of a disappointment when my membership at the country club wasn't renewed. Phillip's mother was a charter member; she'd see to it my name disappeared from the club's roster. There were things in life far more important than who you knew. Maybe the bump on the head had knocked some sense into me.

It was in my best interest to rest, but I kept fighting the feeling I should be doing something. Rather than dwell on it, I pulled the divorce papers from my purse and went out to the patio. The packet was thick and heavy in my hand, like the feeling in my heart. Discarding a major part of my life loomed over me like a shroud. Could I turn the page and move on, or was I destined to repeat my mother's mistakes?

The words ran together in a legalese way over my head. I needed to follow Angie's advice and find a good attorney. Phillip wasn't going to get off the hook easy. He'd cheated, a repeat offender. He'd left. He was going to pay. Since he still had his trust fund and his firm, I expected him to cough up child support, alimony, and the mortgage. Not that I was opposed to working. I'd be happy to foot all my bills, but until I could get a grip on my current expenses and the ones he let slide, he needed to help.

I was trying to digest the intricacies of my pending

divorce when Angie slid through the break in the hedge that separated our backyards.

"Hey, Crash. You okay?" She wore running clothes and sweatbands circled both wrists, her latest effort to stay in shape.

"My head feels like Mount Vesuvius right before an eruption." I set the documents aside and motioned for her to sit.

She tapped the packet. "Divorce papers?"

"Yep. Know any good lawyers?"

"Dave's sister recently divorced her dumb-ass husband. I'll find out who she used. Took her ex for everything he had." Angie picked up the papers. "Mind if I look?"

Angie had my back, and I needed another opinion.

"Go ahead. I started reading it, but my concentration is nonexistent." I leaned back and closed my eyes, wishing my headache away. The faint rustling of papers disappeared into the background. There was something about letting your mind wander, because while I was resting my eyes and not trying to concentrate on anything, I remembered what I'd been thinking when I ran off the road.

The hat! I jerked and bumped my knee on the table. "Ouch!" For a moment, the pain trumped the ache in my head.

Angie raised her head. "You okay?"

"Yeah. I remembered something I have to do." I sprinted through the patio door with Angie trailing behind.

"What's up?" She dropped the divorce papers on the counter.

"I have to go out." I snatched up the packet and shoved it in my purse. I didn't want Michelle finding out about the divorce before I could talk to her.

"You need to take a serious look at those papers," Angie scolded. "There's no provision for insurance for Michelle, or even college."

"I will. Promise. Find me a good lawyer. Okay? Right now, I've got to go."

"Are you sure that's a good idea? You shouldn't be driving." Angie followed me from room to room while I hunted for Michelle's car keys. "Are you taking medication?"

"Oh, for pity's sake. You're worse than Jessie. It's not like I had brain surgery."

"Why don't you let me drive?" she asked.

Yeah, right. "No, I'm good." Like I needed a cop driving me to question a suspect. Somehow, I didn't think she'd see the humor in it.

It dawned on me I had already put Michelle's keys in my purse to keep her from taking her car when I wasn't home. Maybe I had amnesia.

Angie stood on my porch as I backed Michelle's car down the driveway. I could see Angie's mouth moving, but I cranked up the volume on the stereo to drown her out. On second thought, it wasn't such a good idea because my head pounded in time to the music. When I made it to the end of the block, out of Angie's shouting range, I turned the radio off.

Why hadn't I remembered before now? Maybe it was the bump or the confusion of Alder kissing me. And God knew menopause made me forgetful. It didn't matter. The important thing was I remembered why Amanda looked familiar. I had seen her before Sarah introduced us, and not at the salon.

Chapter 27

"Cece Cavanaugh is a nosy woman. Probably a gossip. All those women at Wickford Country Club are."
Amanda Chandler

I went straight to Amanda's apartment. *She* was the sunglasses-wearing woman I tried to follow into the church the day of Brian's funeral. It was the hat I remembered. When Sarah and I visited with Amanda she had moved the hat off the sofa along with a pile of clothes.

Mourners usually showed their respect the old-fashioned way, going in the front door and sitting through the service. If there was nothing between her and Brian, why was she sneaking in the church after the service? Why did she alter her appearance, and more importantly, who was she hiding from? The possibilities made me dizzy.

Arriving at her building, I drove around searching for the red sports car I'd seen at the church. It didn't take long to locate it. I found a vacant space and sat for a minute, practicing what I'd say to her and making sure Alder hadn't followed me. He had a history of showing up at the most inopportune moments, and I didn't want to have to explain myself. He already thought I was crazy. Maybe I was. I mean, here I was in the middle of another 'what-the-hell-am-I-doing' moment.

I knew nothing about Amanda, other than Sarah worked with her and thought she was okay. People who looked and acted normal had their faces plastered on wanted posters all the time. Confronting her in her own apartment gave her the advantage.

If she was Brian's killer, it was unlikely she'd pull a knife and try to kill me in public. The person who killed Brian used one from the inn. Probably not a good idea to meet her at a restaurant, in case utensils were her weapon of choice. While I pondered the best way to lure her out of the apartment, she exited the building right in front of me and drove off in her car. I did what any quick-thinking lunatic would do. I followed.

While I weaved in and out of traffic, trying to keep an eye on her, my cell phone chirped.

I pushed the speakerphone button and left both hands free to drive. "Hello?"

"Where are you?" Jessie's voice sounded an octave higher than normal.

If I had looked at the display, I wouldn't have answered it. But, as I have proven, I don't always think before acting.

"Running an errand. Don't worry." I ran a yellow light and kept right on going.

Amanda sped up. Not to be outdone, I pressed the gas pedal harder.

"Don't worry? Are you insane? You shouldn't be driving," Jess yelled.

At the next intersection, Amanda turned left. I managed to make it through before the light turned red.

"Be home shortly. I need to pick up some odds and ends." I slowed behind a dump truck lumbering along. Either the driver was paid by the hour, or else he had all day to get to his destination. My philosophy was, if you can't keep up, move it off the road. I gunned the car and flew past him.

"I was at the store. You should have called." Jess didn't bother to hide her aggravation. "Mother, you're on medication."

If I kept this up, they'd be medicating me in the loony bin. A van swerved in front of me. I slammed the brakes to keep from rear-ending it. "Damn."

"What? Why do you sound out of breath?"

"Jess, I can't talk. I'll be home soon." I disconnected and tossed the phone in my purse.

After a moment, it rang again. I ignored it and concentrated on driving.

Traffic was heavy for a Sunday, and I had a hard time keeping up with Amanda. She darted in and out ahead of me, but since her car was red, I managed to keep it in sight. When she turned right into the grocery store parking lot, I said a prayer. She'd have a hard time killing me in the store, unless she whacked me with a jar of pickles, the big industrial size. I made a mental note to avoid the condiment aisle.

She parked and went inside, unaware I was following her. I hoped. I found a space several rows over in the crowded parking lot. My bright yellow car didn't stick out, much. My own would have blended in better. Not an option, though, since it was now a hunk of crumpled metal.

At the front door, I could see her struggling to free a cart from the rack. If she only wanted a quart of milk or loaf of bread, she would've grabbed a basket. I gave her a head start and waited until she'd gone through the produce section and turned the corner. Then I snatched a cart and made my way past the lettuce and tomatoes.

One of the security features at the rear of the store was a huge mirror installed to thwart shoplifters. I used it to keep tabs on Amanda. My strategy was to stay one aisle behind her until she was halfway through the store, then casually bump into her, say hi, and start a conversation. Not imaginative, but it might work. What was she going to do, run screaming from the store with a cart full of groceries? I didn't think so.

My plan was working until I encountered one small hitch. I was fondling a cantaloupe when I looked up into the remarkably blue eyes of one Detective Case Alder. *Damn, damn, double damn.* If he wasn't following me, then I was one incredibly unlucky person.

"How's the bump?" he asked. "Hope I didn't cause trouble for you last night."

Of all the times for him to show up. "Everything's fine." I continued to squeeze the cantaloupe, trying to contain my aggravation. "Yesterday did not happen. None of it."

He smiled his charming smile. "I seem to remember yesterday very well, especially the part where you wrapped your arms around my neck."

I focused on the produce to keep from looking at his moustache and the way it framed his upper lip. "Look, Angie wasn't honest with you, and I made things worse last night." I turned to face him. "I think she might have led you to believe I'm divorced. I'm not."

Alder's eyebrows scrunched together. "Ouch, then I made a real big mess for you, not to mention making an ass out of myself."

I wanted to reach out and touch his arm, but I didn't dare. The sparks between us were real, and physical contact would be like igniting an oil spill. "Don't worry about it. We're separated. When you saw him the other day, he'd just given me the divorce papers."

"That explains why you were pissed when you answered the door."

I shifted my gaze to the cantaloupe I still had in a death grip.

A short time passed with neither of us talking. Alder broke the silence. "Nice melon you have there." He grinned. "But you're going to bruise it if you keep mauling it."

I dropped it on the pile and suppressed a giggle before changing the subject. "Why are you following me?"

"Nice segue. I was about to ask you the same thing."

Amanda! Alder had succeeded in distracting me from my mission. If I missed this opportunity to talk to her, then I'd have no choice but to go to her apartment again. That wasn't something I wanted to do. I pushed by him and started down the aisle. "I've gotta go."

Alder aligned his cart with mine and stayed with me. "You're a long way from your neighborhood. The only reason I can come up with is that you're following me." He waggled his eyebrows.

Of all the nerve. I wheeled my cart to the next aisle and prayed Amanda wasn't there. I tried to catch a glimpse of her in the mirror before I turned, but didn't want to take a chance Alder would catch me.

"You're impossible."

"I'll take that as a compliment." He stopped and reached for olives.

I raised my eyebrows. *Damn, I was in the condiment aisle. Stay away from the super-sized pickle jars.* My cell interrupted, and I poked around in my purse until I located the phone. "If you'll excuse me, I have to take a call." I answered and turned in the opposite direction.

"Mother, where are you?" Jessie demanded.

I gritted my teeth. "I'm at the store, honey. Do you need anything?" At the end of the aisle, I disconnected, but continued to talk to throw Alder off track. I stole a look in the mirror and noticed his eyes glued to my back. He must have figured I wasn't going to hang up anytime soon because he continued making selections and disappeared around a display. I scanned the mirror for Amanda and saw her approaching the dairy case. Another glance revealed Alder standing in the checkout lane, helping an elderly woman unload her groceries. Nice guy.

I wheeled over to the dairy case and pretended to be engrossed in the skim milk selection.

Amanda stopped right next to me and reached for a quart of two percent. "Excuse me. I need—"

"Hi." I handed her a carton of milk and pushed my cart toward the cheese display. Sliced cheddar was on sale. I threw two packages in my cart and acted coy.

"What are you doing here?" she asked, reaching for the mozzarella.

"I saw you at the church in your big hat and sunglasses." I stepped in front of her cart and stopped. "Only I didn't know it was you, but then I figured it out. I saw the hat on your couch."

Her face went pale. "What?"

Now that I had her attention, I jumped in with both feet. "At Brian Anderson's funeral. You snuck in the side door after the service. I tried to catch you, but you didn't stay long. I wondered why you were acting stealthy."

She jerked her cart around and went toward the front of the store. "You're too nosy for your own good."

I chased after her, almost sideswiping a harried young mother with two dirty-faced kids in tow. Both toddlers were whining.

"Sorry." I steered around them and zeroed in on Amanda. "Hey, wait up," I yelled.

She stopped mid-aisle, her back ironing-board stiff. Then her shoulders gave way in a slump, and she spun around. "What is it with you, lady?"

"I'm trying to understand your involvement with Brian Anderson. If he meant nothing to you, then why go to the funeral? And why the sneaking around?" I caught a glimpse of Alder unloading his groceries onto the belt and crossed my fingers he wouldn't see me. The mirror had become my enemy.

"I wasn't involved with Brian, regardless of what his crazy wife says," she said, bitterness saturating her voice. "She didn't even know I knew Brian. To her, I would have no reason to be there. I was afraid she would cause a scene when I came in. She had seen me at the inn. If I showed up at the funeral, she might get suspicious, and I didn't know what Sarah might have told her. I waited until the service was over to pay my respects to his parents and left. No big deal."

"Why would Kim be upset if she saw you?" I maintained eye contact with her. She was doing a good job of talking. I didn't want to give her an excuse to stop.

"Because she's crazy. She accused her best friend of sleeping with her husband. What kind of friend does that?" Amanda crossed her arms across her chest and paused. "Then she started in on me. Calling day and night and harassing me. Calling me names. Horrible ugly names I didn't deserve. She didn't seem to need a reason."

"I thought you weren't seeing him," I said.

"He was tutoring me, okay? Are you happy?" She closed her eyes and sighed. "I needed his help to pass my algebra final. Sarah introduced me a couple of months ago when he came in for a haircut. She mentioned he was a teacher. He came to the salon a few weeks ago, and I asked if he would help me with my class."

"All the cloak and dagger at the funeral was because he was tutoring you?" I must be thickheaded, because I didn't understand the connection.

"No, because he was married."

"If you weren't having an affair with him, what difference did it make?" My cell chirped. *Damn. Not now, Jessie.* I ignored it and kept talking.

"Your phone is ringing." She nodded toward my purse.

"Nothing important." She wasn't about to ditch me. I paused and waited for her explanation.

"I'm in the middle of a divorce." She slid a manicured hand through her bleached hair.

"Because of Brian?" I felt an eye-roll coming and caught myself.

"No. My marriage failed long before I met him. I'm trying to get custody of my son, Kevin." She reached in her purse and extracted a photo. "My husband will use every dirty trick he can to sabotage my chances."

The picture was an adorable blond tyke. "He's precious. How old is he?"

She smiled and tucked the photo in her purse. "He turned five last week."

"What does your custody case have to do with Brian?" At the front of the store, Detective Alder exited. I relaxed.

"I have to be careful. Jim, my husband, will twist anything. I wouldn't put it past him to have me followed." She stopped and looked around. "And with Brian's wife harassing me . . ." Her words trailed off and then she seemed to get a second wind.

"I couldn't chance she would do something to hurt my case. But I needed Brian's help to pass my final. I don't make a lot at the spa and can't count on tips for steady income. When I finish my degree, I can find a better job."

"So you weren't having an affair with Brian?" I asked, realizing she was an unfortunate victim in this whole mess, an innocent person trapped between two failed marriages.

"How many ways can I tell you no?"

"What about the night Brian died? Did you see anything out of the ordinary?" I asked.

"No. I didn't even know Brian was there." Amanda's hands shook as she gripped the cart. "You've got to believe me. I cannot jeopardize my custody case. Brian understood my dilemma. That's why he didn't tell anyone he was tutoring me. I knew Sarah was friends with his wife."

"How did Kim react when she saw you at the inn?" If Kim had been hounding her, then why would Amanda even agree to do a massage? If she was trying to get custody of her son, money was the issue. Nurses made good money on private jobs. It stood to reason masseuses would, too.

"She didn't know I was the one she was harassing. All she had was a phone number she found in Brian's wallet. I didn't want to have to explain to Sarah." She peered over her shoulder and then up the aisle. "If you don't have any more questions, I have to go. Jim will be bringing Kevin back. If I'm late, it's one more thing he can use against me."

"Amanda, wait. I have one more question. I know you said you weren't having an affair with Brian, but *was* Brian coming on to you? Was he trying to make your relationship more than it was?"

She laughed. "No. Why would you think that?"

"Sarah thought he might be making unwanted advances."

"No, not at all. He was a nice person trying to help me with a tough situation."

I touched her arm. "Thanks for talking to me. And I hope your custody case works out." I eyed the cheese still in my cart and returned it to the dairy case, before pushing my cart to the front of the store and parking it.

I was even more perplexed than before. Amanda was protecting her son. Sarah was protecting Amanda. Jessie was protecting Kim. Brian had been protecting Amanda and despite all the protecting going on, Brian ended up dead. And I was right back where I started. No suspects with motive and opportunity except Kim.

My cell warbled again. The damn phone was grating on my last nerve. I'd think twice before paying the bill next time it showed up. That would put an end to the pitiful chirping. I zipped my purse shut and hoped the phone would suffocate.

On the way to my car, I saw Detective Alder posed in his best cop stance, leaning against my car. Just what I needed. He was becoming a nuisance, and not in a good way. His tanned face held no expression, but his neatly trimmed mustache hugged the outline of his upper lip in a sensuous sort of way. My knees went rubbery.

"Didn't find anything that struck your fancy?" His sedan idled in the adjacent parking spot.

"Left my wallet at home." I patted my purse, edged past him and opened my car door.

"Ummm. You don't have your license with you?" He shifted his stance and looked toward the store in time to see Amanda emerge. He turned his gaze on me. "I knew you were up to something. Didn't I tell—"

"Gotta go." I jumped in my car and raced out of the parking lot. I checked the rearview mirror, but he was gone. My breathing didn't return to normal until I arrived home. Half expecting him to follow me, I waited in the car a few minutes to make sure he hadn't. With my luck, he was on his way to the station to swear out a warrant for my arrest.

Now to face my daughter. Tangling with her might be worse than dealing with Alder. She was pacing the foyer when I walked in.

"What is wrong with you?" Jessie rushed over and grabbed my keys. "Why didn't you answer your phone? I've been worried sick."

"I'm fine," I lied and hurried to the kitchen to sit down. "Will you make more tea?" My head was spinning, but I didn't dare tell her. She'd have me in bed with a hot compress plastered to my forehead.

I watched as she gathered cups and teabags and set the water to heat. Time for a change of subject. "Hey, I never told you about my trip to the inn. I didn't find anything. It's not as if I had a clue what to search for. But Eve Taft got angry when she found out I knew you." A blanket of heat descended on my body. I picked up a napkin and fanned myself, hoping to stir up a breeze of tornadic proportion. "I found some things you left behind the cops didn't take."

"It was crazy after we found Brian. The cops came, and we all had to go to the station. We left some stuff there."

"Taft went ballistic, and I had to leave everything," I said.

"The woman's got a screw loose."

"Tell me about it. One minute she's praising my work and the next she's screaming."

"When we first checked in, she was nice. We thought after she served the cheese and wine she would leave, but she kept hanging around. She bragged about how successful she is and how her grandparents left her the house and a pile of money." The kettle whistled and Jess fixed our cups and brought them to the table. "She asked where we worked and made fun of Sarah for being a hairdresser."

"Doesn't seem like something a businessperson should do." The woman was bizarre. I was glad I was finished with her job. "Let's not judge. We don't know her. Her sister told me she suffers from migraines. She had rows of pill bottles in her room."

Jess nodded. "She was rude. Even Kim and Sarah commented about her attitude. She won't stay in business long if she's mean to her customers." Jess blew across the top of her tea, sending wisps of steam tumbling from the cup. "And she gave me the creeps. She seemed familiar, but I can't figure out why. I was glad when it was my turn for the massage. I couldn't get away from her fast enough."

"She's around your age. They moved here after their grandmother died and left the house to them. I forgot to ask who their grandmother was," I said. "There's something odd about her. Her sister is a few years younger and the two of them don't look a bit alike."

"Why's that unusual? Michelle and I don't resemble each other. She has more of Dad's features. And I got the Buchanan genes from your side."

True. "Ah, but you and your sister never looked alike. I found pictures of two girls in the study, and they looked like twins, except for the age difference."

Jessie leaned forward. "What does that prove?"

"I don't know," I conceded. "It's strange. Eve is an attractive woman and Carrie is . . . Well, Carrie is plain."

"I rest my case. I got the looks in our family," she said, not even batting an eye.

I smacked her arm. "Jessie Cavanaugh, your sister is every bit as attractive as you are." I shuddered and shook my head. "Eve and her sister give me the creeps. Let's change the subject."

Jessie's eyes narrowed to slits. "Yeah, like why don't we discuss where you've been?"

"That's not important." I waved her off. "All the time I've spent at Harmony Inn was a big waste of time. I haven't found anything."

"There has to be something you're missing."

"Jess, we have to face the possibility Kim may have killed Brian."

"You can't believe that," Jessie said.

I sipped my tea and leaned forward. "She told me she'd been calling a number she'd found in Brian's wallet. She suspected it was the woman he was having an affair with."

"Mom, Kim figured her marriage was over. It doesn't mean she killed him. I've never been married, but if I'm ever lucky enough to find someone to share my life, I'll do whatever it takes to keep my marriage intact. Anything." She toyed with the edge of the saucer and then pushed it away. "I've got to go. I have to work this afternoon."

I tried to digest what she'd said. Was she talking about Kim and Brian, or was she talking about her dad and me? There was no way she could know the lengths I would have gone to in order to save my marriage. If I had been twenty years younger, it wouldn't be beneath me to follow Phillip or call his girlfriend on the phone and warn her to stay away from my husband.

For all the good it would have done, if I had known Phillip was having affairs, I would have stooped to all the dirty tricks. Now, it didn't seem worth the fight.

I decided to keep Amanda's secret. There was no use telling Kim or Jessie. Amanda still had her custody case to deal with. I didn't know what Kim would do if she knew it was Amanda she'd been calling, but I figured it best not to take the chance. Either way, I didn't think Amanda murdered Brian. At least, she didn't seem to have a motive.

Chapter 28

"Cece is not only attractive, she's smart."
Grant Hunter

Michelle had retreated to her room earlier in the day to finish a project for school. I curled up on the couch with a new book I'd bought last month. It looked interesting at the time. Striking cover, great reviews, but I couldn't get beyond the first page. I kept thinking about everything but the book. Phillip, Kim, Detective Alder. Tossing the novel on the coffee table, I settled on some backyard time. Since I had no money to pay the lawn service, there was always yard work to do. The daffodils were in need of deadheading, but thinking about bending over made me dizzy. I grabbed my clippers and the phone and headed to the patio. Before I snapped off the first wilted bloom, the phone rang. Ready for a diversion, I answered.

"Hello?" I said.

Michelle picked up the extension. "Hello?" Rap music blared in the background.

"I've got it," I said.

"Cece, it's Grant Hunter."

"Michelle, hang up the phone," I said.

The music ceased.

"Hi." I hadn't expected him to call this soon, but I hoped he'd gotten a firm schedule for his project.

"Did I catch you at a bad time?" Grant asked.

"Not at all," I said.

"Do you have time to meet me for a cup of coffee?"

I studied my flowers, wanting an excuse to ignore them. "Sure." Again with the coffee. But if it helped me get a job, what the heck. "Great timing."

"It is?"

"Yes, it is." If he had work for me next week, I was more than ready. "When?"

"Is now too soon?" He hesitated. "It's short notice. I'll understand if you can't make it."

According to my schedule, I didn't have anything to do other than wander around the house. The throbbing in my head had subsided, so why not? Fletcher hadn't called, and since Hazel's tirade, I was more determined than ever to take control of my life. "Now's fine. Where do you have in mind?"

"I think you might enjoy Café du Soleil. It's on Main Street," Grant said.

"Sounds great. I'm ten minutes from there." I loved the old town charm of Main Street, and a spring day made it better.

"I'll meet you there," he said and disconnected.

I shook my finger at the daffodils. "I'll be coming for you, my lovelies. Just not today."

I changed into a brown pencil skirt, topped it with my favorite cream-colored sweater set, and slipped on a pair of peep-toe pumps.

Café du Soleil was a new bistro on the banks of the Missouri River. I'd read all kinds of reviews on it but had never been there. A cup of coffee probably cost six bucks. If I ordered a sandwich, I might have to give up a first-born child. If they'd take a second-born, I might spring for lunch and dessert.

Two weeks ago, I wouldn't have thought twice about spending money on 'frou-frou' drinks. Now, the idea of paying six bucks for a coffee which I didn't even like made me rethink my hasty decision. Maybe Jessie could write it off on my taxes as a business expense.

Wickford oozed scenic and quaint, right down to the cobblestone streets. Every tourist and then a few were already rambling up and down the main drag, taking in the sights. Traffic was thick with tour busses and gawking drivers. It took me three times around the block before I noticed a car leaving. I kept a safe distance, put my turn signal on, and damned if one of those Smart Cars didn't race around me and pull in right as the car exited. I laid on the horn, but the driver ignored me. I restrained myself from giving the tiny car a nudge.

Ten minutes later and several turns around the block, I found a place to park. I checked my makeup in the mirror. Before leaving home, I had covered my bruise under layers of foundation. Then I'd combed and sprayed my bangs to cover the lump on my forehead, hoping Grant wouldn't notice. I jumped out of the car, caught the heel of my shoe between two cobblestones and turned my ankle. When I had steadied myself, I tested my footing to make sure my feet wouldn't crumple beneath me. The uneven cobblestones made walking difficult, but when I reached the sidewalk, I realized I'd broken the heel off one shoe.

Crapola!

Grant Hunter was waiting, and I looked like a peg-legged pirate limping along. Some impression I'd make on my future boss. I hobbled to the car and crossed my fingers. If I knew my daughter, she'd have a pair of shoes in the trunk and twelve changes of clothing.

She did, and my choices consisted of pointy-toed silver cowboy boots, pink plaid rubber boots, or black satin stilettos covered in glitter. Why the hell did Michelle have stilettos? It didn't matter; I needed shoes. I nixed the cowboy boots on principle. It wasn't raining, so the pink plaid didn't seem appropriate.

Stilettos it was. Black glitter with a brown skirt, not chic, but it would have to do. Never in my life had I worn a heel higher than two inches, much less a toothpick-thin one. I shoved them in my purse and limped across the street. At the door to the café, I wiggled my feet into the shoes and did a test run to see if I could even stand.

Since Nancy wore shoes like these and chewed gum at the same time, I shouldn't have a problem. Holding my arms like a tightrope walker, I tried a couple of strides down the sidewalk. I reminded myself of a drunk trying to navigate a straight line for a sobriety test. I turned the other ankle and lunged forward. If I hadn't grabbed onto a bench, I would have found myself sprawled on the pavement.

Score one for the stilettos and none for me. Nancy must have had more smarts than I gave her credit for. Scary thought. I limped to the car. The cowboy boots and galoshes both had flat heels. Neither one would win a fashion award, but they both made statements. The only question was what my choice of footwear would say about me.

Inside Café du Soleil, the hostess greeted me and did a double take. If I had chosen a simple pantsuit, the silver boots wouldn't be obvious. She used good judgment, refrained from making a comment, and asked my name. "Your party is already on the veranda," she said with an air of self-importance before leading me through a set of atrium doors and onto the deck.

Grant rose from his chair. His eyes traveled down to my boots. "Hi Ho Silver."

I grimaced. "I broke my heel on the cobblestones and these were the only shoes in the car besides a pair of rain boots." I didn't mention the stilettos. He would think I was weird enough.

He smiled. "I like 'em. They're not meant for a trail ride, but they look good on you." He paused. "And hey, they match your watch."

I glanced at my wrist. "Okay, they do. I planned it that way."

He looked at my arm, and before I knew what was happening, he lifted my hand and placed a gentle kiss on it. "Thanks for coming."

His forwardness caught me off guard, and I gasped.

He blushed and dropped my hand. "Sorry, didn't mean to startle you."

He had a Texas drawl. The kind of voice that made me yearn for brisket and a cold beer. I hadn't noticed it the other day. "No one's ever kissed my hand before. It was nice." I sounded like a complete imbecile—in shiny, silver boots.

Grant pulled out my chair. After I sat, he returned to his seat and motioned for the server. That was when I noticed his shoes, hand-tooled cowboy boots.

"We'll have two Café Spécials and two Napoleons," he said to the waitress.

After she left, he said, "Do you ride?"

"Ride what?" I noticed the sun glinting off my silver boots, shooting a reflection across the patio.

"Horses. I thought with the boots you might be a horse lover."

I laughed and tucked my feet under my chair. "Never been on one in my life. Unless you count my daughter's Ford Mustang."

I added, "But I've always liked horses. I loved *Mister Ed* reruns."

"Then you'll have to come visit my ranch."

"I'd like that." I sat back and relaxed.

Hunter wore khakis and a blue-striped western shirt, quite a change from the work clothes he'd been wearing when I first met him. I was glad I hadn't worn jeans, even if they would have gone better with my footwear.

"Have you been here before?" he asked.

I shook my head. "I've been meaning to, but never seem to find the time. It's charming."

A covered pergola shaded the deck. Dozens of ruby-throated hummingbirds darted between feeders tied at intervals along the crossbeams. It was a spring day paradise. The only thing lacking was a sailboat bobbing in the distance. Instead, we heard the churning of a barge making its way up river.

Hunter cleared his throat. "There's something about a river town. Hannibal is my favorite. I'd like to spend a few days up there exploring the area, but work keeps me busy."

I hoped he was getting ready to change the subject to work, particularly how much more work he had for me.

The waitress brought two steaming mugs of coffee and the pastries.

"Have you been there?" he asked.

I found myself zoning out and thinking about Kim. Did she have it in her to kill Brian? Probably not, but all my possibilities were turning into brick walls. With Amanda off my list, Jo Stewart pinged my radar.

"Cece?"

Grant's voice brought me back to the here and now. "Sorry? What were you saying?" I asked, noticing a familiar burn heating up my cheeks.

"Nothing, not important. Looks like you have a burden on your mind." He dunked a piece of pastry in his coffee and brought it to his lips.

"You've seen the headlines about the recent murder?" I asked. "The victim was the husband of a friend."

Grant slowly placed his fork on the table and wiped his lips with his napkin. "I did read about it. Happened at the new bed and breakfast in town."

I nodded. "My daughter was there when it happened."

"You want to talk about it?" He forked another piece of pastry and held it suspended over the plate.

"Nothing to talk about. Let's get off this subject." I tried the coffee and moaned. "This is good. Does it have cinnamon?"

"Cinnamon, chocolate, and a pinch of nutmeg." He cut off a wedge of pastry. "Try your Napoleon."

Between flaky bites, we discussed the river, Hannibal, and the pastry. I steered our conversation toward business. "How's the project coming along?"

"Good. I should have a few units for you in a week or so." He polished off his coffee and waited for me to finish. "Would you like to take a walk by the river?"

My cup slipped from my hand and crashed onto the wooden decking. "Good Lord. I'm sorry. I don't know why I'm such a klutz today."

Did I have desperate divorcee written all over my face? First Alder and now Hunter. I should have been pleased, and I would have been if I were twenty-five and single. Instead, I was confused and not yet divorced. Was I emitting pheromones or what? Moreover, if I was, what could I do to stop it? I knew Angie wasn't behind Hunter's advances. She hadn't even met him—and wouldn't, if I had my say. My so-called friend had already caused me enough trouble with Alder.

Grant scrambled to pick up the broken pieces. "Guess I was a bit forward. Hope I didn't offend you."

"No, you surprised me. I thought you invited me to talk about your condos."

His face clouded over. "Wasn't thinking of work at all. You must think I'm a dope."

"I'm flattered." I smiled, pushed my plate away, and stood. "I'd love to take a walk." I did it again. Opening my big mouth when I should have shut the hell up. Complications seemed to follow me like a ribbon of toilet paper clinging to my shoe, and I kept making it worse.

The smile returned to his face, and he reached for my hand. "Terrific."

When we turned around, Hazel stood in the doorway. I shook my hand out of Grant's, but it was too late. I was busted.

"You don't waste any time." Her sarcasm bit through the air.

"Let's go," I said to Grant. "It's a bit frosty in here."

"Cece, you will regret your actions," Hazel said between clenched teeth.

Grant paid the bill, much to my relief, and we headed toward the river.

The Katy Trail, former route of the MKT railroad, stretched across Missouri more than 200 miles, much of it alongside the Missouri River. Almost the same trek Lewis and Clark had forged over 200 years ago. On almost any day of the week, you'd find an assortment of hikers, bikers, joggers, and pedestrians.

Today was no exception. The month of April in Missouri found the dogwood and redbud in full bloom. The trail was loaded with sightseers hoping to catch a glimpse of color.

We meandered along, watching a group of bikers unload their gear.

Grant broke the silence. "Who was the ice queen at the restaurant?"

I hedged. "No one worth mentioning."

"Okay, then, how'd a nice girl like you hook up with the likes of Bruce Fletcher?"

I flinched. "It's a long, convoluted story. I'd much rather hear about you."

"I came here a few years ago from Dallas," he said. "Planned to build my retirement home and spend my spare time raising horses."

"You don't look retired to me."

He slowed his pace. "No, my wife died, and my life sort of tumbled downhill. When I climbed out of my funk, I threw myself into my construction business."

"Was it hard? Getting your life together, I mean. I know it had to be rough to lose your wife."

"Hardest thing I've ever done. I miss her like hell, but it's time to move on."

His revelation didn't surprise me. I couldn't see his face, but I could tell by the tone in his voice he was smiling. The ache in my heart tripled. I stopped and turned to face him. "Grant, I'm married."

"A pretty lady like you should be. Having someone who completes you is what life is all about." His eyes darted to my left hand. "You don't have a ring."

"I'm separated," I said. "Soon to be divorced, if my husband has his way. The woman we saw at the restaurant is my mother-in-law."

"I'm sorry. Divorce is a beast. My folks separated when I was twelve." He tilted his head and grinned. "But if you leave the door open, I might have to slide my foot in."

I considered a moment and said, "I have to face one hurdle at a time. But, you do know where to buy a great cup of coffee."

"So there's a chance? Would you go out with me again?" He threw his arm around my shoulder in an easy, non-threatening way.

"No promises. My life is pretty much in the toilet, and that explains why I went to work for Fletcher."

"You have more than one child?" he asked.

I laughed. "Two girls. One grown and on her own. The other is sixteen and still mooching off me."

"You keep an eye on Fletcher. He's a crafty old gelding. If he gives you any trouble, you call me. In the meantime, I'll keep you in work."

A knot of tension began to unwind in my stomach. "Thank you."

Grant guided me to a bench near the old depot, and we watched another barge make its way up river.

When a breeze kicked up and I shivered, Grant said, "Let's get you back."

At my car, he said, "I respect whatever you decide, and I don't want to complicate your decision. Don't ever question your self-worth. I think you're worth waiting for, Cece Cavanaugh, even if it's to be friends until you're ready to move on."

Grant hugged me and waited on the sidewalk until I had driven off. His words about my self-worth zeroed in like a short-range missile. This chick was in dire need of a self-improvement plan, and I knew where to start.

Chapter 29

"It's good to see Cece getting out. Angie worries about her fixating on Phillip."
Dave Valenti

Jo Stewart had been on my mind since I'd talked to Kim. Now the weekend was here and I had a good idea where I could find Stewart. Before I changed my mind and gave the novel another chance, I drove home and pulled on workout clothes. My head felt better, and talking with Grant had lifted my spirits. A slow, easy run would do me good and help work out the soreness I'd acquired the last few days. Plus, I needed to counteract my recent fling with Ben and Jerry's.

"Michelle, I'm going to the gym," I called out before I raced down the steps. "Don't worry about dinner. We'll figure it out tonight."

By the time I arrived at the gym, I was ready for treadmill action. My muscles were on the verge of rebellion, and I needed to whip them into shape. I beat a hasty path to the locker room to deposit my purse and keys.

Several women averted their eyes when I walked in. Their whispers echoed in the enclosed space. I couldn't blame them for not wanting to engage in conversation and run the risk of me blubbering about my cheating husband. I didn't need people feeling sorry for me. I handled that job quite well. I lifted my chin, grabbed my towel, and strutted to the cardio area. I defied them to make me a victim.

My favorite treadmill was vacant. I stretched and climbed on. Before I'd gone a quarter mile, the two women who usually rounded out Stewart's trio walked in. When they entered the locker room, I climbed off my treadmill and followed. The anorexic blonde was pulling on running shoes and the dark-haired one was preening in the mirror when I sidled in. *Seriously? Getting glammed to exercise?*

I feigned interest in my locker until blondie headed for a bathroom stall.

"Hey," I said to the primper. "Where's Jo?"

She pulled a comb through her hair and ignored me, focusing instead on making sure her curls bounced and bobbed when she tossed her head.

I slammed my locker, and it disconnected her gaze in the mirror. "Where's Jo?" I repeated.

"Oh, you're talking to me." She giggled and pulled a tube from her makeup bag.

"Jo Stewart," I said. "Haven't seen her in a while. Hope she doesn't have the bug that's been going around."

She laughed and brushed the mascara wand over her eyelashes, her mouth forming a circle. "No, she's . . ." Losing her concentration, she smeared a wiggle of black across her cheek. "Damn." She pulled a towel from her gym bag and dabbed at her face.

"She's what?" I prompted.

"In . . . Um, I don't remember where she is."

"You ready to go?" Toothpick girl had flushed and returned. "O—M—G, why are you putting on makeup? You're going to sweat it off."

Primper stowed her cosmetic bag and pulled off her workout jacket. "I'm not going to be working that hard."

I tapped my foot.

"Oh yeah. Tara, where did Jo go?"

"Seattle," Tara, the anorexic answered.

I frowned. "Oh, how long's she been there?"

"Who wants to know?" Tara asked.

Think quickly, Cece. Kim never said what class Jo taught, but I had to take a chance. "I wanted to talk to her about my son's grade?" White lie flashed in my brain like a neon marquee.

Tara pulled her hair into a ponytail. "What are you, some kind of teacher stalker?"

I laughed. "No, she's always been approachable whenever I had a question. I'll call the school first thing tomorrow."

"Won't do you any good," Tara said. "She won't be back for a while."

"Is everything okay?" I planted on a fake smile and shook my head.

"Her mother broke a hip. Jo is out there until she can find someone to come in and help out."

"My son never said a word about having a substitute. Wait until I get a hold of him," I said, laying it on thicker. "How long has she been out?"

"She went out the end of March, I think," Make-Up Girl said.

"So, she's been gone a couple of weeks at least?" I asked.

Tara nodded.

"Thanks," I said. "I'll be having a talk with my kid. Thinks he can goof off with a substitute teacher and get away with it. I'll show him." I shook my fist in the air for emphasis and continued to mumble to myself on my way back to the workout area.

I climbed back on the treadmill and crossed Jo Stewart off my list. Damn, if she had been gone a couple of weeks, she had an alibi. That still left Kim floating at the top of the suspect pool. If I eliminated anyone else, I'd have to admit Kim might be guilty, and I wasn't ready to do that. Jo's friends made a wide circle around me and headed over to the free weights. That was where I noticed a couple working out on the universal machine. Their infectious laughter carried across the room. The man had his back to me. The woman was small with dark curly hair and wore a tank top that clung to every curve like it had been custom-fitted. She flashed a radiant smile and hung on the man's every word. His tan, muscular legs caught my attention. I watched while he demonstrated how she should be using the equipment. He exaggerated his motions, and she erupted in a fit of giggles. Everyone in the room watched the exchange between the two.

When the man turned around, I missed a step and lunged for the handles to regain my balance. It was Detective Alder in running shorts and a sleeveless athletic shirt that accentuated his muscles.

What the hell? Was he still following me? I'd never noticed Alder at my gym before. But then, I hadn't been to the gym in a while. I stole another glance.

The woman was at least thirty years his junior. My stomach lurched as if I'd been sucker punched.

Maybe it wasn't what it looked like. She could be his trainer. A training buddy? Why did I even care? After all, his kiss hadn't meant a thing. Not a damn thing. He wasn't following me, his attention clearly centered around Miss Twenty-something.

I scrambled off the machine and fled to the locker room. How stupid could I get? One of these days I'd learn. Took me half my life to learn what a scumbag Phillip was. At least it had only taken a week with Alder. I searched for an exit. In the movies, there was always a back door for the heroine to make her escape. But no, not even a tiny window. The front door was my only option.

I peeked around the corner and drew in a breath. Damn, he looked good, even with the sheen of perspiration. Damp hair, rumpled from his workout, curled at the nape of his neck. *Get a grip, girl. He's a player.* I reminded myself I had pledged not to let a man, any man, interfere with my self-improvement plan. Minutes ticked away while I stood there gawking.

When Alder and the woman moved to a piece of equipment on the other side of the cardio area, I made my break. I would have succeeded if it hadn't been for Angie's husband walking in the front door. Have I mentioned Dave's voice carries like a fart in a bucket? I prayed he'd go mute before he saw me or that I'd suddenly vanish. He didn't, and neither did I.

"Hey, neighbor." He drew me against him in a bear hug and squeezed until my eyes felt like they would pop.

I squirmed out of his embrace before he cut off the blood flow to my brain and positioned myself on the opposite side of his brawny frame. "Can't talk. Gotta run."

"What's the hurry? You haven't even worked up a sweat." His voice boomed across the room.

"Dave, I have to go." I backed toward the door, trying to catch a glimpse of Alder and his girl toy.

The big grin on Dave's face crumbled. "Sure, I'll catch ya later."

Now I felt like a heel. He and Angie weren't just neighbors; they were my support system. If not for them, my whole Phillip situation would be unbearable.

"Why don't you and Angie come over for a beer tonight? We can catch up."

He resurrected the grin. "Sounds good."

A group of jabbering women dressed in sports bras and skimpy shorts entered and headed for the cardio area.

"I better find a treadmill before they're all taken." He cuffed me on the shoulder. "We'll bring the beer if you provide the snacks." Before I could respond, Dave embarked on his mission to secure a piece of equipment. Angie was lucky. Dave was a one-woman man. Not even skimpily-clad women turned his head.

Alder made eye contact before I could get to the door. I willed myself to look away, but he held me in his gaze. He said something to the woman and sprinted over.

Damn!

"Now who's following who?" Alder asked.

"Whom," I said.

"Huh?" His blue eyes sparkled.

"It's whom. Who's following whom? And don't flatter yourself." I let my eyes drift past Alder to his femme fatale.

He noticed. "Oh. That's Becca. Let me introduce you."

Of all the nerve. I leveled a killer stare at him. "Your love life doesn't matter to me."

Another group of women entered. Was it Ladies' Day at the gym or what? When Alder shifted to let them by, I snuck out the door.

"Hey, wait," he yelled. "What the hell are you talking about?"

I ran to my car as fast as my shaking knees would carry me. After I'd belted in and pulled out of my parking space, I allowed myself one last look. He was standing in the doorway, watching me drive away.

Why did he get to me? Why did I let him? I smacked my hand on the steering wheel. My agitation grew as I drove. I turned onto Jefferson near the park. The city had constructed a new jogging trail, complete with exercise stations scattered along the path. I could still get my run in thanks to my tax dollars.

I parked near the start of the path and pushed my keys into my pocket. After a few stretches, I eased into a relaxed gait. The ribbon of pavement meandered past the playground area, around the lake, and skirted the ball fields. Trails veered off to various exercise stations where joggers could perform chin-ups, sit-ups, walk a balance beam, or take their pulse. All part of the fitness trail concept.

Picking up speed, I ran past two young women pushing big-wheeled strollers. The trail ahead lay empty and trees bent in, forming a canopy. A feeling of dread washed over me. I slowed and peered over my shoulder, but didn't see anyone. The stroller moms were gone. Then a couple of kids on skateboards came out of nowhere and whizzed by, nearly knocking me down. They disappeared around a bend. Hesitation slowed my step. I stopped at a park bench to catch my breath, hoping to catch a glimpse of the stroller moms or anyone for that matter. When I heard footsteps coming down the hill behind me, I hit the pavement and didn't look back.

I told myself I was being paranoid, but considering my recent accident and getting hit in Sarah's parking lot, I didn't want to wait around for another mishap. I slowed down and fished out my key ring with the pepper spray. Muggers beware. I pushed open the safety. The strolling moms caught up and passed me. Every few steps I looked over my shoulder. My palms turned clammy.

I made it around one lap and sprinted to my car, my breath coming in gulps. Being spooked erased the relaxation right out of jogging. When I pushed the key in the lock, a hand brushed my shoulder. My arm jerked up, I spun around and emptied the canister.

My assailant let loose with a wail, slammed his eyes shut, and doubled over in a coughing fit.

I'd recognize that chubby man anywhere.

"Oh, my God." I dropped my keychain and grabbed him. "Mr. Fletcher, are you okay?"

He continued to cough while trying to catch his breath.

A man ran out from a nearby exercise station. "What happened?" He was already punching numbers in his cell phone. "I'll call the police."

"No!" I yelled. "I mean, yeah, call 911. He needs help. I sprayed him with pepper spray."

The man narrowed his eyes and stared at me.

"I thought he was following me."

We managed to move Fletcher to a bench, but we were helpless to ease his pain.

"Go grab my water bottle." The stranger pointed to a nearby gym bag. "We need to flush his eyes. Stop some of the runners and get as much as you can."

He stayed with Fletcher while I ran to gather up water. By the time I returned, a crowd had assembled. Fletcher thrashed about while the stranger poured copious amounts of water on his face.

A siren blared in the distance. I paced and prayed I hadn't done permanent damage. Fletcher wasn't a young man, and I feared I'd taken a few years off his life. If he had a heart attack or a stroke, it would be my fault.

I watched powerless, while he writhed in distress, hands flailing as he rubbed his eyes. It seemed like hours before the ambulance made its way onto the parking lot. The medical crew shooed away onlookers and went to work. Fletcher coughed and gasped as they loaded him in the ambulance.

"Are you a family member?" A geeky-looking EMT asked.

My voice caught, and a squeaky babble of words escaped my lips, which had parched from chewing on them. "I . . . Uh . . . He's . . ."

He stared at me. "Well, are you or aren't you?"

"No. I . . ."

He shook his head and slammed the door, giving it two whacks with the palm of his hand.

Chapter 30

"The Cavanaugh woman is trouble. I knew it the minute she walked into Bonafide CSC."
Nancy-Secretary

According to the head nurse, Fletcher was resting and comfortable. I tapped on his door and pushed it open. Nancy sat beside his bed, lips smacking her gum faster than a woodpecker drilling for bugs. Her head jerked up when I walked in.

"Shh. He just dozed off." Concern filled her eyes. "They gave him a sedative." She stood and smoothed the sheet over his massive middle.

"I won't stay long. Wanted to check to see if he was okay." I stepped closer, watching his chest rise and fall.

The monitor alongside Fletcher's bed beeped a steady cadence. I peeked at his vitals, an old nursing habit. Satisfied his respirations were good, I motioned for Nancy to come into the hall.

"Sorry to cause such a ruckus." I let the door close behind us and collapsed against the wall. "I had started jogging in the park and someone was following me. Fletcher spooked me when he came up behind me."

Nancy's eyes grew wide. "Oh, my God! You're the one who maced him? I wondered how you knew he was here."

I wasn't proud of my actions, but I nodded. "It was pepper spray."

"Same difference. He's going to be pissed when he wakes up and figures out what happened." A smile crept across her face, but it stopped as fast as it had appeared. "Why would someone want to follow you? It's not like . . ." The expression on her face made it clear she thought no man in his right mind would hit on me.

"There's more than one reason to defend yourself, you know." I felt my temperature rising, tendrils of heat shooting up my neck. Just what I needed to preserve my self-respect. I fought the urge to fan myself. Gritting my teeth, I willed my hormones into submission.

"Oh, like he was going to mug you in broad daylight in a public park? In Wickford?" She snickered at the idea.

"There was a homicide here last week. A family friend was murdered, and I've been jumpy since then," I told her. "And then someone sideswiped my car, and I've been run off the road." *So there, Miss Know-It-All.*

"And you think Fletcher did it? He goes to the park every Sunday to feed the ducks and wander around the lake." Nancy rubbed her arms and shivered. "I bet he saw you and wanted to pay you. I told him you were in a big rush to get your money." She reached inside her purse and unfolded a check. "It was in his pocket when they brought him in. You better take it before he wakes up and fires you for being stupid."

The needle on my guilt meter jumped a notch. Of course, I didn't think Fletcher murdered Brian. Fletcher wasn't responsible for the prank calls either. And he surely didn't cause my car accident. My nerves had a hold on me I couldn't shake. I stared at the check, but hesitated. My face must have given me away.

Nancy pushed it toward me. "Take it. He won't fire you. You're the only one who'll take the yucky jobs." She winked and placed her hand over her mouth, like she'd let a big secret slip.

"I figured as much." I folded the check and shoved it in my pocket. "Thanks."

She opened the door to Fletcher's room.

I cleared my throat. "Nancy."

"Huh?"

"How'd you know he was here?"

"I live with him."

I gasped.

"Not like that." She shook her head at my blatant stupidity. "He owns a duplex on Jefferson. His wife died a couple years ago. I make sure his place stays clean and cook a few meals. In exchange, he lets me live on the other side. It's . . . What do they call it? A symbolic relationship."

"Symbiotic," I said.

She waved her hand in the air. "Whatever."

My opinion of Nancy wavered. Unless . . . I jumped in headfirst. "Why do you let him ogle you?"

"In case you haven't noticed, he's a harmless old man." She clicked her tongue and pointed a manicured finger at me. "Oh, wait. You're the one who tried to kill him with pepper spray. I guess you haven't noticed."

Touché.

"Mr. Fletcher hired me when no one else would. He gave me a place to live, a decent paycheck, and not that it's any of your business, he's helping me study for my G.E.D." She pushed out her chin. The fire in her eyes dared me to open my mouth. "I know what you're thinking, but you can shove those ideas. His horse has been out to pasture for a lot of years, lady. If I can brighten his day with a wiggle or a glance at my girls, what's the harm?"

"Oh." I backpedaled. I'd never considered she might be capable of helping someone. I admired—*gag*—her for working on her diploma. But her people skills were lacking. "I thought—"

"I don't care what you thought." She pushed through the door to Fletcher's room and let it close in my face.

I felt bad I'd misjudged Nancy. I wasn't any better than my mother-in-law or her posse of Wickford wives. Hazel, Mavis, and Bitsy judged people for where they came from or how much money they had, not the stuff that mattered: who they were inside. Maybe Nancy wasn't all that bad.

~ ~ ~

When Dave and Angie came over, we polished off Dave's beer and a bag of pretzels. It felt good to relax and set my worries aside. By the time they left, I had the name of a divorce attorney who Dave promised would squeeze Phillip's assets until he squealed like a girl. Sounded like my kind of lawyer.

While I straightened the gathering room, Michelle gathered her dirty clothes and started a load of laundry. I thanked her and told her I'd strip the beds if she'd put a load of towels in the washer. To my surprise, she agreed. I hadn't done laundry since Esther left, and I had extra beds to strip since Jessie and Kim had stayed over.

The phone rang while I was in Jessie's room. Michelle had it on the second ring. I started for the stairs, but she beat me to the landing.

"Mom, it's Gran. She wants to talk to you." Michelle handed me the phone, grabbed the sheets I'd piled in the hallway, and hurtled down the stairs.

"Hello."

"Phillip told me he stopped by," Hazel said in her interfering mother-in-law voice, the voice that caused my stomach to knot and twist.

"Yes, he did." My divorce wasn't any of her business, but it didn't stop her from sticking her nose where it didn't belong.

"When are you going to talk to the girls?" she asked.

"I think Phillip and I need to discuss this." It was my chicken-shit way of telling her to butt out.

"Have you talked custody?"

Whoa! "He just gave me the divorce papers. As far as custody goes, Michelle stays with me." My eyes felt like they were going to bulge out of their sockets. Who was she to negotiate the terms of my divorce? "Phillip left us, remember? Both of us."

Again, I wanted to slam the phone, but instead mashed the "off" button good and hard. I thought about buying an old-fashioned phone with my next paycheck. It seemed like being able to bang a receiver in the cradle might be a satisfying form of therapy right now.

Something crashed behind me and I jumped. Michelle had come up behind me and dropped the laundry basket she'd been carrying and it tumbled end over end down the stairs.

"You and Daddy are getting divorced?"

I hadn't seen Michelle come back upstairs, but there she was.

"Oh, honey, I didn't mean for you to find out this way." I sat down on the top step and pulled her down beside me. "I'm sorry."

"Mom, why don't you give him another chance?" Her mouth scrunched into a pout. "You saw how he acted when you were hurt." Tears sprang to the corners of her eyes.

"Honey, Daddy asked me for the divorce. Those were the papers you found on the hall table the other day." I stroked her hair in an effort to comfort her. It always worked when she was younger. I hoped it still would.

The expression on her face remained serious. "Is he going to marry Willow?"

Now that was the question, and one I couldn't answer. "He hasn't said. We haven't even talked about the divorce. He just brought the papers to the house. I haven't even looked at them yet."

"Does Jess know?"

"Not unless he told her. I was going ask her to come over tomorrow. We can discuss it as a family."

I didn't want to deliver this kind of news over the phone. When I called Jessie to ask her over for dinner, she seemed none the wiser about the divorce. I felt confident Phillip hadn't said a word to her.

To be fair, I knew I had to call Phillip. Even though it aggravated me, we needed to talk to the girls together. With a whole wad of reluctance, I picked up the phone and made the call, praying Willow would not answer. If she did, I couldn't guarantee I wouldn't pull her skinny ass through the phone and beat her senseless. Hazel had stepped way over the line this time, and I was prepared to hold a grudge. Forever.

Chapter 31

"If my mom can get Sarah and Kim talking to each other again, she can do anything."
Jessie Cavanaugh

During the night, determination planted itself in my soul. I jumped out of bed with renewed vigor, my mind set on beating Hazel on at least some level. Since I didn't have a job today, I decided to try my hand at domestic bliss. Umm, housecleaning and cooking. Not my best attributes.

Phillip and Jess were coming for dinner to discuss the divorce and the future of our family. What should I cook for a cheater? Chicken livers, with a big side of crow? Or a meal he could choke on? I wished he was allergic to something, but that would be too easy.

I hadn't had time to organize my thoughts. Splitting my family apart left me cold. But then again, Phillip sleeping around didn't make me feel all warm and fuzzy, either. Tact was not a strength I possessed, and I didn't want to embarrass myself in front of my children. My solution? Rehearse while cleaning house.

"Girls," I'd say, *"your dad is a no-good, lying cheater."* No, try again.

"Girls, since your father can't keep his pants zipped . . ." My delivery left something to be desired. Winging it might be my best bet. I'd worry about my car instead.

I hated how I'd wrecked it. The repairman from the body shop called while I was glancing over the morning paper and said he expected the insurance company to total my car. It meant I'd be in the market for a new ride. Something practical and affordable. A solid vehicle, roomy enough to haul supplies. For now, Michelle's Mustang would have to work until my insurance paid off. Thank goodness I hadn't let the policy lapse.

I had stripped the sheets from all the beds the previous night, but after Michelle overheard my phone call, I postponed my cleaning mission. Housekeeper or no housekeeper, this was my house, and I would take care of it. Take that, Hazel. When Beatrice showed up there would be no work for her. What did I care if she sat around and watched TV? Hazel could pay the housekeeper for being a house-sitter.

I opened the door to Jessie's room and sighed. Every time I went in there, a part of me traveled back to her childhood. It made me sad to think someday I'd be reminiscing in Michelle's room, and she'd be grown and on her own like Jessie.

And I'd be alone.

I eased myself onto the edge of the bed and let thoughts that I might be facing a future alone creep into my head. Phillip wanted to move on. It was time for me to get a grip and make a life for myself, one that included him as the father of my children and nothing else. I knew, regardless of my situation, I would never give up my home. This house held years of memories. I was here to stay. No matter where my girls made their homes, I wanted a familiar place for them to come, a place where they had a past. This was their home, their rooms, and their history. I would never deprive them of that sanctuary.

My own mother had denied me security and stability, not to mention memories. Oh, I had them: sheer moments of panic, shoving boxes and garbage bags from a second-story bedroom window and racing down a rusty fire escape still in my pajamas in the wee hours of a bone-chilling morning.

Scenes etched in my mind of Mom's boyfriends, the faces blurred into a contorted collage. Was it Donald or Stan who threatened us with a pistol while in a drunken rage?

The result was always the same—running. Leaving with only the necessities to start over. No photos, no stuffed animals, nothing but a few pieces of secondhand clothing and Mom's important papers. She always managed to keep our birth certificates and immunization records in a safe place. Wherever we ended up, she could still enroll me in school.

My life was again on the verge of change. This time I couldn't blame my mother, it was my own doing. Call it melancholy or strolling down memory lane, whatever, but sitting in Jessie's room, I thought about how different my life might have been if Phillip had been the man he was when we married. We should be preparing for an empty nest or hounding Jessie to marry and produce grandbabies. Instead, he'd pulled up stakes and slammed the door on our future. All I had was our past and an uncertain outlook.

My thoughts didn't sound like a woman embarking on a self-improvement plan. I jerked myself out of my blue moment and scanned the room. Childhood keepsakes filled every nook and cranny. Walking in here today wasn't much different from ten years ago, except Jessie didn't live here now.

Many of her favorite books still filled the shelves, passing the time until someone picked them up and turned the pages again. Characters left alone to doze, waiting for untold adventures to burst forth.

Jessie's senior yearbook caught my eye and a flash of recognition jolted through me. I had seen one like it recently, but where? And why did it give me an eerie feeling?

I slid the yearbook from the shelf and held it, hoping to resurrect the memory. Where had I seen it? Had I seen it at Amanda's? I didn't think so. I hadn't made it beyond the living room, which was littered with too many clothes and accessories. No, I had not seen any books, as far as I could recall. I hadn't been inside Sarah's and I hadn't been to Kim's, both logical places where I would see the yearbook.

I thumbed through the pages and all the highlights of Jessie's high school years lay before me: Homecoming, Prom, football games, even the lame talent show where Jess, Kim, and Sarah had dressed in 1950s attire and sang "Leader of the Pack." I had rehearsed with them for weeks before the show.

As I paged through the book and looked at the pictures, a familiar face kept popping up. In a choir shot, she was in the front row. In one of the pep rally photos, the girl sat at the edge of the bleachers. In every picture, she blended in with the crowd, but when I looked closer, she was alone on the fringe, an onlooker—not a participant. I flipped through the book until I found her senior picture: "Lyn Porter." The name was not the least bit familiar, but I'd seen that face in the photos at the inn, the older girl next to Carrie.

And like that, the memory surfaced. I'd seen a yearbook at Harmony Inn when I cleaned the bookshelves. One or both of those sisters had gone to Wickford High. I skipped ahead to the T's, hoping to find a photo of Eve Taft. No such luck. In the sophomore and junior section, I scanned the T's looking for Carrie or Eve and didn't find a match. On a whim, I checked Porter, and there, under the sophomores, I found Carrie's photo. How did Eve Taft connect to Carrie and Lyn Porter? Sisters? Cousins? Half-sisters?

I slammed the book shut and dialed Jessie's cell. When she answered, my tongue tied itself in a knot and I couldn't form words.

"Mom, slow down," Jessie said, panic rising in her voice. "What's wrong?"

"Where are you?" My heart raced with anticipation and fear.

"I'm home," she said. "I don't work tonight."

"Call Sarah and Kim and meet me at Kim's in an hour." I knew Sarah wasn't working because Monday was her late day. Kim worked from home.

"What's going on?"

"Just do it," I said. "I think I know who killed Brian."

I heard her gasp. "What? Who?"

"I'll tell you when I see you."

"Mother, who is it?"

"Jess, you're wasting time. Call them and meet me at Kim's. I'll tell you all at the same time."

"Why all the cloak and dagger?"

"I figured out *who*. You guys need to tell me *why*. Get a hold of the girls and then call me back." I disconnected and raced down the stairs, clutching the book.

I toyed with the idea of calling Detective Alder. I was sure Lyn Porter was somehow involved in Brian's death. I had no idea why and didn't have any proof. Given the fact that I'd denied snooping, I wanted to make certain before I involved him. If I was wrong, there was no telling what he'd do.

Chapter 32

"Mrs. Cavanaugh is my kind of people. The young one, not the old one."
Beatrice Giovannetti

When Jess called back, she said everyone could meet me at two. It was early, and I was antsy to share my discovery.

I had made Jessie's bed, dusted, and started another load of endless laundry when the doorbell rang.

Beatrice stood on the porch, feather duster and a pail of cleaning supplies at her feet. "I'm here to finish what I started Saturday," she said.

I checked around to make sure Hazel hadn't brought her again. A nondescript sedan, held together by primer, was parked in my driveway. Probably leaking an oil spill the size of Rhode Island. Hazel wouldn't be seen within two miles of that rust heap.

"No, you don't understand," I said. "I don't need a housekeeper."

"That's what you think, Missy. You should of seen the ring around your bathtub." Her eyes crinkled as a smile broke out across her face.

I gripped the doorknob. "You don't understand. Hazel is wasting her money. I don't want a housekeeper."

The smile melted. "That mother-in-law of yours, she wears the pants in this house?"

"No," I objected. "Not anymore. This is my house."

"Not according to The Barracuda." She winked and made quotation marks with her fingers.

I narrowed my eyes. "The what?"

She put a hand to her mouth and snickered. "That's what all the girls at the agency call her."

"What agency?"

"Maids A-Plenty. Almost everyone has had to work for her at one time or another. Eleanor Felder lasted the longest—almost three days—before The Barracuda lit into her about leaving a dust cloth on the counter."

"My mother-in-law has a reputation as a barracuda?" This was too good to be true. I could like Beatrice, and I liked the fact she didn't like Hazel. At least I didn't think she liked her.

She touched a finger to her lips. "Don't tell her, please. I need this job."

"Oh, don't worry. I've always thought she resembled a predator," I said. "How long did you last?"

"Oh, Missy, this is my first time. When she called and asked for a long-term domestic, everyone else begged off. I got stuck." She coughed. "I mean, they assigned the job to me."

"Beatrice, why don't you come in, and please, call me Cece." I picked up her supplies and ushered her into the house.

While the water for our tea heated, I found out Hazel had definitely hired Beatrice to spy on me. I knew my instinct had been right. Too bad my instincts had failed me with Phillip.

"She wants details. I'm supposed to tell her who comes and goes, and in her exact words, 'Just what the devil my daughter-in-law is up to.'" Beatrice wiggled a foot out of her orthopedic shoe and massaged a bunion on her big toe. "Damn feet kill me all the time."

An evil plan materialized, but I didn't have time to think it through. If I was going to meet Jessie and the girls by two, I needed to step on it.

I didn't know how much to trust Beatrice. If she despised my mother-in-law as much as I did, we'd make a good team. But, I didn't want to run the risk of getting Beatrice fired.

"I have an appointment at two. Go ahead and stay. I'll deal with Hazel myself later."

"She's gonna want me to tell her where you went." My new housekeeper swigged down her tea and grinned.

I thought for a second. "Late lunch. That's it. I'm meeting my daughter for lunch."

Beatrice removed a memo pad and tiny pencil from her pocket and scratched out a note. "Got it."

"Any chance you can cook?" I asked.

"I'm a Giovannetti. I came out of the womb with a spoon in one hand and a bottle of olive oil in the other. Do I know how to cook?" Her eyes twinkled.

"My family is coming for dinner at six thirty. Will you whip up something simple? Please?"

"How many?"

"Four, counting me. Doesn't have to be fancy."

"Will your mother-in-law be joining the festivities?" she asked, using an uppity tone.

"Nope, but feel free to share the news with her. Especially the part about it being a dinner party. Don't give her the idea she's invited."

She sniggered and jotted another note in her book.

I left my house in the capable hands of Beatrice and prayed she wasn't a kleptomaniac. I mean, what did I know about her? Wait. She didn't like Hazel. Beatrice moved up a rung on my ladder. And I did miss Esther. Best of all, my mother-in-law was paying someone to clean my house.

The girls had assembled in Kim's kitchen by the time I arrived. I hadn't seen Kim and Sarah together since before this whole mess started, and they didn't act pleasant toward each other now.

I dropped the yearbook on the table, pointed to the picture I had circled earlier and said, "What do you know about her?"

Sarah spoke first. "Who is Lyn Porter?"

"Someone else coming on to Brian?" Kim didn't blink as she raised the question.

"I wasn't coming on to Brian. Shut your trap," Sarah said.

Kim curled her upper lip. "Whatever."

"Look," I said. "As far as I can tell, Brian wasn't having an affair with anyone."

Kim started to open her mouth, but I jumped in. "Don't start. Speculating won't help."

I took both girls by their hands. "You two have got to stop this. Kim, you're hurt, and I understand, but taking your anger out on your best friend is uncalled for."

Sarah pulled her hand free of mine and extended it to Kim. "She's right, you know. I swear to you, I would never sabotage our friendship."

Kim clutched my hand tighter, and then her grip eased. Tears rolled down her cheeks as she reached for Sarah and drew her into a hug. Sarah's eyes started to water, and I breathed a sigh of relief.

Jessie smiled and mouthed, "Thank you."

I noticed her eyes didn't look dry, either.

Ten minutes and twenty 'I'm sorries' later, I pointed to the picture. "I need you to tell me, could Lyn Porter be Eve Taft?"

Sarah shook her head. "No clue."

Kim turned the yearbook to get a better view. "You're telling me this is Eve Taft, the woman at Harmony Inn? You think she killed Brian?"

"Maybe," I said.

"Wait a minute. I know her." Kim went pale. "Prom Queen Porter."

Jess swallowed. "I had forgotten about her."

Sarah cocked her head and nodded in a knowing way. "Oh man."

"Is someone going to tell me?" I sat down between Sarah and Jess.

Kim slammed the book and pushed her chair back. "Mrs. C., are you sure Eve Taft is Lyn Porter? There's no way. Lyn was plain. Eve Taft is model gorgeous."

I pulled the book over and turned to Carrie's picture. "No, I'm not positive, but I found pictures of Carrie and this girl in photos at the inn. Carrie and Eve are sisters, and I never saw a third girl in any of the photos. Is there another sister?"

No answer.

"Well?" I asked.

"Beats me," Jessie said. "None of us even knew about Carrie. I don't remember her from school. I guess there could be more Porters."

Kim and Sarah didn't disagree.

"But how do you account for their differences?" Kim asked.

"Step-sister, half-sister, or cosmetic surgery. Any number of things might explain her appearance," I said.

Jessie paused as if contemplating the idea. "She's right."

"I know I'm making a big assumption, but from the way you three are acting, you know why Lyn Porter might have a motive."

Kim sighed. "This is bizarre. If you're right, then she's held a grudge all these years."

"For a prank?" Sarah asked. "A stupid high school prank."

"You two don't honestly think Lyn would kill Brian over a stupid practical joke," Jessie said. "The jocks were always doing stupid stuff."

I slapped the table to get their attention. "Hello, un-informed bystander here. Would someone tell me what you're talking about?"

Kim spoke up. "Our senior year, Brian and a couple of his buddies faked an announcement and sent it to Lyn saying she'd been voted Prom Queen."

"That's not a reason to kill someone, especially years later," I said.

Sarah piped in, "Except it went further than they expected. None of us knew the boys were planning to embarrass her." She looked at the other girls for support. They both nodded. "It was as much a surprise to us as it was to her."

"Kim, weren't you Prom Queen your senior year?" I asked.

"Yes. I swear none of us knew what the guys were up to," she said. "When it came time to crown the queen, Lyn strutted up on stage. They called my name, and she kept smiling and waving at everyone. I don't think she knew what to do."

"Everyone laughed. She froze on the spot. Two teachers had to go up there and drag her off. It was like it happened in slow motion," Sarah added.

When word spread about Phillip and Willow—more than it already had—and the news leaked about my new job, I'd get my turn learning about humiliation. I'd find out firsthand what it was like to be the laughingstock of the neighborhood. Part of me sympathized with Eve, or Lyn, or whatever her name was.

"We still had two weeks of school left, but she never came back. Didn't even show up for the honor's ceremony or graduation," Kim said.

"Someone started the rumor she had a mental breakdown." Sarah twisted a strand of hair around her finger. "Another rumor said she'd gone off to live with an old-maid aunt somewhere."

"This is so far-fetched. Listen to yourselves." Jessie squirmed in her chair and shook her head. "And coincidental. We show up at Harmony Inn and what, she goes berserk and kills Brian? How would she even know he would be there?"

"Jessie's right. All we have is an old high school prank. What does that prove?" I said. My rationalization had pretty much unraveled, leaving me no closer to figuring out who killed Brian. I slammed the book. "There's got to be an explanation."

"Oh. My. Gosh." Kim jerked her purse from the back of the chair and dug around until she found a large postcard. "She knew we were going to be there. At least she laid the groundwork to get Brian and me there, not knowing it would be the three of us instead." She placed it on the table, and we all moved in for a better look. "She set us up, and when Brian came over he gave her the opportunity. Remember how she kept hanging around like we were all besties with her?"

The front of the card had a beautiful color photograph of Harmony Inn. I flipped it over to reveal an invitation for the inn's grand opening, complete with a complimentary wine and cheese celebration, hand addressed to Mr. and Mrs. Brian Anderson.

"Now what?" Sarah asked, looking at me.

Biting my lip, I tapped the invitation against the table, plotting my next move. "Kim, can I keep this?"

"Sure."

I touched her arm. "Hang in there."

What if this postcard could clear Kim, and she'd had it the whole time? Alder didn't know the connection between Brian and Lyn Porter. Did he? Could I link her to the murder? Could I link her to Eve Taft? Alder needed the information, even if it meant facing his wrath for interfering. I'd snoop again if it meant clearing Kim. Thinking of Alder made my blood run cold. I couldn't face him, not after yesterday at the gym. I grabbed my purse and headed for the door.

"Jess, will you pick Michelle up from school?"

"Where are you going?"

I clutched the yearbook to my chest. "I don't know, but I need to talk to Angie. She'll know what to do."

"Be careful."

"Don't worry. Pick up your sister and be at the house by six. Tonight is our family meeting."

"What's the meeting about?" Jessie asked.

"Dad and I want to talk to you and Michelle about what's been going on." I averted my eyes.

I had prided myself on teaching my girls not to be quitters. In the Cavanaugh family, giving up was never an option. Now I was the quitter.

Chapter 33

"**I know why Brian was killed. Now I must prove it to Alder, so he doesn't think I'm interfering. It won't be easy.**"
Cece Cavanaugh

The only task on my mind when I left Kim's, besides calling Angie, was double-checking to see if the yearbook I'd seen at the inn matched Jessie's. If I could get that book and check the inscriptions to make sure Eve actually was Lyn, then I'd have some evidence other than a postcard. Jessie's book had all kinds of notes from her friends scribbled on the pages. I hoped Lyn's did, too. I needed an excuse to get back in the study at Harmony Inn.

Before I pulled onto the highway, I called the number on the postcard Kim had given me.

Carrie answered on the first ring.

"Hi," I said, trying to make my voice sound chipper. "It's Cece Cavanaugh."

"What do you want?"

"I lost my debit card and think it may have fallen out of my pocket while I was cleaning. I hate to be a nuisance, but would you mind if I swing by and check?"

"I'll look for it," she offered.

"Oh, don't bother." I started to panic. "It'll be easier for me to retrace my steps. I'll be there in a few minutes."

"Whatever. Eve's leaving for an appointment, but I'll be here all afternoon." She disconnected before I could respond.

Perfect! I wouldn't have to face Eve. She gave me the willies, and I'd just as soon not deal with her.

Before I chickened out, I called Angie at the station.

"Hi," her voice mail said. "I'm away on business. Leave a message, and I'll call you when I return."

What kind of business does a cop have besides chasing criminals? I tried her cell, and it went straight to voice mail. "Where the hell are you? I think I can prove Eve Taft killed Brian, and I'll be damned if I'm calling that skirt-chasing Alder. Angie, call me."

I sat for a minute and willed my phone to ring. "Come on, Ang."

The voice in my head told me to suck it up and call Alder. Kim's freedom was at stake, and I was acting like a jilted lover. I dug around in my purse for the card Alder had given me and practiced what I would say when he answered.

"Hi, I know who murdered Brian Ander . . ." No.

"Umm, hello, Detective Alder this is Cece Cava . . ." Not that he didn't know who I was.

Okay, then, how about I come right out and say it. *"Eve Taft killed Brian Anderson, and I have proof."* Right. Between an old yearbook and the postcard, I had proof. Or did I?

I could do an anonymous tip. He didn't have to know it was me. I'd call in and tell him Taft killed Brian. Let him do the detecting. Would he figure out the link? Not without the dang yearbook.

I punched in his number and braced myself for his wrath.

"This is Detective Alder. I'm not able to answer your call . . ."

Don't cops ever answer their phones? Now what? I smacked my forehead. *Dummy.* I had the perfect solution. Leave a message and I won't *have* to talk to him. By the time he gets around to me, he'll have solved his case and be ready to thank me for my help.

This time when the call went to voice mail, I didn't hesitate. In my most professional tone, I said, "Detective Alder, it's Cece Cavanaugh." What the hell was I doing? I disconnected.

I punched in Angie's number. When her recorded voice answered, I yelled, "Where the hell are you? Call me. It's important." My phone died before I could tell her the rest.

I knew better than to poke around in the glove box for the car charger. It was in my car at the auto body shop. Maybe in the car crusher by now, if the insurance company had totaled it. Once I checked the yearbook to see if it belonged to Lyn Porter, I'd smuggle it out in my purse and call Alder when I got home or better yet, I'd give it to Angie. She could deal with the jerk.

Carrie was waiting when I pulled into the driveway.

I threw the car in park and rushed up the sidewalk. "Thanks for letting me come over." I pasted a smile on my face and hoped I sounded sincere.

"Come in." She stepped back and allowed me into the hallway.

I wanted to run straight to the study and peel the yearbook from the shelf, but I needed to restrain myself. Knowing Carrie, she'd be right on my heels to make sure I wasn't lifting the heirloom silver.

"I'll take a look upstairs." I headed up the steps and called over my shoulder, "Shouldn't take me long."

I cursed my aching knees as I climbed to the second floor.

Carrie followed right behind me. "I'll give you a hand. The sooner you find it, the sooner you can be on your way."

Now I had to pretend to look for the stupid card. Why couldn't I come up with a better excuse?

I led Carrie through all the bedrooms I'd cleaned, making a show of looking under beds, behind chairs, and inside closets. Surprise, surprise, no card in sight.

"Well," she said, pulling the last door shut, "that leaves the study. Let's check there."

"I've wasted enough of your time. Go back to what you were doing." I stayed one step behind her as we descended the stairs. "I know my way around, and I'll let you know when I leave."

Somewhere in the back of the house, a phone rang. Carrie tilted her head and frowned. "Oh, go ahead. I should get that. But let me know when you leave."

"Will do."

After she disappeared, I sprinted to the study, slid the doors closed behind me and made a beeline to the bookshelf.

Even though the furniture had been moved around and a new area rug covered the spot where I'd removed the blood-soaked one, the room still felt creepy. Maybe knowing who had killed Brian, and why, was what set my teeth on edge. Or it could be the fact that I was sneaking around and hoping to not get caught.

I'd made sure to leave the drapes open the last time I was here. Now they were closed. The room wouldn't have seemed sinister with sunlight splashing across the hardwood floor. Fine hairs stood at attention on the back of my neck and a feeling of dread enveloped me as I reached for the yearbook. Part of me wanted to be wrong about my suspicions. I didn't want to be standing in a killer's house. But if Eve wasn't the killer, that meant Kim still had the best motive for Brian's murder. I wanted more than anything to prove her innocent.

I found the yearbook and it matched the one from Jessie's room. Same year. Inside the cover in tiny block print the name Lyn Porter stood out. The rest of the pages yielded no clues. They were blank. I mean, there were pictures, and everything looked normal, except no one had signed the book. Not one note about being *best friends 4ever* or *seniors rule* or any of the other ridiculous promises classmates make about keeping in touch. But the girls said Lyn left the night of prom and never returned to school. It was possible Carrie or a parent had gone to pick up the book.

I heard footsteps approaching and slid the book in place just as the doors to the study opened.

"Why did you shut the doors?" Carrie eyed me and crossed to where I stood.

"Oh," I said, grasping for an excuse. "Umm, didn't want to disturb your call. This room has an echo, and I figured all my searching might cause a ruckus, especially if I moved any furniture. But I see you bought a new rug. Sound shouldn't be an issue. It's nice. The rug, I mean. Goes nice with the décor."

"So, did you?" she asked.

"Did I what?" I slid by her and headed for the door.

"Did you move any furniture?"

"No, but I'm not finished. Still need to check the desk. Might have to move it away from the wall." I slithered by her and crouched down to check under the desk. "Nope, nothing here. I bet my debit card wound up in one of those bio collection bags with all the trash. I'll call the bank, report it missing, and order a new one."

"Then I guess you're finished here. I'll see you to the door."

Remembering the frantic message I'd left for Angie, I cringed. If she got it before I called her off, I'd be toast. "Would you mind if I use the phone? My cell died, and I could report my card now before anyone wipes out my bank account." *Right! Like I had anything to pilfer.*

Carrie's mouth scrunched in a grim line. "Can't it wait until you get home?"

What was up with the broad? I only asked to use the phone for Pete's sake. It's not like I asked for a personal loan or something. "Sure, I guess so. I hope my account isn't wiped out before I drive across town. One transaction and 'poof,' everything I have could be gone."

"Oh, for God's sake. Go ahead." She handed me the cordless from the desk.

"Thanks, I won't be long." I grabbed it and dialed Angie's number.

Carrie didn't budge.

"Umm, could I have some privacy?" It was a gutsy move, but Angie could be on her way. How embarrassing would that be? "They'll need my bank account number, and it's not that I don't trust you, but we don't know one another."

"Let me know when you're done." Carrie exited the room, but left the door open.

The muscles in my neck relaxed. While waiting for Angie to answer, I saw the preliminary invoice I'd left with Carrie and froze. She'd signed the invoice as Carrie Porter. I hadn't noticed before. I'd assumed their last names were the same: Taft. The handwriting looked familiar. I recognized the *r*'s and the *a*'s. I'd seen them a short while ago at Kim's.

Setting the phone down, I dug around in my purse until I unearthed the invitation Kim had given me. It didn't take a handwriting expert to determine Carrie's signature matched the handwriting on the invitation. Were Carrie and Eve in this together?

I reached for the phone again and felt a whack across the back of my head. The phone flew out of my hand, and my lights went out.

When I came to, I was in the study, lying on my side in almost the same spot where Brian had died. I didn't know what the hell had happened, but my shoulders ached, and a prickle of numbness tingled my fingers. My hands and feet were bound. If there was an upside, it had to be that my feet and hands weren't tied together like in the movies. A wave of icy fear raced up my spine, replacing my customary hot flash.

For the second time in less than a week, my head had been subjected to trauma. Not good. The contents of my purse lay scattered across the rug. I scooted around and scanned the room. My eyes landed on the portrait of Eve's ancestors. Everything clicked into place. Evelyn Porter, the name of their great-great-grandmother.

It fit. Eve . . . Lyn . . . Evelyn. Eve and Lyn were the same person.

Chapter 34

"Holy moly, if I die, I'm going to haunt Phillip for the rest of his life. It's his fault I'm in this mess."
Cece Cavanaugh

"What the hell are you doing?" From somewhere behind me, Eve's voice pierced the silence.

I froze in mid-scoot and braced for another smack across the head. It didn't come.

"Stay out of it," Carrie said. "Just leave and let me take care of this."

The voices sounded like they were coming from the hall. I rolled over and saw both women standing outside the study.

"Take care of what?"

Carrie stepped toward her sister. "Go upstairs and let me handle this."

"I will not. Why is there a woman lying on the floor?" Eve backed up a step.

Neither appeared to be paying attention to me. I wiggled my hands to see if I could pull them free. The end of a piece of fabric dangled in my hand. I grabbed it between my thumb and finger and tugged. The binding became tighter. If I could get a grip on the knot, I might be able to loosen it. I twisted my hand and arched my back, trying to free myself without making noise.

"You idiot. It's the nosy Cavanaugh woman," Carrie hissed.

"And you tied her up? Are you nuts?" Eve turned and rushed to me.

I stopped fiddling with the knot and plastered on a pathetic face. Between the hot flashes and the icy panic, I guessed I was pathetic. It was difficult to read Eve's expression. If she had killed Brian, she would be happy to do me in. But on the off chance she hadn't, maybe she'd untie me.

Carrie followed her. "She knows who you are."

Eve bent and picked up the invitation, which had landed on the floor next to me. "What's that supposed to mean?"

I wiggled my hands, and the knot loosened.

"All she has to do is tell that detective, and it wouldn't be long before he figured it out."

Eve dropped the postcard. "What are you talking about?"

"When you saw his picture in the paper, you flipped out. Teacher of the Year, what a joke. The man was an ass. He deserved what he got." Carrie's voice wavered.

Eve sank to a chair. "You think I killed Brian Anderson. Is that what this is all about?"

"You don't get it, do you?" Carrie laughed. "I killed the bastard."

Eve gasped. "You did what? Why?"

And to think I'd thought Eve murdered Brian.

"Because of you. I lost my sister the day he humiliated you." Carrie crossed the room and placed a hand on Eve's shoulder. "No matter how you've tried to change yourself for the better, the cosmetic surgery, the name change, you lost the old Lyn. The Lyn I loved. My big sister. The person I admired most of all."

Cosmetic surgery, no wonder Jessie and the others hadn't recognized her. What I hadn't counted on was that one sister would be willing to kill for the other. I should have known. Sisters have a bond. I'd seen it in my own two girls, but I hadn't recognized it in Eve and Carrie.

Tears streamed down Eve's face. "How could you? That was a lifetime ago."

"Don't be such a wimp. He deserved what he got." Carrie hovered over me and kicked my leg. "Come on. You're going with me."

I cringed. How the hell was I supposed to go with her? I couldn't stand up. And I'd trip over my feet if I did.

Eve wiped her face. "Where are you taking her?"

"To Daddy's old cabin. We'll dump her so far out in the woods no one will ever find her." Carrie motioned to Eve. "Come help me get this heifer up."

"Heifer? Who the hell are you calling a heifer?" *Why the heck did I say that?* The batty broad had enough reason to kill me, and I'd given her another one.

"Shut up." Carrie grabbed my hands. "On your knees."

I glared at her and remained still.

"Now!"

I complied, and Eve helped her pull me to my feet.

"This isn't a good idea. Let's talk about it before you go and do something we can't undo," Eve pleaded.

Sounded like a plan to me. Here I'd figured Eve was the nutcase, and it turned out her sister had a screw loose.

"It's a little late for that, sister. We need to finish what I started. Come on and help me," Carrie said.

The hope I'd been holding on to fizzled. Eve's facial expression told me she had no intention of standing up to her sister. I wobbled and started to fall, but they grabbed my arms.

"Untie my feet. I can't move," I said. My feet and legs felt like I was wearing cinder blocks for shoes.

"Not on your life. You walk or we'll drag your sorry ass all the way." Carrie cuffed me on the shoulder.

I saw the empty canister of pepper spray I'd used to drench Fletcher. It lay on the floor right next to my dead cell phone and my purse. Some detective I'd make. Why hadn't I followed Alder's advice and kept my nose out of his investigation?

My wallet was splayed open, and I saw a photo I'd taken of Jessie and Michelle last Christmas. I squeezed my eyes shut and remembered how happy they'd been. I hoped Phillip would give them a good Christmas. Then the idea of Willow making our traditional holiday brunch in my kitchen flashed into my head, and I lost all sense of restraint. If these women meant to kill me, I'd make them sorry they messed with Cece Cavanaugh. How, I didn't know, but my timing had to be perfect. If we were going to some old cabin, we'd be going outside to their car. Once I was in the open, I'd unleash on them. Not sure what, but they weren't getting me in a car.

"If you're going to kill her, you're doing it without me." Eve folded her arms across her chest.

My pulse beat a manic tune against my temples, but I brightened at the prospect of having an ally. Carrie may have gone too far even for the sisterly bond.

Carrie whispered something to Eve.

"I guess," Eve said.

Carrie stared me down. "Do you like spiders?"

I squared my shoulders in an *I'm-not-afraid-of-you* stance. "Why?"

"My sister doesn't have the guts to kill you, and I can't get rid of you without her help. There's an old cistern out there where you can scream for days and no one will hear you." Carrie grabbed a set of keys off the desk. "It's crawling with spiders. They can lunch on you until they've had their fill."

My good mood crashed. Eve would stick with her sister and do me in.

Eve shivered.

Carrie bent and removed the strap around my feet. "Don't be stupid, or I'll kill you right here."

Blood rushed to my feet, and it felt like a thousand pins poking my toes, the soles of my feet, my ankles.

Carrie pushed me. "Get moving."

I stumbled and caught the edge of a chair to keep from toppling over. "Wait a minute, will you? My feet are numb." What she didn't know was I wanted more than ever to be outside. But first, I wanted my feet in working order.

I hobbled out the door with the sisters gripping my arms. A tall privacy fence surrounded the backyard. A gate led to the garage at the rear of the lot. Unless I could haul my ass over the fence, my escape plan was doomed.

"Don't drag your feet. You weigh a ton." Carrie urged me down the sidewalk and into the garage where a black pickup sat.

I narrowed my eyes at the truck's crumpled bumper. "You're the one who hit me and then ran me off the road."

Carrie grinned. "You're slow to catch on. I hoped the phone calls would scare you off, but you were too dense to figure it out."

Phillip hadn't hired a thug to scare me off, and Willow hadn't made the prank phone calls. At least that was something.

Eve opened the passenger side and helped me in the truck. Her hand slid down my back, and the ties on my hands loosened. "Shhh," she whispered.

I slid to the middle of the seat. Carrie hopped in the driver's side and started the engine. Eve crawled in next to me and pushed the button on the garage door opener.

"Next stop, Spiderville." Carrie giggled and pulled the big truck into the late afternoon sun. When we cleared the edge of the fence, she turned and started down the double driveway. My car sat halfway down the drive with a car I presumed to be Eve's behind it. The best sight of all was Alder's blue Crown Vic crossways blocking the exit to the street. Angie must have gotten my message and acted. I sent up a silent prayer and waited for the drama to unfold.

The clock on the dash read quarter past five. In less than an hour, Phillip and the girls would be waiting for me. If Carrie was smart, she'd stop the truck, give up, and I'd be home in plenty of time for our family meeting. On the other hand, if she wasn't, I'd be spider chow by the time my family figured out I was missing.

Crazy ideas meandered through my brain. I wondered if the police department had a hostage negotiation strategy. Did they consider me a hostage? Would they bargain with Carrie? Or shoot and maybe kill me in the process. I chewed my lip and considered all the options. My cheating husband problem seemed small-time compared to the possibility of losing my life.

Forsythia bushes lined the driveway on the south side. A terrace built with landscaping blocks covered the north. Much to my glee, Carrie had no place to go.

Alder stood behind my car. Three squad cars sat at various angles in the street. Six uniformed officers had their guns drawn and aimed at the truck.

"You're screwed," I said.

Carrie banged her hand against the steering wheel. "Shit. Shit. Shit."

"Put your hands up and get out of the truck," Alder yelled.

Eyes straight ahead, Carrie didn't move.

"What are you going to do?" Eve asked.

"Get the hell out of here. What do you think?" Carrie twisted the steering wheel and aimed the truck toward the gap between my car and Alder's.

"Don't you even think about it." I gritted my teeth and eased my hands out of the straps, wiggling my right one so Eve would see.

Casting a glance at her hand in her lap, Eve nodded slightly. "Don't do it, Carrie. You'll kill all of us."

Eve ticked off three fingers and knotted her fist. After a few seconds, I grasped the meaning of her signal. I hoped it meant she had a plan and on the count of three she was going to do something.

Carrie slammed the truck in reverse and gunned the engine. The truck shot backward. She jammed the shifter into drive. She was lining up to take a run at the Mustang. Eve nudged my shoulder and held up one finger in her lap. She held up a second, and my breath caught. I didn't know what she had in mind, but I'd follow her lead.

Carrie was busy staring down Alder, not watching the drama unfolding on the passenger side. When Eve's third finger went up, she shoved open the door and jumped. I started after her, but Carrie stomped the gas pedal. The door slammed shut blocking my exit. I scrambled to open it right as we crashed.

The raucous sound of crunching metal filled my ears. It was the second time in a week I'd had a face full of air bag. I punched it out of the way. Cops scrambled across the lawn, guns drawn. I didn't know what to do. Carrie had wedged the truck between my Mustang and Alder's car, making an escape out the door impossible. I slid down to the floor and hoped she wouldn't try anything stupid.

Carrie began to cry. Soft at first, but the sobs turned frantic. She wheezed and then gasped for air.

"Help me, I can't breathe," she whimpered. The gasping became more insistent.

Working in the hospital for as long as I had, I'd witnessed plenty of asthma attacks.

"Stay calm," I said. "Do you have an inhaler?"

I felt the truck rock from side to side and heard the grating of metal against metal. Someone was backing Alder's car away from the truck.

"In my purse," she gasped.

I felt along the floor, groping for the inhaler. Carrie's door swung open. In mere seconds, she was on the ground facedown, with cops kneeling over her.

Her wheezing grew louder. My fingers curled around the inhaler.

"Stop," I screamed.

No one listened. Alder handcuffed her and pulled her upright. Her face had a purple tinge. My anger melted away, and Nurse Cece emerged. The woman who'd held my life in her hands now depended on me. She could suffocate if I didn't help her soon.

I stumbled out of the truck, ran to Alder, and grabbed his arm. "She's having an asthma attack."

All eyes focused on me.

I held up the inhaler. "She needs this."

Alder pinned me with a stare.

"Step away, ma'am." A uniformed officer grabbed my shoulders and pulled me back.

Carrie continued to wheeze and gasp for air.

I twisted free. "Alder, she's not able to breathe. Give her this." I held the inhaler to let Alder see it. "She needs to go to the hospital."

"Go ahead," he said.

I stepped forward and held the inhaler to Carrie's mouth. She labored to catch a breath.

I searched for her sister. "Where's Eve?"

Alder motioned to a squad car parked at the curb. Eve sat in the back, face pressed to the window.

"She's innocent." I pointed to Eve. "She tried to help me, not hurt me."

Alder exchanged glances with the officer who had pulled me away, a kid who didn't look old enough to be wearing a uniform, much less out of high school.

"Go get the sister," Alder said to the officer and then turned to me. "You're bleeding."

In all the excitement, I hadn't noticed the blood on my shirt or the gash above my eye. When Carrie rammed my car, I must have hit my head.

Alder's face softened. "When the ambulance shows up, we'll have a paramedic check you over." He reached a hand toward my face.

I bristled at his attention and ducked away. Two-timing jackass. If he wanted his sweet young thing at the gym, good for him. Another man chasing after young twits was more than I could handle. His sympathy wasn't necessary. Even if he was doing his job.

"Don't touch me." I didn't try to hide my disgust. "I'm fine. I can take care of myself."

The glint in his eyes faded. "What's the mat—?"

The wail of an approaching ambulance pierced the cool evening air, drowning out his words. I shivered and wished I'd brought a sweater. Phillip and the girls would be waiting. Of all days to have our meeting. I wondered if Phillip had waited for me or if he'd gone ahead and had the divorce discussion. If he even dared to bring Willow, I'd give him a piece of my mind.

~ ~ ~

As it turned out, I needed stitches. While the ER doc patched me up, the nurse, a friend of mine from when I'd worked, called Jessie. Sometimes it paid to have hospital connections. Since I'd suffered another head injury when Carrie whacked me, I wouldn't be driving myself home. Besides, my car was still at the inn. I wasn't sure how much damage it had suffered, but I'd take care of it tomorrow. My insurance agent would be putting out a hit on me if I didn't quit smashing vehicles.

When I trudged out to the waiting room, Eve and Alder were sitting side by side, engrossed in conversation. I assumed he was questioning her about Carrie and what, if any, involvement Eve had in Brian's murder or what had happened with me. I wanted to intervene, to know Kim was off the hook, to know Carrie's asthma was under control, and to know she would pay for what she had done to Brian. But I didn't trust myself to talk to Alder. Not yet, anyway. When he saw me, he rose from the chair and excused himself to Eve.

I held up a hand and shook my head. "I don't want to talk to you. Not now. Not ever."

I didn't see his reaction because Michelle and Jessie came in, followed by Phillip. My daughters ran over and hugged me.

Phillip eyed Alder and frowned, but it didn't stop him from enfolding me in his arms and whispering in my ear, "Are you okay?"

"I think so." My body trembled as I sagged against him.

Alder started toward us, but Phillip waved him off. "Stay away from my wife." The air crackled with anger, and I was too shaken to care. Right then, the only thing I cared about was going home. Someplace safe, surrounded by my children.

Out of the corner of my eye, I watched Alder sink into the chair. The tiniest bit of regret niggled in my brain. I wanted to believe in happy ever after, but my chance had already been torpedoed. I didn't need to wait another thirty years for it to happen again.

In the parking lot, Jessie announced she and Michelle were going to the inn to see if the Mustang was drivable. Michelle was not happy when she learned Carrie had rammed her car. Phillip led me to his car and told the girls we'd be at home when they returned.

I climbed in and fastened my seat belt. I knew we were in for a bumpy ride.

Chapter 35

"I will be my own person, make my own decisions, and decide what perfume to wear. I am Cece Cavanaugh, and I matter. Watch out, Wickford."
Cece Cavanaugh

Phillip didn't speak for the first few miles. I laid my head back, closed my eyes, and pretended to be resting, but Alder wormed his way into my head. My lips still remembered his kiss, as if it had happened yesterday. What if Becca *was* his workout partner? Right! Like that was a possibility. And Grant? He was a wonderful man who understood my need for space and was willing to wait until my life settled down. Then, there was Phillip, the man I had been married to, who had one tiny, unforgiveable flaw. He was a cheater. Would I ever trust him again? Did I owe it to my marriage to give it a second chance, to find out what went wrong and try to fix it? Did I owe it to my kids? Could I stand up and be my own person and still be Phillip's wife?

"I've been thinking," Phillip interrupted my musing.

The familiar sting of tears began to work their way to the surface. I squeezed my eyes tighter and feigned sleep.

Phillip touched my arm and stroked it. "You awake?"

I stirred, but didn't trust myself to open my eyes. "Yes."

"What are we doing?"

Eyes still closed, I shook my head.

"It's over with Willow and me. I've been doing a lot of thinking." Phillip's voice sounded shaky. "I almost lost you today."

I squeezed my eyes to keep tears from coming. Surprisingly, there were none.

"We have a lot to work out. You'll have to learn to trust me again. And I'll have to learn to trust you again."

I swiveled my head so fast I thought it would torque off. "What?"

"The cop. There's something going on with you two. I think I can forgive you if you slept with him." Phillip paused. "I mean, you were on the rebound, and he was there. I get it."

Neurons sizzled in my head, a bolt of lightning or maybe an aneurysm, but I saw my life flash before me. I was drowning, not literally, of course. But, I was going down for maybe the final time, suffocating in my own stupidity.

I gritted my teeth. "You forgive me?"

"Um, sure. I understand how it happened. I was self-absorbed. I didn't see you had needs. The cop comes along and wham bam."

"What do you mean?"

"I just explained myself. Did your head injury affect your hearing?" Phillip turned into our driveway and parked. "Damn, I'll have to get my garage door opener back. I hate leaving the Porsche parked outside. When Jess and Michelle get home, let me be the one to tell them our good news, okay?"

The girls weren't home yet. I pushed open the door and stomped into the house.

Phillip closed in right at my heels and followed me inside. "What's the matter? I thought—"

I saw the flash again and dug in for a fight. "Let me tell you something. The only good news we'll be telling anyone is how rapidly our divorce will be final."

I looked around for my purse and remembered it was still on the floor at the inn. "As soon as I get my hands on those divorce papers, you are history. I want you out of my bed, out of my hair, and out of my life."

Jess and Michelle arrived in the middle of my speech.

Phillip didn't miss a beat. "I think your mother needs to rest. She's been through a lot today."

"Get out!" I yelled. "Go back to Willow or your mother or your girlfriend *du jour*, because we're through." I turned to my daughters. "I'm sorry you had to see that. Your dad and I wanted to tell you in a civilized manner that we're getting divorced, and I seem to have blown that. But it's out, there's no taking it back."

Jess put her arm around Michelle and glared at her dad. "It's best if you leave."

Michelle stood there, tears running down her cheeks.

"Girls, let's be reasonable," Phillip said.

"Dad, don't." Jessie's voice trembled. "You were right when you said Mom's been through a lot today. You need to go. Now!"

"I'll call tomorrow." He eased the door shut.

Michelle ran up the stairs crying. The slam of her bedroom door made me cringe.

"She'll come around, Mom. Give her time." Jess hugged me again. "Are you going to be okay? I can stay if you want."

"I'll be fine. I need to rest." I started for the stairs and turned. "About your dad . . ."

"You don't have to explain. He's still my dad, and I still love him, even though I don't like him much right now." Jessie's eyes grew misty. "Get some rest. I'll check on you in the morning, and we can talk."

"Thanks for understanding, honey."

"Oh, when we picked up Michelle's car, one of the officers at the scene gave us your purse." She placed it on the hall table. "It's kind of a jumble, but I think we found everything."

I hadn't even noticed her holding it, nor had I asked about the car.

~ ~ ~

Long after Jessie had left, I rambled around the kitchen. Beatrice had left a note saying she'd finished the laundry and put a pan of lasagna and a salad in the fridge for our dinner. She'd also written that Hazel had called, but not to worry.

The anesthetic they'd used when they stitched me up had worn off, and my head throbbed. I decided to try a different numbing agent and poured a glass of wine. If it didn't work, I'd hit the hard stuff. I had scooped a serving of salad onto a plate and started grazing when the phone rang. I started to ignore it, but Caller ID revealed Angie's cell number.

"Hello," I said.

"I just listened to your message. What the hell is going on?"

"You don't know what's happened?" I asked.

"It's been a day from hell. Nothing has gone as planned. Nothing."

That was an understatement. "Where are you? I tried you at work and on your cell." I refilled my glass and carried it to the gathering room.

"I'm in Kansas City. Had to pick up a prisoner. But when we got here, he had appendicitis or something. I'm stuck here until a doc checks him out. What's this about Eve? I told you to quit snooping. Alder is going to kill you."

"You didn't call Alder?" I asked.

"No, I told you I just got your message and wanted to see what you were up to."

"Damn, he's still following me then," I said. Part of me wanted to be aggravated, but the logical side of me thanked the heavens he was, or else I'd be a salad bar for spiders.

"What are you talking about?" Angie asked.

I told her the whole story while I finished off the bottle of wine. My head no longer throbbed, but I drank enough not to care even if it did. It wasn't a full bottle, only the leftovers I dug out of the wine cooler. I might imbibe a little, but I wasn't a lush.

"Wow, guess you had quite a day. I'm glad it cleared Kim. You're okay, aren't you?"

I hadn't even thought about Kim. First thing tomorrow, I'd drop by to see her. On second thought, I'd call, in case Alder had more questions for her. I didn't want to risk seeing him again.

"I'm fine. Don't know how many more head injuries I can take. My brain cells are already dying from old age, I don't need to hasten their demise." I laughed for the first time in a long time.

"Now," Angie's voice grew serious, "tell me about Alder?"

"Oh," I gulped. I'd forgotten I'd left that message. "Nothing. I saw him at the gym with a girl half his age named Becca. You can quit wasting your time trying to fix me up. I'm done with men."

Angie sighed. "You dope. Becca is his daughter."

My eyelid started to twitch. "You didn't tell me he had kids."

"Did you ask?"

When would I learn to keep my big mouth shut? "Who cares? I'm through with men."

Angie gave me a severe tongue-lashing for jumping to conclusions, but we made a date for lunch when she got home from Kansas City, with the promise she'd buy, of course. My finances had a long way to go before I'd be able to put on country club airs again.

I was picking at the lasagna when Michelle slipped into the kitchen.

"That looks yummy," she said. "Can we heat it up? I'm starved."

"Sure." I pushed the stool back, but she motioned for me to sit still.

"I'll do it. You need to rest." She scooped two squares of pasta onto plates and nuked them in the microwave.

I watched as she gathered utensils and arranged placemats on the bar. She poured two glasses of tea and eased herself onto the stool across from me.

"We saw him today," she said almost in a whisper.

"Who?" I was rolling the edge of the placemat, thinking maybe I should let her off restriction.

"Daddy," she said matter-of-factly. "And Willow."

I sat up straighter and leaned forward on my elbows. "When was this?" I felt the skin on my neck prickle, but reminded myself to stay calm.

"When Jess picked me up at school, we went by Daddy's office and saw him coming out." She didn't meet my gaze, but I saw a tear roll down her cheek. "He had his arm around her, and they were laughing and acting stupid.

"Jessie and I decided we were going to let him have it when he came to dinner tonight, but then the hospital called right when he got here. Jessie told him we'd drive ourselves. We didn't want to be in the same car with him."

I reached across and grasped Michelle's hands. "Listen to me. What your dad did has nothing to do with you and your sister. Do you understand me?"

"I guess," she mumbled.

The microwave buzzed, and Michelle slid from the stool and retrieved our dinner. When she set my plate down, I squeezed her shoulders. "I'm serious, Michelle. You and Jessie are the world to him."

"But, Mom, I was horrible to you," she blubbered. "I'm sorry for being such a brat."

I kissed the top of her head. "Does that mean you're on your best behavior from now on?"

She gave me the familiar eye-roll.

I knew we'd be okay.

Alder, on the other hand, was a different story. He deserved an apology. I had over-reacted when I saw him with his daughter. My decision to go ahead with the divorce left me in a vulnerable position. Not that I thought Alder would take advantage. No, I didn't trust myself, and I certainly couldn't rely on myself to deliver an apology in-person. No telling what kind of mess I'd get into. I fished his card from my purse and hesitated. *Do you really want to do this?*

Before I could talk myself out of it, I dialed his number. On the third ring, he answered with a gruff, "Hello?"

I swallowed, then said, "It's Cece."

"I know," he said, softening his tone. "Caller ID."

"Oh."

He didn't say anything.

"Thanks for coming to get me at Harmony. I owe you," I said.

"Doing my job," he replied.

Crap, he wasn't going to make this easy. "I'm sorry for the day at the gym. I. Uh. I misunderstood." The words stuck in my throat.

Silence.

"Dammit, I'm trying to apologize for being an idiot," I said.

A low chuckle came through the receiver. "You were jealous of my daughter?" Alder asked.

"No," I shot back. "Okay, yes. A little. It's just—"

"I was kidding. You've got more important things to focus on. Looks like you and your husband patched up your differences, so don't worry about it," Alder said, the gruffness returning.

"What?" I asked. "No, it's not like that."

"Cece," Alder said. "I'm not going to get in the middle of you and your husband."

Well, you sure didn't mind when you kissed me in front him, I thought, but I said, "There's nothing to get in the middle of. I'm signing the divorce papers."

Alder did not respond. Again? *When would I learn to keep my big mouth shut?*

"I mean," I said. "I wanted you to know is all. Not that it means anything. Or anything. You know?" Damn, I kept stumbling over my words. "Okay, well I'm going to say goodbye and get off the phone."

"It's not goodbye, Cece," Alder said softly. "Let's say goodnight. When you're ready, we can see what happens."

"Goodnight then," I said and disconnected.

Long after I had gone to bed, I lay awake, remembering what Grant Hunter had said about me being worth it. That had been my problem; I had never valued myself. Phillip lived the life he wanted, at my expense.

It was my turn now, and I intended to listen to the voice in my head.

Tricia L. Sanders:

Tricia L. Sanders writes about women with class, sass, and a touch of kickass. A former instructional designer and corporate trainer, she traded in curriculum writing for novel writing, because she hates bullet points and loves to make stuff up. And fiction is more fun than training guides and lesson plans.

When she isn't writing, Tricia is busy crossing dreams off her bucket list. With all 50 states checked, she's concentrating on foreign interests. She's an avid St. Louis Cardinals fan, so don't get between her and the television when a game is on. Currently she is working on a mystery series set in the fictional town of Wickford, Missouri. Another project in the works is a women's fiction road trip adventure.

Her essays have appeared in Sasee, ByLine, The Cuivre River Anthology and Great American Outhouse Stories; The Whole Truth and Nothing Butt. She is a proud member of The Lit Ladies, six women writing their truths into fiction. To find out about her future releases:

Visit her website: www.triciasanders.com

Find her on Facebook:

www.facebook.com/authortricialsanders/

CPSIA information can be obtained
at www.ICGtesting.com
Printed in the USA
FFHW012037111118
49312213-53593FF